Praise for *The Titanic Murders* . . .

"Collins does a fine job of insinuating a mystery into a world-famous disaster . . . [He] manage[s] to raise plenty of goosebumps before the ship goes down for the count . . . Whether your interest is disasters, forgotten writers, or good murder mysteries, Collins is able to deliver the goods." —*Mystery News*

. . . and for Max Allan Collins

"No one can twist you through a maze with the intensity and suspense of Max Allan Collins." —Clive Cussler

"Max Allan Collins blends fact and fiction like no other writer." —Andrew Vachss, author of *Flood*

"A terrific writer!" —Mickey Spillane

"Max Allan Collins masterfully blends fact and fiction . . . Transcends the historical thriller." —Jeffery Deaver

"Collins displays a compelling talent for flowing narrative and concise, believable dialogue." —*Library Journal*

continued . . .

The
HINDENBURG MURDERS

Max Allan Collins

BERKLEY PRIME CRIME, NEW YORK

This is a work of fiction. Names, characters, places, and incidents are
either the product of the author's imagination or are used fictitiously,
and any resemblance to actual persons, living or dead, business
establishments, events, or locales is entirely coincidental.

THE HINDENBURG MURDERS

A Berkley Prime Crime Book / published by arrangement with
the author

PRINTING HISTORY
Berkley Prime Crime edition / June 2000

The Penguin Putnam Inc. World Wide Web site address is
http://www.penguinputnam.com

ISBN: 0-425-17409-3

Berkley Prime Crime Books are published
by The Berkley Publishing Group,
a division of Penguin Putnam Inc.,
375 Hudson Street, New York, New York 10014.
The name BERKLEY PRIME CRIME and the BERKLEY PRIME CRIME
design are trademarks belonging to Penguin Putnam Inc.

PRINTED IN THE UNITED STATES OF AMERICA

10   9   8   7   6   5   4   3   2   1

To Joe Pittman—
for helping keep
the Collins balloon aloft

Though this work is fanciful, an underpinning of history supports the events depicted in these pages. The author intends no disrespect for the real people who inspired the characterizations herein, nor to take lightly the disaster that took so many lives, and brought an end to the golden age of the airship.

"A finger of intense radiance appeared suddenly on one of her sides, unfolded upwards with a swift blossoming, and pointed into the sky with a burst of glare. . . . "

—Leslie Charteris

"It must have been an infernal machine."

—Ernst Lehmann,
Hindenburg captain, from his deathbed

DAY ONE:

Monday, May 3, 1937

ONE

How the Hindenburg *Voyage Began in a Hotel, and Leslie Charteris Made New Friends*

Despite the elegant surroundings, it had all been vaguely demeaning—thirty-six well-heeled passengers scheduled to board the airship *Hindenburg,* herded into the main dining room of the Frankfurter Hof by Zeppelin Company representatives, quasi-military in their midnight-blue uniforms. There amid the hotel's tall mirrors and burnished mahogany columns, under the unforgiving eyes of customs officials in Nazi-style black-and-gray uniforms, baggage was screened by bulky X-ray machines, suitcase linings frequently knifed loose; sealed packages were rudely unwrapped, shaving kits disassembled, bon voyage candy boxes slitted open, perfume bottles uncorked, flashbulbs and flashlights and other dry-cell battery-operated gizmos seized like contraband.

The suspects at the end of a murder mystery were treated with more dignity.

That was a subject with which Leslie Charteris was well acquainted—murder mysteries—as the dapper Englishman was the creator of the popular "Saint" stories. At a muscular six-foot-two, with his monocle, Clark Gable mustache and jet-black, brushed-back hair, Charteris could easily have posed for book-jacket representations of his fictional Saint—Simon Templar, the "modern Robin Hood" who extracted booty (and vengeance) from criminals.

Despite the urbane veneer, however, the man in the chalk-line oxford-gray herringbone two-button suit conveyed an unmistakable air of the exotic. His thirtieth birthday little more than a week away, Charteris had been born in the British colony of Singapore, his mother English, his father a wealthy Chinese surgeon, which lent his handsome features a distinctly Eurasian cast.

He'd been born Leslie Charles Bowyer Yin (a descendant of Shang dynasty emperors) but had legally changed his name to that of his literary pseudonym, ten years or so before; "Charteris" was an expansion of "Charles," but also a nod to notorious gambler and rake Colonel Francis Charteris, founding member of the Hellfire Club.

Charteris was doing his best not to be annoyed; the day outside the hotel was a dreary, overcast one, drizzling intermittently, discouraging excursions to the Altermarkt or the Liebfrauenkirche or other Frankfurt tourist attractions. Several hours ago, the passengers had been gathered here and required to read and abide by a compendium of regulations far more restrictive than those of any ocean liner. And it was now four o'clock P.M., as this humiliating procedure dragged on—interesting treatment for passengers paying $400 one-way passage to America.

His two suitcases passed inspection, but there'd been a tense moment at the inspection table when the young Aryan customs agent had asked the author in perfect but stiltedly spoken English, "Are you a Communist or anarchist?"

And Charteris had replied, "Are there any other choices?"

This seemed to puzzle the lad, who was in the process of checking the author's passport and tickets, and Charteris had done his best to amplify: "Communists rarely wear suits from Savile Row, and as for anarchists, everybody knows they can be identified by their untidy whiskers and the round black bombs behind their backs—the ones with the sputtering fuses?"

The young Aryan was frowning now, but a trim, somber gentleman in his early forties, his graying blond hair combed back on an oblong head, stepped forward.

"This gentleman is a friend of mine," said the formidable fellow—whom Charteris had never seen before in his life.

The young customs agent nodded curtly, as if to a superior officer, though Charteris's rescuer, despite an obvious military bearing, wore a nondescript three-piece brown business suit.

As the pair of bags were tagged and stickered (a bold "C" for Charteris), the author was passed through. He sought out his savior—some passengers were pacing, others had taken seats at the linen-covered tables—and spied the gent standing by himself near an ornately gilt-framed mirror.

"Thank you," Charteris said to the man. "Comes in

handy having a friend in high places, doesn't it? By the way, what's your name?"

"Erdmann, Mr. Charteris." He extended a hand and the two men shook, firmly. "Oberst Erdmann . . . but my friends call me 'Fritz.' "

"Well, thank you, Fritz, for the assistance."

Charteris offered Erdmann a Gauloise from a silver cigarette case; the German accepted the smoke, Charteris plucked one out for himself, then—his lighter having been confiscated by the customs agent—reached for a book of Frankfurter Hof matches off a nearby table, lighting first Erdmann's cigarette, then his own.

"That young man doesn't have much of a sense of humor," Charteris said, exhaling smoke. "You'd think a civil servant in a country run by a man with a Charlie Chaplin mustache might enjoy a laugh."

The somber face creased in a smile, though the lines around the man's pale blue eyes did not tighten. "Mr. Charteris, your wit may be wasted on this trip. Things aren't as gay as they were on the maiden voyage of the LZ-129."

The LZ-129 was the *Hindenburg,* and Charteris had been among the celebrities on the maiden voyage just a year earlier. Precautions had been few, tickets and passports handled expeditiously.

"I appreciate the advice, Fritz, though it's a shame— that really was a lovely voyage. Did we meet, then, and I've somehow misplaced you in my memory?"

Smoke curled like a question mark in front of the German's face. "We haven't met, sir, but you are after all a famous man."

"What branch of the military are you in? Or do I have the privilege of speaking to a member of the S.S.?"

Another smile creased Erdmann's face. "What makes you assume I'm with the military?"

"You and those other two gentlemen"—Charteris pointed, discreetly—"are the only passengers whose luggage was not searched, and pockets not emptied."

". . . Luftwaffe."

"Ah. Security?"

"Strictly aboard as observers."

"Oh, of the topography of France and England, you mean?"

Erdmann sighed smoke. "The current political situation makes it a necessity to avoid France, and take a detour around England, by way of Holland. . . . Mr. Charteris, I hope you take my advice to heart. You could have been in a great deal of trouble if I had not interceded. Those 'customs agents' are S.D. officers."

Charteris frowned, glanced back at the customs table. "I know of the S.S., but I'm afraid the S.D. is new to me."

"The S.D. *is* the S.S.—the security branch. That young man you were . . . what's the term? Ribbing? That young man has the absolute ability to forbid embarkation to you or any passenger whose presence might be deemed by him 'detrimental'—without redress or refund."

"Well, I wouldn't have liked that at all. I'm heading to Florida for a birthday party . . . mine."

Erdmann bowed, slightly. "It's been a pleasure to meet you, Mr. Charteris."

"Call me 'Leslie,' please—after all we're old friends, aren't we, Fritz?"

Now at last the eyes joined Erdmann's mouth in a tight smile. "I'll have to read one of your books . . . they must be quite amusing."

With another half bow, Erdmann retreated, joining his two Luftwaffe comrades at a table.

Red-jacketed waiters had begun threading through the dining room, taking orders for, and serving, cocktails—to assuage the restlessness and annoyance of these put-upon passengers.

Charteris ordered a Scotch and water, specifying Peter Dawson, and leaned against a manteled wall, studying his fellow travelers, spotting no apparent Communists or anarchists at all among a group that seemed fairly evenly divided between English speakers—Brits and Americans—and Germans. The author could eavesdrop in these and several other languages, if necessary.

Most shuffled through the indignity of the baggage-check process without much ado, though one little fellow made Charteris's skirmish pale to insignificance.

Wearing a jaunty golf cap, bow tie, powder-blue suit with matching sweater vest and blue-and-white shoes, the small figure was at once dapper and clownish. His diminutive stature was emphasized by a gigantic dog on a leash who seemed to obey his master's every thought, much less command. The brown-and-black Rin Tin Tin–ish police dog was beautifully groomed and obviously highly trained, sitting and standing and moving through the customs line at seemingly subliminal prompts.

Charteris had seen the man, if not the dog, before, though he couldn't place him. The round face, the elfin features, reminded the author of comedian Bert Wheeler, of the Wheeler and Woolsey team, and somehow Charteris felt sure the sporty figure was in show business.

The little man, or anyway his dog, had attracted considerable attention, upon their entrance; but man and beast were unassuming enough as they waited on line. Tucked under the arm that controlled the dog's leash was a paper sack covering a gift-wrapped package, an oblong box probably containing a child's toy, and in his other hand he carted a good-size, battered blond suitcase haphazardly adorned with decals indicating years of European travel.

But upon reaching the head of the line, the little man with the big dog became a huge problem. The customs officials did not know what to make of the beast, whose master shrugged off their concerns by informing them, in German, that arrangements had been made for Ulla, which was the dog's name.

The same humorless young Aryan Charteris had encountered did not take kindly to the little man's dismissive manner. Tickets and passport were reluctantly deemed to be in order; then the customs agent pointed to the paper sack under the man's arm.

"What is in the box, Mr. Spah?"

"It is a gift for my daughters. Put it under your X-ray machine, but please don't spoil the gift wrap."

The young agent took the paper sack from the passenger and, without removing the gift-wrapped box, held it up and shook it.

"Please be careful!"

The agent sneered, ever so faintly, and withdrew the brightly wrapped package and began to tear off the colorful paper, like a greedy child at Christmas. Mr. Spah became agitated, throwing his hands in the air, making eye-rolling expressions of disgust, which his dog noted with stoic indifference—apparently it had seen its master worked up before.

The young agent withdrew the lovely Dresden doll, eyeing it suspiciously; he lifted its lacy skirt and had a peek underneath.

"It's a girl, dummkopf," Mr. Spah snapped.

The agent glared at Spah, then carted the doll to the bulky X-ray machine and had a look at its insides. Finally, the doll rudely dumped back into the ruined gift box, the package was handed back to Spah, who clicked his heels together and thrust his arm forward in a parody of the Nazi salute, replacing the *sieg heil* with a German variation of the Bronx cheer.

That was when Charteris—who was smiling around his dangling cigarette—remembered who the little man was.

The customs agent, embarrassed, infuriated, was glaring at Spah and his dog, clearly trying to decide whether to detain this passenger. Perhaps intimidated by the dog—who could have torn the young Aryan's throat open, quite easily, a sight Charteris at this stage might have relished—the agent curtly passed the passenger on.

"Ben Dova," Charteris said, approaching the man and animal, adding in German, "I saw you at the Crystal Palace in London."

The little man beamed; he had a wide smile that brightened up his entire face, like a switched-on lightbulb. Spah extended his free hand for a shake, which Charteris accepted, once he'd shifted hands with his Scotch and water.

"You prefer English or German?" the little man asked, in the latter.

"English, if you don't mind," Charteris said, in that language.

They sat at a small linen-clothed table, the police dog sitting beside his master at a tiny nod of a command.

" 'Ben Dova' is my stage name," the little man said, stroking the animal's neck. His German accent was faint. "I'm Joseph Spah—Joe. And you are?"

"Leslie Charteris."

Spah's elfin features bunched in thought. "I've heard that name."

"Perhaps you've read a 'Saint' story."

Spah snapped his fingers and his dog looked at him curiously, as if trying to translate that into a command. "The mystery writer. Not a reader myself, but my wife is."

"From that"—and Charteris nodded toward the unwrapped gift Spah had set on the table—"I deduce your family's in America. I might have thought you lived in Germany."

Spah shook his head, his expression one of disgust. "I'm a native of Strasbourg, but I've lived in the States for going on twenty years. Long Island."

"You working that dog into your act?"

The performance Charteris had taken in at the Crystal Palace had consisted of Spah's rather remarkable rubber-kneed drunk act, the comic acrobat doing various gymnastics with a post as his prop, playing an inebriated playboy in a tux trying to get a light from a gas street lamp.

Scratching the dog's head, Spah said, "It's a possibility. I could use a new routine, but first I'll have to pry him loose from my daughters."

"German shepherds are beautiful animals."

"I prefer to call her an Alsatian . . . though I'm still a German national, my loyalties lie elsewhere."

"You took a chance, razzing that customs agent. I've been told he's S.S."

"He can kiss my S.S. I'm never routing through Germany again—no more bookings there, either. Who needs it? I'm at Radio City, starting next week, for a solid month."

"That's an impressive engagement. You're very good, Mr. Spah."

" 'Joe,' please, make it 'Joe.' You prefer 'Leslie' or 'Les'?"

" 'Leslie,' I'm afraid. Anyone who'd suffer an affectation like this"—and he gestured to the monocle—"*has* to be a 'Leslie.' "

Spah laughed at that; the police dog was looking at Charteris, too, with what seemed a smile. "How do you keep that hunk of glass in, anyway?"

"Immense concentration and a dab or two of chewing gum. How do you travel with . . . what's her name?"

"Ulla," Spah said, petting the dog. "She'll be in a 'kennel basket,' they call it, a cargo compartment aft of the airship. I'm told they've had quite an assortment of animals on the *Hindenburg,* including antelopes. I only hope I'll be allowed to see Ulla a few times a day— seems cruel, otherwise."

"I wouldn't count on it. The way this is going so far, I'd say pampering the passengers has fallen off the *Reederei*'s list."

Deutsche Zeppelin-Reederei was the German name for the Zeppelin Transport Company.

Charteris was finishing up his Scotch and water. "Think I'll flag down a waiter for another. Can I get you something, Joe?"

"No thank you, Leslie." Spah rose and his dog snapped to attention. "Actually, I have to take Ulla out to the airport, early, to deal with the cargo people. I've hired a car . . . can't take her on the bus with the rest of you peasants."

"You show-business folk certainly do know how to live."

Spah and Ulla made their exit, other passengers smiling at them and tossing an occasional compliment—as the acrobat's ridicule of the customs agent had done all their hearts good—and Spah bowed comically, doffing his golfer's cap in a sweeping gesture that got him a few laughs . . . though not from the customs agents.

Charteris rose, to seek out a waiter and order another drink, pausing to light up another Gauloise.

"Can I bum one of those matches?" a rough-edged male voice inquired, in American-accented English.

"Certainly," Charteris said, turning to a ruggedly handsome apparent businessman of perhaps forty, seated at a table with another two of his ilk. Brown hair touched with gray, mustache thick but well trimmed, eyes gray blue and knowing, the businessman withdrew a Camel from a pack and allowed Charteris to light him up.

Without standing, the man introduced himself as Ed Douglas, and the other two men at the table gave their names as well—Nelson Morris and Burt Dolan, Americans with the flat slightly nasal tone of the midwest, fortyish, prominent-looking sorts in business suits that hadn't come off a rack. Charteris introduced himself and his name seemed to mean nothing to the trio.

"Join us?" Douglas asked.

"I was just going to commandeer a waiter and get something to drink—alcohol seems to be the only way to make this afternoon tolerable."

"He's on his way over," Douglas said, nodding toward a busy waiter. "Sit, why don't you?"

Charteris sat.

"I'm only in advertising," Douglas said, gesturing with cigarette in hand, "but my friends here are worth knowing—Burt's in perfume, and Colonel Morris's hobby is collecting meatpacking plants and stockyards."

"Perfume and steaks," Charteris said, shaking hands

all around. "Two ways to a girl's heart—I will have to get to know you boys. I may want some ammunition for a shipboard romance."

Morris, sturdy and distinguished looking, probably the oldest of the three, who had been studying Charteris, said, "Your name is familiar to me, sir."

Charteris explained that he was an author.

"Mystery writer, aren't you!" Morris said, grinning. He had the fleshiness that came with prosperity, but grooves had been worn in his face by a certain amount of nonsoft living. "What is it, what's your detective's name, don't tell me—the Saint! My wife reads your books."

Everybody's wife seemed to be reading him.

"Perhaps you know her, Mr. Charteris—Blanche Bilboa?"

"Oh! The musical-comedy star. No, I haven't had the pleasure, though I have seen her perform. You know, Mr. Morris, come to think of it, I believe I've heard of you, too."

"Not so formal, please, sir—call me 'Colonel.' "

Charteris managed not to smile at that, saying, "Well thank you, Colonel."

"Colonel in the army reserves," Douglas explained, with sarcasm so faint only Charteris caught it.

"Ah." To Morris, Charteris said, "And do call me 'Leslie.' Uh, forgive me, but weren't you formerly married to Jeanne Aubert, the actress?"

"That's true," Morris said, a little pride showing. Both his wives had been extremely attractive. *This boy* must *be rich,* Charteris thought.

"Is your lovely wife traveling with you?" Charteris asked. *Your most current lovely wife, that is,* he thought.

"No, Blanche has stage engagements in Paris that will

keep her there till June. She has no love of dirigibles, at any rate."

"I don't love them, either," Douglas said, exhaling Camel smoke, "after this horseshit treatment."

"It's not the *Reederei*'s fault, Ed," Morris said. "Dr. Eckener's at the mercy of these goddamned Nazis."

"I don't know about that, Colonel," Dolan said. The perfume magnate was smaller than his mates, a round-faced man with thinning blond hair. "I hear they've been using the *Hindenburg* to drop Nazi leaflets."

"Yes," Morris admitted, "and they showed off the airship at the Olympics, too, but that's not Dr. Eckener's fault—it's just the foul political waters he's forced to swim in, these days."

"Are you acquainted with Dr. Eckener, Colonel?" Charteris asked.

Dr. Hugo Eckener, avuncular head of the Zeppelin Company, was a world-famous figure whose name was synonymous with dirigibles. He had designed the massive *Hindenburg* to complement the renowned *Graf Zeppelin,* the airship that had over the past eight years established successful service between Germany and Brazil.

The *Hindenburg*—Eckener having been encouraged by his American partners in Akron's Goodyear-Zeppelin Corporation to establish a North American service—had flown ten flawless flights last year between Germany and the United States, plus seven nonstop flights to Rio de Janeiro. This would be the first of eighteen scheduled flights for 1937—transatlantic crossings were becoming routine.

"I'm proud to call Dr. Eckener my friend," Morris said, rather pompously. "I served in France, during the

Great War, and learned to fly, there—I've had an interest in aviation ever since."

"Now you've started him," Douglas said, waving at the waiter.

Morris went on, undaunted. "Dr. Eckener arranged, on one booked-to-capacity flight, for me to share quarters in the keel of the *Graf Zeppelin,* with its captain. . . . I love airship travel—no words can properly express the sensations."

"I met Dr. Eckener on the maiden voyage," Charteris said, flicking cigarette ash into a round glass Frankfurter Hof tray. "Got to know him rather well—and my impression is, no love is lost between him and the Nazis."

"Damn right," Morris said. "He despises his beloved zeps being used for Nazi propaganda."

"Nonetheless," Charteris said, "the *Hindenburg* and the *Graf Zeppelin* are the best weapons in the Nazis' public-relations arsenal. People do love dirigibles."

"Phallic symbols are always popular," Douglas said dryly.

"Will Dr. Eckener be along for this flight?" Dolan asked.

"I don't believe so," Charteris said. "My understanding is he's on the outs with the Reich."

"Kicked upstairs," Morris said glumly.

Charteris didn't know the idiom. "What's that?"

"Given some kind of honorary chairmanship. Captain Lehmann's the anointed one now, I hear—and he's along for the ride, this time."

"Glad to hear it," Charteris said. "They say Lehmann's the best airship captain alive."

Morris shrugged. "He's not captain, this time around. Merely observing—just for show, first flight of the season and all."

The waiter finally came over and said, in German, "Last call, gentlemen. The omnibuses to the airfield are here."

"What did he say?" Morris asked.

Charteris translated, and the men ordered their drinks.

The torturous afternoon of indignity and delay was over, the delights of travel by airship awaiting.

TWO

How the Hindenburg *Disembarked, and Leslie Charteris Met Two Women*

The burly majordomo at the front door of the Frankfurter Hof was as elaborately uniformed as a cast member of *The Student Prince,* rather a relief after the Nazi-ish attire of the customs officials. But the doorman was almost as officious, hustling the *Hindenburg* passengers through the drizzling rain to the three buses, shooing them aboard like schoolchildren late for class.

It was approaching seven P.M. and the lights of Frankfurt did their best to sparkle and twinkle in a dreary dusk. Charteris had managed to select a bus that included a drunken gentleman who was singing German folk songs from a seat toward the back. The author chose a seat toward the front.

The drunk had not been Charteris's only objective in

his forward-seat selection. Across the aisle from him was a rather Nordic-looking dark-blue-eyed blonde, in her early thirties, her frozen-honey locks worn up in Viking braids, a coiffure that only wide cheekbones and classic bone structure like hers could pull off. She was one of those pale beauties whose demeanor conveyed a stately beauty and whose near voluptuousness promised earthier delights. Like Charteris, she wore a belted London Fog trench coat and he was about to comment across the aisle about their mutual taste in rainwear when another woman came between them.

This new woman in his life was younger than sixty but not much, a slender, sparrowlike lady standing (in the aisle of the bus) barely five feet in her practical heels. She had been pretty once, but that prettiness had congealed into a pixie-ish mask, and her stylish attire bespoke both money and a desire to affect youth—white flannel suit narrowly pin-striped black, black gloves, black soupbowl chapeau with a long sheer shadowy veil designed to serve the same function as Vaseline on a movie lens aimed at a beautiful but aging actress.

"Would you mind terribly scooting over?" she asked ever so sweetly.

Charteris had taken the seat nearest the aisle, to obtain proximity to the Viking blonde, leaving the window seat empty.

"Not at all," Charteris said, and did so. He thought he caught the barest amused glimpse from the Viking—which was at least an acknowledgment by her that he was alive.

"Thank you, ever so," his new neighbor said, settling snugly into her seat. "I'm Margaret Mather—Miss."

She extended a ladylike gloved hand, which he took, introducing himself.

"Oh, the mystery writer! I do so enjoy your novels."

"Well, thank you."

She beamed beneath the veil. "The villains always receive their just deserts. Would that real life had the decency to perform the same service."

He squinted at her. "Are you an American, Miss Mather?"

"Born in Morristown, New Jersey, of all places. Now I consider myself a resident of the world."

"Do tell."

"My apartment is at the top of the Spanish Steps in Rome—from the second floor you can see St. Peter's."

"Really."

"But I spend most of my time in travel. I do so adore travel, flying in particular. The *Hindenburg* should suit me perfectly—all the comfort of a luxury liner, and none of the seasickness. . . . What takes you to America, Mr. Charteris?"

He was polishing his monocle on his handkerchief. "I've been maintaining residences in both England and America, for several years now. Large country estate in the former, a bungalow in Florida . . . or rather I *had* a bungalow in Florida."

"But no longer?"

Reinserting his monocle, he replied, "It's my wife's, now. My soon-to-be ex-wife."

"Oh, you're getting divorced? How terrible." But a distinct tinge of "How wonderful" colored her tone. "I do hope this is not too melancholy a time for you."

"Not at all, Miss Mather. My wife and I are parting friends. We have a wonderful daughter together, and we've agreed not to subject each other to any unnecessary unpleasantness."

"How very admirable." The smile again beamed beneath the veil. "How very civilized."

They were in the middle bus, which just now was pulling out behind the lead vehicle. The rumble of the engine joined with the rough music of tires on cobblestone streets, accompanying the drunken folk songs emanating from the rear. None of this racket prevented Miss Mather from filling Charteris in on her life.

Henry James might have written it. Like most spinsters, Miss Margaret Mather—"a direct descendant of Cotton Mather himself"—had a dead fiancé in her distant past, due to a sailing accident on Cape Cod, near her family's Quisset summer home. Her man's-man father had been a successful lawyer in New York who had once gone 'round the world by clipper ship ("So, you see, my seven-league boots come naturally to me"). After her father retired, the family joined her ailing brother in Capri; the brother recovered, became a professor of art at Princeton, while the family stayed behind. Her mother had died in 1920, and Miss Mather had cared for her father until his death in '29 at the ripe old age of ninety-four.

"I'm afraid I'm something of the black sheep of the family," she admitted, "with my two meager years of schooling—but I've learned so much in my travels, and I've written a bit of poetry."

"Ah."

"Perhaps I could impose on you, at some point on the voyage, to read some of my work—the opinion of a professional author would mean so much to me."

"Perhaps you could."

What she really loved to do, as she'd indicated, was fly—from the glimmering Mediterranean to the sand dunes of the Sahara, from the Albanian mountains to the capitals of Germany and France, she'd seen them all from the open cockpit of a two-seater, goggles and helmet against the wind.

"You sound like you could give Amelia Earhart competition," Charteris said. "When did you learn to fly?"

"Oh, I don't know how to fly, myself. I always hire a pilot."

Good-looking young male ones, he'd wager.

She continued her flirtatious chatter, letting him know what a woman of the world she was, as he took in the dusk-softened scenery through his rain-flecked window. Young tree toads sang in the farmlands they glided past; and as they neared the airfield, agriculture gave way to beech groves and pine stands, representative of that timeless bucolic Germany that seemed so incongruous in a country overrun with Nazis.

Miss Mather was noticing the scenery, too. "How enchanting, their green young leaves . . . May I share something rather personal with you, Mr. Charteris?"

"If you like."

She touched a gloved finger to a veiled cheek. "It may seem absurd, for one who loves travel and flight, as I do . . . but all this afternoon, I've felt a certain . . . uneasiness."

"Those thugs at the hotel would make anyone uneasy."

"Oh yes! Do you know they charged me for fifteen kilos of excess baggage? I pointed out that at ninety-eight pounds I weigh considerably less than the average man, and some compensation would seem logical—but I was told, 'It's the rule—only twenty kilos allowed.' "

"Does seem unfair."

"But no, no, Mr. Charteris, I don't think it's the dreadful gestapo that are giving me this sense of . . . what else can I call it but foreboding? Do you believe in premonitions?"

"Sometimes."

"Well, would I seem a silly girl if I told you, that when I gaze out at that lovely forest, I find myself thinking, 'What a beautiful farewell to earth' . . . ?"

She was trembling, almost on the verge of tears. He took her gloved hand in his and held it, rather tightly.

"It will be fine," he told her.

Beneath the veil, she smiled in gratitude and, for a moment, she was indeed a girl again, and a beautiful one.

They were passing through a town, now—or rather a town in progress. Identical white stucco houses, each with a red tile roof, stood along either side of the autobahn, with dozens more in the process of being built. This, Charteris knew, was Zeppelinheim—a planned village for zep crewmen and their families. Finally, beyond the village, over a bridge, as the trio of buses barreled down a slope, the vastness of the new Rhein-Main World Airport revealed itself.

Many new buildings designed for airplanes had been constructed here in recent days, for what was being planned as a combined airship and airplane harbor, to accommodate passengers from all around Europe seeking passage to North or South America.

But what set this airfield off from all others was the immense zeppelin hangar, a virtual Olympic stadium with a roof, a staggering thousand feet long and twenty stories high, seeming ghostly and unreal in the misty twilight. Just beyond the yawning doors of the hangar, floating on its nosecone tethers, was the great seamed silver ship, an impossibly small ground crew scurrying beneath, like ants carrying off some enormous gourd from a slumbering giant's picnic.

Miss Mather gasped in wonderment. "Forget what I said, Mr. Charteris. . . . Such majesty sweeps any of my doubts away."

The archness of his poetic companion aside, Charteris also felt a wave of elation roll through him. They would soon be boarding the largest aircraft ever to trade earth for the heavens, a ship only a few feet shorter than the fabled ocean liner *Titanic*.

Once through the main gate, the buses drew up along-side the hangar, where the passengers were again rudely herded by *Reederei* officials in paramilitary midnight blue, into the cavernous building, the inside of which was illuminated by arc lights—or least partly illuminated: the greenish glow gave way to shadow in the upper recesses of the man-made grotto.

Yet again the travelers were subjected to queuing up at a table where another group of Nazi-uniformed customs agents inspected tickets and passports, and checked one last time for lighters, flashlights or camera equipment (numerous books of hotel matches were confiscated). Dusk gave way to darkness as this tedious process continued, and Charteris approached his new old friend, Fritz Erdmann.

"Why all these precautions, Fritz?"

The Luftwaffe officer in mufti stood with arms folded, a posture more of supervision than observation. "Would you have the Zeppelin Company take chances with its passengers' safety? The *Reederei* have a flawless record; I'm sure they'd like to maintain it."

Very quietly, Charteris said, "It's a bomb scare, isn't it?"

Erdmann's eyes tightened in an otherwise impassive mask. "I told you before, Mr. Charteris . . . I'm merely an observer, here."

"Please, Fritz—it's 'Leslie' . . . and, since we're friends, I must beg you please not to insult my intelligence. Hydrogen is the most flammable, hottest-burning gas in the world . . . and that big silver sausage is filled with it."

"And that is why such careful precautions are being taken . . . excuse me."

But before Erdmann could wander off, Charteris gripped him by the arm. "Why the hell don't you people use helium, instead? Of course, you couldn't make as much money that way, could you?"

With cheap, buoyant hydrogen, the *Hindenburg* could lift an extra sixteen and a half tons of cargo and passengers than with inert helium, a gas so safe you could smother a fire with it.

"I'm surprised at your ignorance . . . Leslie." Erdmann plucked off the author's hand as if removing a bothersome insect that had landed there. "The Americans control the world helium market . . . and their government refuses to export it to us."

"Hell, that's a difficult one to figure. Who wouldn't want to help your man Hitler keep his airships safely flying?"

Erdmann chuckled hollowly. "I believe boarding is beginning, Mr. Charteris . . . Leslie. Perhaps you and your wry wit should make your way aboard."

Stewards in white jackets and dark ties were escorting the ladies the brief distance between hangar and zeppelin. Umbrellas were available for the men, as well, and Charteris snatched one and sidled up to the Viking blonde before one of the stewards could beat him to the punch.

"May I?" he asked, offering her an arm, tipping the umbrella's shelter above her.

She gazed at him with an amusement that wasn't as

detached as it pretended to be. Her full, lushly red-lipsticked lips pursed in a smile that was tantalizingly near a kiss.

But, as she'd said nothing, he repeated his question in German.

"We have not met," she said, in German-accented English.

"Well, then by all means we should. Allow me to introduce myself—I'm the man who's going to keep your lovely braids from getting damp. And you are?"

Now she laughed, lightly, and it was fluid, musical. "I am the woman who is going to allow you to do so."

They began to walk across the final expanse of hangar toward the drizzle and the airship.

"I thought you already had a female companion," she said, nodding toward Miss Mather, who was on the arm of a young steward.

"I think I'm a little old for her. By the way, my name is Leslie—Leslie Charteris."

"Hilda—Hilda Friederich. May I ask a favor, Leslie?"

"I hope you will."

"Could we go for a quick stroll on the airfield? I would like a better look at this balloon that promises to swallow us up."

"Certainly," he said, already liking this woman, who seemed as sharp as she was alluring. "After all, I'm sure Jonah would have appreciated a closer look at the whale."

Rain beating an uneven tempo on the umbrella, they walked out onto the runway, the plump silver airship looming; they couldn't seem to get far enough away from it to get a decent look at the beast. Finally they stopped and he tilted back the umbrella and they both gaped, unable even from this distance to take it all in without moving their heads side to side, a motion that seemed to express their disbelief. Monocle flecked with droplets, Charteris squinted behind the glass and opened his other eye wide as he surveyed the airship he and Hilda would soon be flying.

The overall impression was of a stupendous stream-lined seamed silver specter; but here and there were markings and mechanical manifestations that indicated this was indeed, for all its size, a man-made object. Per-haps a quarter of the way back from the nipplelike moor-ing cone, lower-case Old English lettering spelled out in red the designation: HINDENBURG. Almost directly below, underneath the belly of the flying whale, extended the boothlike control gondola, seeming ridiculously small. Moving aft, fairly low, lay a long narrow bank of obser-vation windows; farther aft, toward the final third of the ship, perched the propellers of an engine car, like a bug hopping a ride. Another such bug was farther aft still, but between it and its prop-driven predecessor, higher up, were bold block numerals: D-LZ129. Toward the tail, a rocketlike fin separated the rudder-bearing fins above and below—both of which wore the Nazi *hakenkreuz*—the swastika.

"It is impressive," Hilda said.

"Size isn't everything," Charteris pointed out, and—as she seemed to ponder this concept—walked her to-ward the ship, skirting puddles.

Despite the drizzle, the *Hindenburg* was not without spectators to see her off, prominent among them a de-tachment of Hitler youth in their Nazi uniforms, and a brass band in blue-and-yellow finery, their instruments festooned with matching streamers. Right now they were playing a German folk song, "Muss I denn?"—which, coincidentally, that drunk had already executed (in several senses of the term) on the bus.

A pair of puny-looking aluminum retractable stairways served as the gangway of the ship; between the two sets of hinged stairs, stewards collected umbrellas—the underbelly of the ship providing a roof away from the rain—as the passengers climbed up the flimsy steps into the *Hindenburg*.

Immediately, ooohs and aaahs of pleasant surprise drifted up the stairwell, as only passengers who (like Charteris) had flown this very ship before could have anticipated such splendid surroundings. Unlike the zeppelins that preceded her, the *Hindenburg* boasted two decks of luxury-liner lavish passenger accommodations. (Even the grand *Graf Zeppelin* had housed its passengers in a cramped gondola slung under the ship.)

At the first landing, Hilda paused—taking in the sleek modernity of the surroundings, the soothing pale peach-linen walls, the rich rust-color carpeting, the gleaming chrome railings—until Charteris guided her toward the stairs that led on up.

As they climbed, Hilda glancing back at him, Charteris said, "The bar and smoking room are that level—B deck. We're headed up to A deck, where the cabins and dining room are, and the observation area, so we can watch the world shrink as we lift off."

Hilda smiled and nodded at this news. She was still snugged into her trench coat, and Charteris admired the pistonlike action of what appeared to be a fine female bottom beneath.

At the top of the stairs, an ample aisle extended laterally across the ship. Charteris was pleased—in fact, relieved—to see that the bust of Marshal Paul von Hindenburg still held its position of prominence on a high central shelf overlooking this foyerlike area, off of which the cabins were accessed; Dr. Eckener had bragged to Charteris, on the maiden voyage, that he'd refused to replace the bust with one of *Der Führer*. Considering the repressive treatment the passengers had received going through customs, the author wouldn't have been surprised to see Hitler's glowering picklepuss in the place of the ship's namesake.

Charteris took Hilda's arm and—following behind several other passengers, who were still moving slow, taking it all in—escorted her to the starboard side, where a spacious lounge was outfitted with modernistic tables and chairs of an aluminum chrome so light a child could lift them.

The lounge—dominated by a huge mural-style wall map with sailing ships, denoting the routes of famous explorers—was bereft of the feature that had been its most popular item on the maiden voyage: the lightweight yellow pigskin-covered aluminum Bluthner baby grand piano, around which Charteris and his wife, Pauline, had so often stood as Captain Lehmann played. He and Pauline would offer slightly tipsy renditions of Cole Porter, to the delight of their fellow passengers. "Cheek to Cheek" had been their showstopper.

"Leslie," Hilda said. "Is something wrong?"

"No," he said, realizing he'd paused in reflection, now moving on, dismissing a pang of loss that he told himself was for the Bluthner baby grand but was in fact for his soon-to-be ex-wife. "Let's find a nice front-row seat."

Separated from the lounge by an aluminum railing, an observation deck ran the length of the starboard side (a similar one would be found portside). A number of passengers—Miss Mather among them—had found positions along this promenade. Padded upholstered rust-orange benches, now and then, sat at a right angle to the wall of big slanted windows, offering an aquariumlike view on the world below.

Right now that view was of the Nazi Boy Scouts and that blue-and-yellow-garbed brass band, as well as several dozen spectators—friends and relatives denied permission to go aboard before castoff, waving their bon voyages in the rain.

Charteris and Hilda had just taken one of the seats—barely room enough for two, but a pleasant sort of crowding, the author thought—when the brass band began to play "Deutschland über Alles."

"Ah," Charteris said, "we'll be casting off soon. . . . Would you like to remove your raincoat?"

"No, thank you. I rather enjoy this breeze."

The slanting windows were open, letting in cool evening air but no rain; even at cruising speed, Charteris knew, nasty weather could not find its way in these ingeniously rigged windows, which had a generous shelf-like sill. Unfortunately the blaring German band—somewhat off-key—was having no trouble getting in.

When the band had completed the ponderous anthem, the crowd applauded and cheered and whistled; above this clamor came a voice over the ship's loudspeakers, a blaring announcement in German that could be heard outside, as well.

"Will the wife of Colonel Erdmann please come forward!"

So Erdmann of the Luftwaffe was a colonel—but unlike the stockyard king from Chicago, Nelson Morris, Fritz hadn't bragged about the fact.

From the crowd stepped a slender woman in a green-and-white gingham dress and large-brimmed green straw hat, protecting herself and her stylish attire under an umbrella. Even at this distance, it was apparent that Mrs. Erdmann was a strikingly attractive woman. A steward ran to greet her and escort her to the ship, the pair walking out of view from the promenade windows.

"Privileges of military men," Charteris muttered, glancing around to see if Erdmann was on this side of the ship.

He was, but not with the others, at the slanted windows—the Luftwaffe colonel had taken a seat, by himself, in the lounge area, which was otherwise unpopulated, his hands folded on the table, his expression an odd amalgam of glum and anxious.

Soon the woman in green and white emerged on A deck, appearing like an apparition; and she was indeed striking, Charteris noted—brunette, slenderly shapely, her face a pale oval, as perfect and lovely as the image on a cameo brooch.

Erdmann sprang to his feet and she rushed to him. They embraced, not kissing, not speaking, just clutching each other with a passionate intensity that caused most of the passengers witnessing this private moment to turn away, out of respect, or embarrassment.

But Charteris watched. As an author, he had trained himself to observe and this farewell was both touching and unusual. Erdmann's wife was grasping her husband so tightly her knuckles had whitened; and when they finally drew away, her face was streaked with tears. He withdrew a handkerchief from his suitcoat pocket, dried her face with it, then pressed it into her hand. They kissed, briefly, and he walked her toward the stairs, both of them disappearing from view.

Charteris caught Miss Mather's gaze, down the promenade; the spinster was frowning as her eyes sent him a question: *Had Erdmann, too, had a premonition?*

"What do you make of such an emotional *auf wiedersehen*?" Hilda asked.

Charteris shrugged. "That gentleman is involved with
ship security. He may know something we don't."

"I cannot say I like the sound of that."

"I can't say you're alone."

Then a voice blared over the loudspeaker, first
German, then English: "*Schiff hoch!* Up ship!"

The band began to play again, a reprise of the national
anthem; figures were scurrying below, loosening mooring
lines, unhooking the nose cone at the bow, searchlights
on the field fanning the great ship as if at a motion-
picture premiere. Diesel engines sputtered to life, but on
the observation deck, the sound seemed muffled, even
remote.

Down on the runway, Mrs. Erdmann had not rejoined
the crowd—she stood closer to the ship than anyone else,
staring up at the windows, waving with the handkerchief
her husband had given her to dry her tears. And indeed
Erdmann stood at the promenade windows, now, staring
down at his wife, his hand raised in a frozen wave that
uncomfortably resembled a Nazi salute.

Then Mrs. Erdmann and everyone else on the airfield
grew smaller.

THREE

How the Hindenburg *Floated into the Night, and Leslie Charteris Shared a Cabin*

At 8:15 P.M. the *Hindenburg,* on a northwesterly course, making for the Rhine River at Cobenz, sailed into an overcast-cloaked twilight. Below, the Hitler youth belied their adult uniforms and became the children they were, running after the silver airship as it rose, as if pursuing a balloon whose string had slipped through their fingers. Nazi caps flew from their heads as they raced after the shrinking ship, until the airfield fence at the pinewoods brought a sudden stop to their carefree chase. The hatless boys gazed up at the great ship, an airfield searchlight holding its circular beam on the tail fin where rode their beloved swastika; then the spotlight switched off, ship and symbol disappearing into the gathering darkness.

In the well-lit world of A deck on the *Hindenburg,*

Charteris and his new friend, Hilda Friederich, were standing at the windows now, the author catching the young woman, when she seemed to lose her balance.

"I am sorry," she said, breaking from the brief embrace. "I'm afraid I am a trifle dizzy. . . ."

"It will quickly pass," Charteris said, knowing this reaction was typical of dirigible departure, a momentary disorientation caused by the sight of the ground swiftly receding and the people below growing smaller and smaller, combined with the absence of any sense of motion, of any awareness of being airborne.

He himself did not experience this sensation, however; to Charteris, there was only a feeling of buoyancy, a lightness, as if gravity had suddenly lessened. The start of a journey by any other mechanical means—airplane, railway, motorcar, tramway—could not compare with the smoothness, the effortlessness, of a zeppelin casting off.

For a few minutes Charteris and Hilda stood at the windows, watching the darkened forests and farmlands of southern Germany glide by, stroked by the airship's single spotlight, like a prison searchlight seeking an escaped felon. The lights of farmhouses and an occasional ancestral castle would flicker through the darkness, and now and then a speeding train would reveal itself, throwing sparks from its smokestack, bidding the zep hello by way of its long mournful whistle. The drone of wind stirred by the airship's cruising speed of eighty knots drowned out any engine sound, adding to the surreal effect of sightseeing by night.

A familiar voice just behind him caught Charteris's attention: Ed Douglas, the advertising man, had flagged down a white-jacketed steward.

"Where's this fabled smoking room, anyway?" Douglas demanded. "And can a man get a drink there?"

Charteris could see Douglas's companions—Colonel Morris and Burt Dolan—seated in the lounge, waiting and watching with anticipation as their emissary went forward.

The steward, a narrow-faced youth of perhaps twenty-two, said, "The smoking lounge is below us, on B deck, sir—and, yes, there's a fully outfitted bar."

"Good! Where exactly?"

"Starboard side, all the way back, sir—"

Douglas had turned away, heading back to his friends, when the steward called out to him.

"But, sir! For certain technical reasons, the smoking room cannot be opened until we've been aloft for three hours."

"What? The hell you say!"

"Safety precaution, sir. The bar *is* open—you see, you enter the smoking room through an air-lock door in the bar."

Douglas's mustache twitched with irritation. "All right, then. Least we can drown our damn sorrows."

"There will be a light supper served, sir, in the dining room, at ten P.M."

"I'll be drinking mine."

The advertising man returned to his comrades to report this dire news, the steward moving on. Charteris and Hilda, who had both overheard this exchange, shared a smile.

"How terrible to be held so under tobacco's sway," Hilda said.

"I have to admit," Charteris said, "I'm little better. But I take solace in knowing that, prior to the *Hindenburg,* there was no smoking at all on zep flights. . . . Would you like me to help you find your cabin?"

"I would."

They were almost neighbors. Charteris had been as-
signed cabin A-49/50 near the portside stairs, and Hilda
was in A-31/32, just down the narrow hall a few doors.
After the spacious promenade and lounge, these window-
less, glorified closets came as something of a shock—
they were no better, or for that matter no worse, than a
first-class railway sleeping car.

Hilda's room—if a six-and-a-half-by-five-and-a-half
cubicle could be so designated—had pearl-gray linen
walls, a rose in a wall vase, cupboards over a fold-out
washstand; her suitcase was on a small fabric-and-
aluminum stand and an aluminum ladder, drilled with
circular holes to lessen its weight, leaned against the top
bunk.

"Bathrooms and shower are on B deck," Charteris said.

"A shower on an airship? That must be a first."

"Oh, it is—but there's only one, so you have to make
a reservation, I'm told."

"Well," she sighed, surveying her tiny world, "at least
I do not have a roommate."

Charteris leaned an arm against the bunk. "Would you
like one?"

She had been just about to finally undo the belt of her
trench coat, but now she paused, smiling faintly, as if
thinking better of it.

"You are rather bold, are you not, Mr. Charteris?"

He leaned forward, just a bit, and kissed her on her
full mouth—a short but promising kiss, which she accepted, if not quite returned.

"At times," he said.

Smirking in a not unfriendly manner, she placed her
hands on his chest and pushed him gently toward the
door. "Perhaps you should check out your own quarters
before trying to replace them."

"Fair enough . . . Shall I stop by just before ten? We could have supper together."

"What, and eventually breakfast?"

"Now who's bold?"

She squeezed her pulchritude past him, reached around to grasp the sliding door's handle and gently nudged him out. "I'll meet you at the dining room at ten."

"It's a date."

"No it is not—it is just supper."

She closed the door on him—and over her wicked little smile—and he walked to his cabin grinning, whistling a jaunty tune (one he'd worked out for the Saint, should those Hollywood people ever come through on their promises). He opened his cabin door with the key provided in a *Reederei* "Welcome Aboard" packet given the passengers at the hotel during the customs process, and found quarters identical to Hilda's, with two exceptions.

First, the linen-covered panels of his cubicle compartment were beige, rather than pearl gray.

And second, he did have a cabin mate.

The man was lanky, blond hair slicked back like an Aryan George Raft, with a pale, narrow, well-grooved, sharp-featured face including eyes so light a blue they almost disappeared. He wore a tan suit and orange tie and was probably pushing forty.

"I guess we are in this together," the man said in German, with a ready smile. He was putting a suitcase up on the top bunk, Charteris's bag already resting on the single luggage stand.

"Leslie Charteris," the author said, extending his hand.

"Knoecher—Eric Knoecher." He took Charteris's hand in an indifferent grip. "I'm from Zeulenroda."

"That's in Germany?"

"Yes. Are you English?"

Charteris nodded. "I live outside London. I'm a writer by trade."

"Really! I'm in the import business. You speak German well. . . . I know some English, if you prefer. . . ."

"German is fine."

"No, please—I can always use the practice." Carefully, thoughtfully, Knoecher asked, in English, "What sort of books do you write?"

"Mystery novels. Thrillers."

Knoecher raised his eyebrows, impressed. "I don't read much fiction but I know such books are popular. Well—what are we to do with these cramped quarters?"

"Sleep. I think we're expected to spend our upright time in those spacious public rooms."

"They are very nice. . . . By the way, you can have the top bunk, if you like. I just was looking for someplace to stow my suitcase."

"No, this is fine." Charteris sat on the lower bunk; Knoecher was standing, arms folded, leaning back against the washstand wall. "I'm a little surprised to have company, though, since I understand this flight is underbooked."

"Is that right?"

Charteris nodded. "I think they're only a little more than half capacity. There should be plenty of cabins."

Knoecher frowned in thought. "Well, perhaps we could complain."

"I don't mind the company, Eric, if you don't. Besides which, I'm endeavoring to make the point moot by getting into the good graces of a lady passenger I recently met. She *doesn't* have a roommate—yet."

"Ah! A shipboard conquest, so early?"

Charteris smiled, shook his head; like Ed Douglas, he

was craving a smoke. "Early stages, and I don't like to think of it as a 'conquest'—that's so ungentlemanly. Rather a . . . new friend that I hope to make."

This remark was not lost on the German, who grinned; his English was good enough to grasp the double entendre.

A sharp knock interrupted their conversation. Charteris rose and opened the door to find a familiar figure—Chief Steward Heinrich Kubis, whom the writer had become well acquainted with on the ship's maiden voyage.

"Welcome, Mr. Charteris," the chief steward said. His German-accented English was impeccable.

"Heinrich! I rather hoped you'd be aboard." Charteris put one hand on his friend's shoulder and extended the other for a warm clasp.

Looking past Charteris to his cabin mate, the steward said, "I hope I am not intruding, gentlemen."

"You're a welcome sight," Charteris said.

In his late forties, about five-foot-nine, dark blond hair brushed back, bright blue eyes perpetually atwinkle, Kubis was a cheerful, suave veteran of such fashionable hotels as the Carlton in London and the Ritz in Paris. He had also been the first steward ever to serve aboard an airship.

Charteris introduced Knoecher to the chief steward, and after some polite small talk, Kubis said, "Captain Lehmann would be honored to welcome you aboard, personally, Mr. Charteris. If you would come with me, sir . . ."

In the narrow hallway, the chief steward said, "I just finished your book."

"Really? Which one?"

"*The Saint in New York.* Exciting, if a bit bloodthirsty."

They walked· single file in the cramped corridor, the steward leading the way, glancing back as they conversed. Charteris was amused by Kubis, who catered to famous passengers, keeping up on all the society columns.

"I appreciate the business, Heinrich. Did you read it in German or English?"

"German. Very good translation, sir."

"Yes, I've taken a look at the German versions—the fellow they're using isn't bad. Is it true Captain Lehmann is merely observing on this flight?"

"Yes, sir."

"How many captains do you need on one trip?"

"Well, this time we have five, sir."

"Five!"

"There are more airship captains available, at present, than airships—but we hope, with this new American sister fleet imminent, that may all change."

Charteris had supposed they were headed to the control gondola, but Captain Lehmann was instead waiting in the chief steward's office on B deck, starboard, near the tiny bar and the much-yearned-for, still-off-limits smoking room.

The office also served as Kubis's quarters, which were about twice the size of a passenger cabin, but nonetheless hardly spacious, with both a cot and a desk, flush against opposite walls. After ushering Charteris into the cubbyhole, Chief Steward Kubis departed, both as a practical matter of space, and out of respect to these two men.

Captain Lehmann rose from the desk to greet the author with a smile and a handshake. The captain looked smaller in civilian clothes—a gray three-piece suit and darker gray bow tie. Suddenly Charteris realized the fiftyish Lehmann was an unprepossessing figure out of his usual snappy midnight-blue captain's uniform—short, stocky, his thin dark graying hair combed back, Lehmann seemed an unlikely candidate for war hero or principal director of the Zeppelin Company, both of which he was.

Lehmann had struck Charteris, on the ship's maiden voyage, as a kindly, soft-spoken father figure, with a surprising wellspring of good humor, as demonstrated by entertaining the passengers with his accomplished piano and accordion playing. Around his eyes and mouth were lines etched by a lifetime of smiles; but in the pale blue eyes in the egg-shaped face, a new melancholy seemed to have settled.

Charteris knew, at once, something was wrong.

"Please sit down, Mr. Charteris," the captain said in German, and the conversation that followed was in that tongue. Lehmann gestured to the cot, adding, "Forgive the limited seating."

Charteris sat. "I'm delighted to see you again, Captain—though I'm disappointed you're not at the helm, this trip."

"That's a luxury an executive like myself can rarely, if ever, indulge in," Lehmann said. "You'll meet Captain Max Pruss, and you'll like him—no nonsense, confident . . . I trained him myself. Former *Graf Zeppelin* captain."

"Do you miss it?"

"Do you think I would willingly trade hands-on airship command for overseeing passenger operations and crew recruitment?"

"No. But I rather supposed Dr. Eckener enjoyed that kind of thing—has he retired?"

Lehmann shook his head, wearily. "It's very sad, Mr. Charteris. Very sad indeed—we worked as comrades for almost thirty years, but politics has ruined all that."

"Dr. Eckener alienated himself with the brownshirt boys, I take it."

"Yes. And he assumes, wrongly, that I am one of them—he calls me a Nazi, and many others in the company, loyal zeppelin men, he condemns as 'collaborators.' "

"Eckener is a wonderful man, but blunt, not to say irascible."

"He is indeed all of those things. I assure you I am not a Nazi, Mr. Charteris, not a party member—I seek only to keep our ships flying in troubled skies."

"The atmosphere has changed, since my previous voyage," Charteris said, and briefly filled Lehmann in on the indignities of the customs process.

Lehmann shook his head forlornly, at this report. "I do so regret that. I remember fondly the good times we had on the maiden voyage, you and your lovely wife. . . . I am sorry to hear that you and Pauline have parted."

"On friendly terms." He adjusted his monocle. "She abided my wandering eye longer than most women would. The fault was mine, entirely."

"Forgive me for prying into personal matters."

"Not at all, Captain. May I do the same?"

"Certainly."

"Your boy was ailing, when last we spoke. An inner-ear infection, I believe. Is he well?"

Lehmann smiled tightly; there was no mirth in it. "Marie and I lost Luv, Easter Sunday last."

"No! Oh my God, Ernst. I am so very sorry."

As a father himself, dealing daily with mere separation from a beloved child, Charteris knew how deeply such a tragedy could wound.

And now the author understood the sadness in this gentle soldier's eyes—how a warrior who had won the

Iron Cross, twice, could become that most pathetic of figures, a heartbroken parent.

"We suffer our sorrows," Lehmann said, "and yet we go on—you write, I fly. There is escape in work."

"There is indeed."

The captain shifted in the hardwood chair. "I invited you here for more than social reasons, Mr. Charteris—much as I enjoy your company. As you know, we have an increased security presence on this ship."

"Yes—I met Colonel Erdmann."

Lehmann nodded. "Colonel Erdmann mentioned to me—in a friendly way, I might add—that you expressed to him some concerns . . . specifically, about the possibility of a bomb scare."

"The precautions being taken suggested as much."

"I'm sorry to hear that, because loutish security men, causing a commotion about possible sabotage, can be as damaging to the Zeppelin Company as the discovery of a bona fide bomb."

"Were you warned that a bomb might be aboard?"

Lehmann sighed. "You should know, Mr. Charteris, that virtually no zeppelin flight, particularly in these difficult days, goes untouched by such concerns. Time bombs have been uncovered a number of times on zeppelins in the past—the *Bodensee,* the *Nordstern,* recently on the *Graf Zeppelin.* Even the Americans had a sabotage problem, with their *Akron.* The S.D. have an increasingly challenging task to protect our passengers from enemies of the Reich."

"I should think," Charteris replied, with mock innocence. "After all, there are so many enemies to choose from, when so many nations are alienated, so many people of various racial, political and religious backgrounds are persecuted."

Lehmann managed another smile—a tired one. "I personally have no problem with such talk, Mr. Charteris, and though I might agree with you in at least some instances, certainly you'll understand my need for . . . discretion."

"Certainly."

Now Lehmann frowned. "What I don't know is if you understand *your* need for it. Discretion, I mean."

". . . I see."

"Perhaps you don't. The gentleman sharing your cabin, Mr. Knoecher—the importer?"

"Yes?"

"What he imports, Mr. Charteris, is information. He is an undercover S.D. agent."

"Oh."

" 'Oh' indeed. The *Reederei* was instructed to provide Mr. Knoecher to you, as your cabin mate."

"Why in heaven's name?"

"Because you are outspoken. Mr. Knoecher is not aboard this ship seeking a bomb—his specialty, I understand, is ferreting out information about both his fellow countrymen and foreigners who do business in Germany."

"What sort of information?"

"Perhaps you can make certain assumptions yourself. But those with skeletons in their closets—racial, political, religious skeletons, to quote you—might do well to steer Mr. Knoecher a wide path."

Charteris shifted on the cot. "Well. Thank you for the warning. He certainly seemed pleasant enough—even innocuous."

"Yes. That is his . . . special gift." Lehmann rapped on the desk, with the knuckles of his right hand. "I hope you will keep in mind that we never had this conversation.

Should Mr. Knoecher and those he works for learn of my . . . indiscretion, in sharing this information with you . . . I could well be added to his list."

Touching his heart with an open hand, Charteris said, "Ernst, I'm grateful to you—though I doubt I have anything to fear, from Mr. Knoecher."

"Mr. Charteris, everyone has something to fear from the likes of Mr. Knoecher."

A knock at the door seemed to put a period at the end of the captain's sentence.

"Yes?" Lehmann called, in a firm, loud voice that reminded Charteris this man had indeed been a captain and a soldier.

Chief Steward Kubis peeked in. "Captain, I apologize for interrupting, but there is a matter I wonder if you would mind handling—I prefer not to bother Captain Pruss at this stage of our voyage."

"Understood. How can I be of help?"

"One of our passengers insists that he must feed his dog himself."

"His dog?"

Charteris, still seated on the cot, said, "I think you're about to meet Joseph Spah, more popularly known as Ben Dova."

And Spah, who'd been waiting in the hallway, squeezed his compact frame past the chief steward and joined Charteris and Captain Lehmann in the cramped cabin. The little man in the powder-blue suit and matching sweater-vest had a wooden bowl lettered ULLA in one hand and a bag of dog food tucked under his other arm.

"Captain, forgive my rudeness," the acrobat said in German, then he noticed Charteris and said, in English, "Ah! My friend the mystery writer! Leslie, perhaps you will help me convince the good captain that only *I* can feed my dog."

"I think you'll find Captain Lehmann a reasonable sort," Charteris said, not wanting to get involved.

Back to German, Spah continued, words tumbling out of him, "This is the *Reederei*'s responsibility, Captain. I wanted to ship my dog to New York by steamer, but your people at the ticket office talked me into shipping Ulla on your zeppelin. They said many, many animals had made the trip, birds, dogs, cats, fish, even deer, no problem. They promised I could feed and handle my dog myself—she's young and skittish and must be frightened back in your dark hold."

"I understand your concern, Mr. Spah," the captain said, "but I'm sure your dog will be well cared for."

"You don't understand, Captain—this dog is royalty! She is Ulla von Hooptel, with pedigree papers!"

"Everyone's a 'von' in Germany these days," Charteris said dryly, catching the chief steward rolling his eyes, "even the dogs."

Patiently, the captain said, "Mr. Spah, your dog is in our animal freight room—that's all the way aft at Ring 62. It's a precarious passage."

"Not for an acrobat!"

"He's right, Captain," Charteris said, and explained who Spah was.

"For months I've trained Ulla for my act," Spah said. "She leaps at me from behind, and I pretend to fall down. She won't know what to do without me! She's such a sweet dog, Captain—please!"

Lêhmann chuckled, as if having a problem so petty were a relief after talk of bombs and Nazis.

"Mr. Kubis, escort Mr. Spah to his dog."

Charteris stood. "Is it all right if I tag along, Captain?

I'm not an acrobat but I think I can maintain my footing. Always wanted a glimpse at the innards of this beast."

Lehmann shrugged, standing, saying, "I see no harm. Mr. Charteris—we'll spend more time together, as the trip progresses."

With another handshake, Charteris said, "I hope so, Captain."

Soon Chief Steward Kubis was leading Spah and Charteris down the B-deck keel corridor, unlocking a door that led onto the lower gangway, which the steward illuminated with a flashlight.

They were traversing nothing more than a blue-painted plank of aluminum. Here within the zeppelin's dark interior, the thrumming of diesel engines was distinct, a powerful presence.

"Passengers are never allowed back here unaccompanied," the steward told them, as his flashlight found the gangway before them. "Afraid there's not much to see at night, Mr. Charteris."

Indeed the bones of the flying whale—struts and arches and wires—could barely be made out in the darkness. There was only a sense of vast black emptiness all around. It took five minutes to reach the stern, where— within a netted-off baggage area—the dog sat in an enclosed wicker basket.

Spah, speaking baby talk to the police dog, let her out and she nipped playfully at him, barking joyfully. Hugging the dog, Spah almost fell backward, acrobat or not, and Charteris caught him, steadying him on the shelflike floor of the baggage area.

Swallowing, holding the animal close to him (she was damn near as big as he was), Spah muttered, "What would happen if we fell?"

The chief steward said, "You would tear through the

linen skin, most probably, and hurtle seven hundred feet into the Rhine."

They fed and gave water to the dog and returned her to her wicker basket, then left to rejoin the well-lighted world of the passenger area. It was almost ten o'clock and humans had to eat, too.

FOUR

How the Hindenburg *Delivered the Mail, and Leslie Charteris Slept Alone*

From the portside promenade, which had slanting windows identical to those on the starboard side, Charteris and Hilda stood looking down at the glitter and glow of Cologne at night. Before long, silhouetted against the manufacturing center's expansive profusion of lights, the Gothic towers of the city's famed cathedral revealed themselves, stretching toward the airship like ghostly fingers.

"It is a lovely sight," Hilda sighed.

"Yes it is," Charteris said, but he was looking at her.

She wore a white silk shantung tunic dress with black buttons that angled across her full bosom and then marched down the side of her skirt in a straight line. He found her utterly bewitching, her braided blonde hair and deep blue eyes and creamy complexion and full lips and full figure, rounding as it did, and narrowing, and flowing, at the precisely correct places. . . .

She caught him staring at her. "Is something wrong?"

"Nothing is wrong. Not on the earth or in the heavens."

"Well, you look very nice, yourself, Leslie—you seem to be the only man who bothered dressing for dinner."

He was in his tuxedo, which seemed none the worse for the half day it had spent folded up in his valise. "Less would have been an insult to such charming company."

She laughed, a throaty, endearingly unfeminine laugh at that. "What is it the Americans say? Baloney!"

He laughed, too. "Coincidentally, I think that's what we're having for tonight's late supper."

Stewards were setting up a buffet of cold meats and cheeses and salads in the nearby dining room, which—like the lounge on the starboard side—was separated from the observation deck only by an aluminum railing.

"Shall we sit for a few moments?" Charteris asked, gesturing to the nearby orange-upholstered bench for two, which made a right angle to the row of windows.

"Why don't we?" she said, and sat.

Settling in next to her, Charteris said, "We don't really know much about each other, do we? Except that we're both terribly attractive."

The teeth in her smile were perfect and white; beneath all her sophistication, she had the beauty and form of a healthy farm girl. "I gather from remarks I have overhead that you are a famous author."

"So famous you've never heard of me."

"Others obviously have. But I am afraid I do not read mysteries."

He slipped an arm behind her along the top of the two-seater. "Since I've already stolen a kiss, I feel rather awk-

ward asking, but . . . who are you, Hilda Friederich?
Germany's biggest movie star, perhaps, or are you her
most lovely Mata Hari?"

"Nothing so romantic. I am a secretary, a private secretary, to a vice-president at Bundesbank in Frankfurt."

"Ah—and you've sampled some of the goods, and
have a bag of hot cash back in cold storage, and you're
heading to America for a new life."

"Nothing so daring. I have a sister in New Jersey—
Trenton. She married an American businessman last year,
and has just had a baby. I am using my vacation to visit
and help out for a few weeks."

He shrugged. "I don't know—that sounds romantic
and daring to me. Are you political at all, Hilda?"

The dark blue eyes flared, eyelashes flying up like a
window shade. "Heavens no."

"You have no opinion on the current upheaval in your
country."

"What good would it do me if I did?"

"A very practical attitude."

Passengers had begun to line up at the buffet; it was
rather crowded.

"Do you mind if we just sit here awhile, my dear?" he
asked her. "And let that queue thin out a bit?"

"I don't mind in the least. The company is pleasant
and you are keeping your hands more or less to yourself."

"I'm not much for buffets. They make me feel rather
like a barnyard animal squeezing in at the trough." He
frowned, sensing something. "I say—have we stopped?"

"I don't know." Hilda narrowed her eyes, cocked her
head. "It is so hard to tell on this ship. But it does seem
as though we are floating. . . ."

"We have stopped. I don't hear the engines."

Again the advertising man, Ed Douglas, flagged down

a steward, demanding to know the reason for the delay. The steward—a different one, but equally young and polite—explained that the ship was parachuting a mail sack down.

"Good Lord, man," Douglas said, a hefty drink in one hand, "we just came aboard! Who the hell's had time to write a goddamn letter!"

The steward merely apologized and the irritable Douglas—*This man needs a cigarette!* Charteris thought—rejoined his business-magnate friends Morris and Dolan, already seated in the dining room.

"Look!" Hilda said, pointing.

A spotlight from the city a thousand feet below had picked up on the parachute-adorned mail sack, floating its lazy way to the ground. It was easy to make out people in the streets gazing up at the drifting mailbag, and at the ship, waving and yelling. The sound of the latter was faint, like a distant radio station fighting to come in.

"What Mr. Douglas doesn't realize," Charteris told her, "is how profitable it is for the Zeppelin Company to make that little mail run."

"How so?"

"Stamp collectors pay pretty prices for cards and envelopes with *Hindenburg* postmarks. Remember when the *Graf Zeppelin* went to the Arctic for scientific exploration? Stamp collectors underwrote the expedition."

"How terribly well informed you are."

He slipped his arm down from the shelf of the seat behind her until his hand was cupping her shoulder. "I'm merely desperate to impress you. We have such a short time for our shipboard romance. We simply must get started."

The red-lipsticked mouth pursed into its kiss of a smile. "Do you have any shame at all, Mr. Charteris?"

"Oh, yes—but it's safely stowed away for the duration of the voyage."

Soon Charteris, with Hilda on his arm, strolled into the long, narrow dining-room area, the buffet table set up just inside and along the promenade railing. The congenial atmosphere was highlighted by colorful images painted directly onto the beige linen wall panels—picturesque views of scenes as seen from a zeppelin flight between Friedrichshafen and Rio de Janeiro. White-jacketed stewards threaded swiftly and silently around tables draped with white linen and carefully arrayed with sterling silverware and elegant gold-edged china bearing the *Deutsche Zeppelin-Reederei* crest—a white zeppelin outlined in gold on a blue globe; individual lamps on each table cast cones of soft yellow light and small vases held freshly cut flowers.

The author and his blonde companion moved past a mother and father with two sleepy little boys sitting at a table for four. Along the wall were cozy tables for two, but other couples had beaten them to these prize spots. Perhaps they'd lingered too long at the observation windows.

The captain—that is, Captain Max Pruss, whom Charteris had yet to meet—sat at the head of a long table with Miss Margaret Mather at his right. A pleasant-looking blond man in his forties, in the crisp midnight-blue uniform that had once been Lehmann's, Pruss was drinking mineral water and nibbling at a sandwich, and seemed distracted. Miss Mather was the only female at a table seating twenty men, including a rather glum-looking Fritz Erdmann, seated toward the end with his two fellow Luftwaffe officers-in-mufti.

Several college-age men were seated near Miss Mather, and she was chattering like a schoolgirl, very animated, eliciting expressions ranging from amusement to horror. The boy next to her was keeping her wineglass full, which reminded Charteris how desperate a young love-starved college boy can get.

Surprisingly, Captain Ernst Lehmann was not seated with Captain Pruss (who within five minutes took his leave, anyway). He was instead ensconced with his new friend Joseph Spah, at a round table set for six. Also seated there was a handsome dark-haired gent in his late fifties, in a dark suit that had been expensive, when purchased perhaps five years before; and next to the gent, in a blue silk gown attractively draped over a nice shape, sat a pretty blonde who (judging by their affectionate, knowing manner with each other) was either his sweetheart or his wife, though she was easily twenty years younger. The group had been served wine but had not gone through the buffet as yet.

"It's the Saint!" Joe Spah called out in English. "Come sit with us, Saint."

Embarrassed, Charteris guided Hilda to the table, not necessarily eager to join Spah's party, but wanting to quiet the little man down.

"Please, you and your lovely friend, please sit, sit, sit!" Spah said as if to his dog. He was on his feet, waving his arms. He'd been drinking, just a bit.

"Do please join us," Lehmann said, standing, with all the dignity Spah lacked.

"Yes, by all means," the dark-haired gent said in a heavily German-accented but eminently understandable English—half rising to show his respect. "Both my wife and I are avid readers of your stories, Mr. Charteris. We would be honored."

"My pleasure, sir," Charteris said to him, pulling out a chair for Hilda. "We gratefully accept your invitation, particularly since these are about the only seats left . . ."

Chuckles and smiles blossomed around the table.

". . . but, Joe, let's strike a bargain: I won't call you Ben Dova, and you won't call me the Saint."

Spah laughed at that, rather raucously—about twice the reaction Charteris figured the remark was worth—and lifted his glass of Liebfrauenmilch in casual toast. "Agreed, my friend! Anyone who helps me feed my dog is jake with me."

"Jake?" a puzzled Hilda asked Charteris in a whisper.

He whispered back, "Never mind."

The couple introduced themselves as Leonhard and Gertrude Adelt, from Dresden.

Spah chimed in, "You should take their compliments seriously, Leslie—they're both writers, too!"

The genial director of the Zeppelin Company gestured toward Adelt, saying, "Leonhard here has been collaborating with me on my autobiography."

"We have publishers in London and Cologne," Adelt said, "and in a few days we'll be meeting with prospective houses in New York. . . . It will be called *Zeppelin*."

"Short, sweet and to the point," Charteris said, with an approving nod. "And you're a writer, too, Mrs. Adelt?"

" 'Gertrude,' please," she said.

She had enormous blue eyes; all these damn Germans had blue eyes, but she had the best and biggest on the ship, with the possible exception of Hilda's.

Gertrude was saying, "I'm working on a film script about zeppelins."

"I'm advising," Lehmann said with a smile.

She continued: "I have a first draft I hope to show to certain Hollywood people, while we're in America."

"They should admire the subject matter," Charteris said, testing his own glass of white wine. "Most Hollywood people I know are giant bags of gas."

That roused some general laughter, and a male voice behind Charteris said, "I wonder if I might join you? Mr. Charteris here is my cabin mate, after all."

Charteris glanced back, where angular Eric Knoecher stood in his tan suit and orange tie with a big friendly smile on his narrow face.

"More the merrier," Charteris said. "This is Eric Knoecher—importer, from . . . where is it?"

"Zeulenroda," Knoecher said.

"Ah," Gertrude said, "we have family there. Pleasure to meet you, Mr. Knoecher."

Knoecher made his way around the table, shaking hands, taking names . . . the latter a process at which he was no doubt skilled.

Charteris resisted the temptation to let his fellow diners know that the affable Mr. Knoecher was an undercover S.D. agent. He glanced at Lehmann, the man who'd given him this information, but the *Reederei* director— who was at the moment shaking Knoecher's hand, as if they'd never met—betrayed nothing in his expression.

"Shall I sit down," Knoecher asked, "or shall we all fill our plates first?"

As the little group made their way to and through the buffet line, Charteris continued chatting with the Adelts, and learned that both husband and wife were journalists, or at least they had been. Leonhard had covered the Austrian front during the Great War, and went on to work for several well-known newspapers and magazines in Germany. Gertrude had been an arts editor for the Dresden paper. All of this was couched in the past tense.

"What made you move into books and film scripts?" Charteris asked them, as they all settled back into their chairs with their plates of cold meat and salads before them. "It sounds as though you had very successful careers in journalism."

Surprisingly, it was Knoecher who responded. "You must forgive my cabin mate—he is naive in the ways of the New Order."

"I am?"

Knoecher nodded. "These are two very fine journalists. Mr. Adelt, I followed your work as Munich correspondent for *Tageblatt,* and your aviation column in the *Deutsche Allgemeine*."

"Thank you, sir," Adelt said, nodding, applying butter to a fresh-baked biscuit, unaware he himself was being buttered up.

Nibbling at a piece of Swiss cheese, Knoecher said, "Several years ago, Mr. Charteris, the press in Germany was declared a public institution. Journalists like the Adelts were ruled to be government officials—answerable to the state, not their publishers."

Gertrude Adelt paused between bites of salad to say, "Dr. Goebbels, our esteemed propaganda minister, has a list of subjects that are to be kept out of the press—because they might weaken the Reich at home or abroad."

"What exactly is on the list?" Hilda asked.

"Let us just say it's ever-expanding," Adelt said.

"The contents of the list aren't public knowledge," Knoecher said. "And any reporter who reveals anything on the list is considered to have committed treason. And the penalty for treason . . . well, not while we're eating."

"Beheading," Gertrude said.

"Fortunately you both seem to have retained your heads," Charteris said. "In your case, Gertrude, quite a lovely one."

"Thank you, Leslie. I have my head, but not my press card. Like my husband's, it was lifted."

"I lost mine because I'm a Catholic," Adelt said.

"I lost mine," his wife said, "because I had the bad form to point out to my editor that banning mentions of the 'Jew' George M. Cohan was nonsensical, due to 'Co-han' being an Irish name."

The silliness of that made them all laugh—but just a little; it was the kind of laughter that caught in the throat.

Smiling, Knoecher asked the Adelts, "Aren't you friends with Stefan Zweig?"

"Close friends," Adelt said. "Brilliant writer."

"Brilliant writer," Knoecher echoed.

"The universities threw his books on the fire," Gertrude said. "He's a Jew, so his words must be burned."

Charteris was quietly burning, too. This fellow Knoecher was as smooth as he was sinister—getting into the good graces of the Adelts, and prying from them admissions of continuing contact with a banned, Jewish writer.

"These biscuits are delicious," Charteris said, nibbling one, changing the subject innocuously.

"I understand they're a *specialité de la maison*," Gertrude said, spreading grape jam on another.

"I think you'll find the cuisine on this ship," Lehmann said, quietly proud, "comparable to that of any first-class hotel or restaurant."

"Well, nevertheless, I do have a complaint," Charteris said, lifting one of the numerous cups, goblets and glasses provided for coffee, wine, cola and what have you.

"Yes?" Lehmann asked.

"Can't we rid ourselves of a few of these glasses?

What is in this one, anyway—water? What are you trying to do, Captain, poison us?"

Light laughter followed, and Charteris then did his best to steer the little group away from overtly political topics, at least not dangerously political ones—the upcoming wedding of the Duke of Windsor and Mrs. Wallis Simpson, and the coronation of King George VI, seemed a safe subject. Captain Lehmann mentioned that the *Hindenburg*'s return trip was fully booked, many of the passengers prominent Americans who would be guests at the coronation.

But Knoecher, from time to time, would try to shift onto the sort of political topic that seemed to Charteris designed to reveal any anti-Nazi tendencies among those at the table.

"Perhaps Captain Lehmann will disagree with me," Knoecher said, "but I find this business of the Luftwaffe obliterating that little town in Spain . . . what's it called?"

"Guernica," Gertrude said, frowning, nodding.

"Thank you, my dear," Knoecher said, nodding back. "I find this bombing attack most disturbing."

Hilda seemed to be trembling, Charteris noticed; though she said nothing, he felt sure this line of conversation was bothering her. Her eyes seemed to be tearing up. . . .

"Strafing civilians, blowing up buildings," Adelt said, shaking his head, "it's shameful."

Spah was nodding. Between sips of wine, he put in his two cents: "The English say the Luftwaffe destroyed that town for practice. Barbarians!"

"I think the English should concentrate on their own problems," Charteris said easily. "This bus and tram strike, for instance—the Lambeth Walk will be more than a dance step if they don't settle it soon."

"Shall we have dessert?" Captain Lehmann asked, rising. "The stewards have added some awfully sweet surprises to the buffet table, I notice."

Lehmann traded the barest glance with Charteris; the Zeppelin Company director knew very well what Knoecher was up to, and seemed eager to conspire with Charteris to keep off any dangerous political course.

As the table was being cleared, the chief steward came through and loudly announced, in both German and English, that the smoking room was now open. Many of the men in the dining room practically bolted from their tables, and Charteris would have killed for a cigarette, himself.

Hilda seemed to sense this, saying, "I am afraid all of this food has made me sleepy. Leslie, would you walk me to my cabin?"

"Of course," Charteris said.

Gertrude was making a similar request of her husband, and the men had soon agreed to meet up in the smoking room.

As they passed the promenade windows, the view froze Charteris and the lovely blonde, and around them other passengers were reacting the same way.

While they had dined and talked, the *Hindenburg* had turned in a wide northwesterly arc, flying over the canals of Holland, crossing the narrow waterway that was the Wester Schelde, loping over the sandbars and cold, rugged waters of the North Sea, into an electrical storm.

Out the observation-deck windows, black clouds swirled and swarmed, billowing like ink cast into water, alive with crackling lightning, the jagged veins of energy periodically lighting up this darkest of nights.

Hilda clutched his arm, alarmed, pressing herself up against him. It would almost have been worth it, if Charteris weren't equally alarmed at the thought of what lightning might mean to the seven million cubic feet of hydrogen gas keeping this blimp afloat.

Captain Lehmann's voice rang out: "No cause for alarm! You are as safe here as if you were walking down Unter den Linden in Berlin!"

Charteris hoped Lehmann didn't mean as safe as a *Jew* walking down Unter den Linden in Berlin. . . .

But the airship itself seemed unfazed by the storm; a steamship in this gale would be rolling, its framework groaning, screeching, creaking; but the *Hindenburg* was gliding through the black clouds, as smoothly as though this were a serene, starry night. The storm sounded like a gently rolling surf, as rain pelted the ship's linen skin.

As Charteris walked his beautiful companion to her cabin, the stillness, the quiet, was remarkable. The only sound was a faint drone of diesel, providing a muted, soothing pulse.

"Difficult to believe the world out there is so torn apart," Hilda said, as they paused at her cabin door.

Did she mean the storm, or something else?

"You were upset at dinner," he said.

She frowned. A few other people were passing by in the narrow corridor.

"Come in a moment," she said.

Within her cabin, she bid him sit on the lower bunk. She sat next to him, slumped a bit, hands folded.

"I did not realize you had noticed," she said.

"You were trembling. I thought you might cry. Did you have friends in Guernica?"

"No . . . but I lost someone in the war in Spain."

"A friend?"

". . . A lover."

"When?"

"Just this January past."

"Hilda, I'm so very sorry."

She squeezed his hand.

"But, my dear . . . I thought you weren't political?"

She stared into nothing. "Losing him . . . That is why I have no time for politics. Do you understand?"

"I think I do."

She gave him a small, tender kiss and sent him on his way.

As she was closing the door, Hilda bestowed him a smile, just a little one, and said, "Knock at nine—we will have breakfast."

"Good night, Hilda."

Heading to the stairs down to B deck and its renowned smoking room, Charteris noticed Knoecher and Spah standing at the promenade windows, the dark storm clouds swirling beyond them. The two men were chatting and it seemed friendly enough. Charteris wished he could warn Spah of the S.D. agent's true intentions—at the first discreet opportunity, he would.

The smoking room, way aft on the starboard side, was entered through the cramped bar, an antechamber little bigger than a passenger cabin. Charteris turned down the bar steward's suggestion of an LZ-129 Frosted Cocktail (gin with orange juice) and acquired a Scotch and water, double, Peter Dawson of course.

The bartender granted him admission through the one-customer-at-a-time revolving air-lock door into the pressurized compartment, which Charteris guessed measured at around twelve and half by fifteen feet. The room seemed larger, though, thanks to the arrangement of black leather settees built into three walls, facing black-and-chrome tables and chairs. The fourth wall paralleled the side of the ship, and a railing allowed passengers to gaze down at a bank of Plexiglas windows set flush in the floor along the edge of the ship. Yellow pigskin leather covered the walls, which were illustrated with images of various hot-air balloons.

Hot air was apropos, with all the smoking and talking going on by the exclusively male populace of the room, who shared one lighter, housed in the wall on a draw cable. Advertising man Douglas and his little group sat chatting in a cloud of cigarette and cigar smoke—the room was well ventilated, but these were serious smokers. Leonhard Adelt was standing at the rail, a drink in hand, a cigarette drooping from his lips, as he studied the black clouds churning below.

Charteris was glad to catch the journalist by himself.

"Mr. Adelt," the author said, very quietly, "I must advise you to watch what you say around this Knoecher character."

Adelt's handsome, intelligent features tightened, then loosened as he grinned. "Oh, he seems nice enough."

Charteris shook his head. "Don't ask me to say more, because I shouldn't. Just don't talk politics around him, no matter how he prompts you."

Adelt frowned, and his face fell as he grasped the author's meaning. "What a fool . . ."

"Pardon?"

"Not you, Mr. Charteris, no not you . . . I must have allowed myself to be seduced by the elegance and civility of this airship. . . . This is like another world, is it not? A better world than the one down there—suspicion, fear, jealousy, self-hatred, these are the cancers at the heart of the Reich."

"I just thought you should know. But I never said this, understood?"

"Understood, Mr. Charteris. Easily understood by one who lives in a land of midnight knocks at the door . . . who exists in a country of rigid structure, rotting from within, morally bankrupt . . . Excuse me. I'm a little drunk."

"You're articulate, nonetheless."

"I only hope . . ."

"Yes?"

Adelt's eyes were tight with concern. "Did we say too much at the table tonight? I know we spoke of our friend Stefan Zweig. . . ."

"I can't judge that. I don't have to swim in those waters."

"Someday you may, Mr. Charteris. Someday you may. . . . If you'll excuse me, I think I'll join my wife in our cabin."

Charteris finished his own drink and headed up to A deck. In the hallway, shoes had been placed outside most doors, for elves to polish in the night. No shoes outside Charteris's cabin, though.

No sign at all of his cabin mate.

Shrugging, Charteris undressed, hung up his tuxedo, set his Italian loafers in the hall, slipped into silk pajamas and slid between fine linen sheets and light woolen blankets, falling quickly, soundly asleep, lulled by the murmur of distant engines.

Blissfully unaware of the storm outside, or that his cabin mate, one Eric Knoecher, would not be joining him on this—or any—night.

DAY TWO:

Tuesday, May 4, 1937

FIVE

How the Hindenburg *Misplaced a Passenger, and Leslie Charteris Walked the Plank*

By dawn of what would be the airship's first full day of travel, sailing along at 2,100 feet on a course designed to outmaneuver the churning storm system, the *Hindenburg* cruised above the English Channel, past the Scilly Islands. The swastika-tailed silver ship flew somewhat south of Ireland and the familiar landmark that was the Old Head of Kinsale, heading toward the endless lonely gray-blue expanse of the Atlantic. Aboard were ninety-six people (passengers and crew), as well as a considerable cargo including mail, fancy goods, airplane parts, tobacco, films, partridge eggs and Joseph Spah's dog. As the time for breakfast neared—serving began at eight A.M.—the airship gradually lowered to the accustomed altitude of one thousand feet.

Surprised and vaguely concerned when—upon awaking—he discovered himself alone in the cabin, Charteris shaved and washed up at the tilt-down basin, frowning all the while.

An innocent reason for Knoecher's absence might present itself. Perhaps the undercover S.D. agent had followed his cabin mate's suggestion and requested one of the numerous unoccupied berths on the airship.

But Charteris knew that was unlikely: the S.D. man had been placed in the author's quarters specifically to keep tabs on a potential troublemaker.

The other obvious possibility—that Eric Knoecher had gotten lucky with a female passenger, spending the night in another cabin—seemed equally unlikely. The only two unattached females aboard were Margaret Mather and Hilda Friederich. Charteris felt Miss Mather made an improbable paramour for the handsome bounder, and besides which, if the spinster had spent the night with anyone, it would have been that college boy who'd been plying her (and himself, in loin-girding preparation) with white wine.

As for Hilda, Charteris was confident that he was the only man in her shipboard life.

A remaining prospect was that Knoecher had stayed up all night, either in conference with Erdmann and the other two Luftwaffe "observers," or perhaps sat up talking, maybe falling asleep, in a seat in the lounge or on one of the observation decks (the bar closed at three A.M., so that was not a possibility).

Charteris slipped into comfortable, sporty attire—a single-breasted gray herringbone sport jacket with white shirt, plaid tie, darker gray slacks, gray-and-white loafers—and followed the seductive scent of coffee to the portside dining room, like a cobra heeding a snake charmer's flute.

He was able to collect a cup of steaming aromatic coffee from a steward (taking it black), but breakfast proper wasn't to be served for another forty-five minutes. A number of passengers were already seated having coffee and rolls, and others were seated on the two-seater benches jutting from the wall of windows, enjoying light conversation or writing a letter or postcard. They were mostly ignoring the view, which wasn't much: a gloomy overcast sky, when the ship wasn't caught within a gray cloud.

Knoecher wasn't among them.

Sipping at his coffee, the author strolled around to the starboard lounge, where he found himself alone, the other passengers preferring to be nearer the pending food. The long row of slanting windows and the gray landscape of the sky was all his, if he wanted it. Idly, a thought nibbling at the back of his brain, he went to where he'd seen Knoecher and Spah standing, chatting civilly, last night. He didn't know what he expected to find.

But he found it.

Not at first. At first, having set the coffee cup on the ledgelike sill, he leaned against the aluminum bar separating one window from another and looked down through the closed Plexiglas portal at the stirred-up sea, the agitated swells trailing tendrils of foamy white. For the sea to be that angry, the wind had to be strong—but up here, in the Never-Never Land of the *Hindenburg,* all was calm. No steamship propeller shafts to vibrate you, no handgrips needed to protect you from the lurch of the ship as it rode the choppy waves.

The aluminum window frame was polished and

smooth under his palm, which was how he came to notice the tickle of silk threads.

Frowning, he lifted his hand and spied—caught alongside and between aluminum window frame and its jamb—orange threads, silk threads. . . .

No, more than just threads, a tiny piece of cloth had been caught there. Holding the edge of the trapped scrap of silk in the thumb and middle finger of his right hand, Charteris used his left to lift the handle on the window, which raised like a lid on the world below.

This freed the scrap of cloth, wind-fluttering in his grasp, perhaps an inch across and about as long, tapering to a point, the point having been caught in the window, and the rest torn away, the threads standing up like hair on a frightened man's head.

He knew at once what it was, and in moments a scenario explaining its presence in that window jamb had presented itself.

Closing the window, slipping the silk fragment in his sport-jacket pocket, Charteris glanced about to see if he still had the starboard promenade to himself: he did. Quickly but casually, he returned to the portside promenade and the dining room, which was filling up. He deposited his empty coffee cup on a passing busboy's tray, looking around for Chief Steward Kubis, who he knew would be supervising the staff, and mingling with the guests.

And there Kubis was, near a table where sat that wholesome-looking German family with their two well-behaved, properly attired boys (one was maybe six, the other possibly eight). The younger boy—bored, as they waited for breakfast to come—was seated on the floor near the table, playing with a tin toy, a little car with

Mickey Mouse driving. When the child ran it quickly across the carpet, the toy threw sparks.

"Lovely boy," Kubis, leaning in with clasped hands, told the parents, who nodded back with proud smiles over their coffee. "And I do hate to play the villain . . . but I must confiscate that vehicle."

"What?" the father said, not sure if Kubis was joking.

Kubis tousled the child's hair; the boy frowned up at the steward, who with one big hand was lifting the tin car from two small hands.

"Please tell your son," Kubis said, "why we take no chances with sparks on a zeppelin."

The father gathered the boy onto his lap and was quietly explaining—the child didn't cry—as Kubis handed the car to a busboy, whispering instructions.

"My apologies," Kubis said to the family, "and I'll see the lad gets it back before we land."

Charteris ambled over and placed a hand on the steward's shoulder. "Heinrich, you're a hard man."

"Sometimes I have to be, Mr. Charteris."

"Me, too. I need to talk to Captain Lehmann—it's important."

"He's not come up for breakfast yet, sir."

"Take me to him."

The chief steward's eyes narrowed but he did not question Charteris's demand—and it had been a demand, not a request.

"I believe he's in the control gondola, sir."

"Fine."

No further conversation followed, not even small talk. The friendliness these two usually shared fell away, the tone of the author's voice having conveyed a seriousness that the steward responded to dutifully.

Kubis led Charteris down the stairs to B deck and for-

ward through the keel corridor, trading the modern luxury of the passenger deck for the spare reality of a narrow
rubber-padded catwalk that cut through a maze of wires
and controls, bordered by massive fuel and water tanks.
With the gray choppy ocean hazily visible directly beneath, the precariousness of this approach was dimin-
ished by the steadiness of the ship in flight, as well as
cables and ropes strung along either side, providing ten-
uous railings.

Rain-flecked windows were spaced along the arching
pathway, looking out onto the charcoal cloud in which
the airship was currently enveloped, and the trek was
rather like crossing a jungle crevice on a rope bridge. But
no jungle was so eerily silent: the wind failed even to
whisper as it rushed by, thanks to the streamlined design
of the ship, and the engines way aft were not even faintly
audible.

Then the gangway emptied onto a rubber-floored platform, on either side of which were doorless mail and
wireless rooms, a single blue-uniformed crew member at
work in either. Just beyond these work areas, and prior
to where officers' cabins began, the platform was
breached by an aperture from which a ladder yawned,
providing the inauspicious means of entering the control-
room gondola below.

"A moment, sir," the steward said, and climbed down
an aluminum, hole-punched ladder not unlike the ones in
the passenger cabins.

After some muffled conversation, Kubis climbed back
up, returned to the platform and gestured grandly toward
the ladder as if presenting Charteris to the Queen.

"Captain Lehmann says he'll be walking you back,
sir," Kubis said. "So I'll take my leave."

Charteris nodded his thanks, and climbed down the

rather shaky ladder into the aft portion of the gondola, a three-chambered shoe-shaped control car whose aluminum framing might have been the work of an industrious youth with an Erector set (which Kubis would no doubt have confiscated). Surprisingly small, only the openness of the flimsy construction and the tall, slightly slanting Plexiglas windows on all sides kept the long narrow affair from seeming a claustrophobe's nightmare.

Or the windows would have served that function had they not been rain-pearled views on a gray cloud.

Captain Lehmann—again in civilian attire, a brown three-piece suit with a darker brown bow tie—helped Charteris down from the ladder, greeting him with a smile and tight, puzzled eyes.

"What a pleasant surprise, Mr. Charteris."

"Well, a surprise, anyway. I need to talk to you and Captain Pruss."

The eyes tightened further, then eyebrows in the fatherly face lifted in a shrug. "Come with me, please."

The center section was the chart room, a uniformed navigator on duty there. Lehmann led Charteris into the next and largest segment of the aluminum pod, which held the zeppelin's equivalent of a steamship's bridge, with its mass of telegraphs, gauges, control panels and other gizmos, including of course a pair of wheels, standing almost at right angles to each other, the elevator pilot at one, the rudder pilot at the other.

Lehmann introduced the author to Captain Pruss, the pleasant-looking blond man in his middle forties an unexceptional figure made impressive by the crisp dark blue of his uniform and cap.

Still, just as Lehmann carried melancholy in his eyes, the new captain of the *Hindenburg* had tiredness in his, the features of his oval face touched with a surprising softness.

"A smooth ride, Captain," Charteris said in German, and the conversation that followed remained in that language.

"One of the worst trips we have ever made," Pruss said, his voice a pleasing, mellow baritone at odds with his words. "We like to give our passengers better sightseeing weather than this."

"Weather charts determine our course," Lehmann put in. "But it's a science very much in its infancy—the captain had a long night."

Both men, polite and even solicitous as they were, were waiting for Charteris to explain and justify his intrusion.

Glancing about him at the various blue-uniformed officers in the control car, Charteris said softly, "I wonder if we might repair to some private area? I have a subject to discuss, gentlemen, that is unlikely to improve Captain Pruss's opinion of how this voyage is going."

Soon they'd gone back up the ladder and forward to the officers' cabins, ducking into Lehmann's, which was somewhat larger than a passenger cabin, with room for an aluminum desk; a small, sloping window looked out on the grayness of sky and sea. Lehmann's trademark accordion—which had so enlivened the maiden voyage—rested on the floor, leaning against a beige-linen-paneled bulkhead. On the single cot lay unrolled architectural drawings.

"Been working on our house," Lehmann said, rolling up the plans, slipping a rubber band around them, setting them aside to make room for Charteris on the cot.

"Ah," Charteris said, sitting. "You and Marie moving

to Zeppelinheim with the rest of the *Reederei* family, eh, Ernst?"

"We have a lovely parcel of land," Lehmann said, nodding, gesturing for Captain Pruss to take the chair at the desk, which Pruss did. "Beautiful beeches and firs all around us . . . Now, what has you concerned, Leslie?"

Lehmann remained standing, a quiet assertion of his authority.

Charteris asked, "May I assume Captain Pruss is aware of Eric Knoecher's true background?"

Pruss glanced sharply at Lehmann, who nodded, saying, "You may speak freely."

Charteris told the two poker-faced captains of Knoecher's overnight absence in their cabin, and ran through his reasoning as to the unlikelihood of the "importer" having spent the night with one of the airship's two unattached ladies.

"Of course, if Mr. Knoecher likes boys, rather than girls," Charteris said, "that might require a new line of thought."

"Impossible," Lehmann said.

"Ah," Charteris said. "I forgot: there are no homosexuals in Germany. It's against the law."

Pruss said, "What are you suggesting, Mr. Charteris?"

"I don't think I've suggested anything just yet, gentlemen. But before I do, is there something pertaining to Mr. Knoecher of which I'm unaware? Do you know of his presence elsewhere on the ship, perhaps in the crew's quarters, or in another passenger cabin, or even in sick bay?"

The two captains exchanged a solemn glance, and both shook their heads.

Lehmann said, "Where do *you* think he is, Mr. Charteris?"

"Not on this ship—not anymore."

Lehmann's eyes widened and Pruss's narrowed.

Charteris reached in his sport-jacket pocket and displayed the fragment of silk, holding it between thumb and middle finger like a little bell to be rung. "I found this caught in a window jamb on the starboard promenade."

Lehmann took the silken tidbit, examined it briefly, passed it on to Pruss, who did the same. Then the two captains looked to Charteris with a shared unspoken question.

"It's the tip of Mr. Knoecher's tie," the author said.

"Are you certain?" Lehmann asked.

"Certain enough. I don't remember anyone else wearing an orange silk necktie, yesterday. It's not exactly the rage, is it?"

"It does appear to be the tip of a tie," Pruss said quietly.

"You can keep that," Charteris said. "I don't really have any use for an inch of neckwear."

Lehmann said, "Are you suggesting he jumped?"

"Hell, no! That manipulative, arrogant son of a bitch was anything but despondent. I do think someone may have done the world the favor of pushing him out a window."

"Good God," Pruss said, whitening. He dropped the fragment of necktie onto Lehmann's desk, as if the fabric had turned suddenly hot.

Lehmann didn't whiten: it was more a greening.

"It's possible he was killed on board, then disposed of," Charteris continued cheerily, as if describing the plot of a Nöel Coward play, "but my money would be on a scuffle that got out of hand. In the middle of the night,

in the early morning hours, those observation prome-
nades are no doubt deserted."

"That's true," Lehmann admitted.

"No witnesses, no problem. A quick shove, and slam
shut the window—muffling any scream, but unfortunately catching the tip of the tie . . . The drop itself
would've killed him, don't you think? If not, he'd have
certainly drowned in the Channel, or maybe frozen to
death. I say, are there sharks in those waters?"

"You don't seem terribly upset at the prospect of Eric
Knoecher's murder," Lehmann said dryly.

"I believe Western civilization will survive the loss—
though the sharks are probably in for some nasty indi-
gestion. Still, I felt a responsibility to let you know. Besides which, however deserving a victim Knoecher may
have been, this does mean we have a murderer aboard."

Lehmann leaned against the bulkhead; he appeared
woozy, a rare occurrence on a ship famed for not causing
seasickness.

"And having a killer among us certainly could make
for a less relaxing trip than advertised," Charteris added.

"We don't know that Mr. Knoecher has been murdered," Lehmann said, rather numbly.

Pruss swallowed, nodded. "He may well still be on this
ship."

Charteris shrugged. "He might. So I would suggest
your first course of action is a search."

Lehmann sighed heavily, then straightened; his expression was businesslike but not unfriendly. "We will
do just that. Mr. Charteris . . . Leslie . . . we . . . I . . .
would ask a favor."

"Certainly, Ernst."

"I ask it as a friend . . . but also, as director of the
Reederei, I can offer you free passage, every year hence,

a lifetime 'pass,' so to speak . . . if you will cooperate."

"Cooperate how?"

"Keep this to yourself. Share this information with no other passenger—until we indicate otherwise."

Charteris smiled half a smile. "All right. I can understand that you don't want to alarm your passengers."

"Yes."

"And I understand how damaging this could be to the reputation of the Zeppelin Company . . . not to mention how embarrassing to Nazi Germany."

Lehmann said nothing; he was looking at the floor.

Pruss stood. "We will have to discreetly search the ship, beginning as soon as possible." To Lehmann, the captain said, "We will instruct our stewards and our stewardesses, in their daily housekeeping duties, to check every cabin for this stray passenger."

Lehmann nodded firmly. "And we'll search the interior of the ship. . . ." To Charteris, he added, "Which will not be as difficult as you might think. For all its size, the *Hindenburg* has scant hiding places."

"Balloons tend to have relatively few nooks and crannies," Charteris said. He slapped his thighs and rose. "Well, that's all I have to report, gentlemen. Just one passenger mislaid; everything else would seem in place, as best I can tell."

Pruss was frowning, a little. "No offense, Mr. Charteris—but your flippant attitude does seem inappropriate. A man, apparently, has died."

"A man who was in the business of causing misery for others has died. Besides, Captain, it's my general philosophy that in a world rife with absurdity and cruelty, an arched eyebrow and an ironic aside are sometimes the only defenses against going stark raving mad."

Pruss considered that remark, for a moment, but chose

not to comment on it, saying instead, "Should anyone inquire about your cabin mate's whereabouts, please say that he is staying in his cabin, with a cold, and does not wish to be disturbed."

"All right. But I would have preferred to make up my own lie—that's what they pay me for, after all."

Pruss ignored that, saying to Lehmann, "A moment with you?"

Lehmann nodded, then asked Charteris to step outside the cabin, which the author did, and perhaps a minute later, the two captains emerged. Pruss nodded to Charteris and walked to the aperture in the platform and the ladder to his control car.

Lehmann waited until Pruss was out of sight, then whispered to Charteris, in English, "Did you tell anyone what I told you? Did you warn anyone of who Knoecher really was?"

"Of course not," Charteris lied. "Did you?"

"Of course not!"

The two men continued to speak in English, carrying their conversation onto the catwalk as they made their return trip to B deck.

Charteris, following Lehmann, said, "You watched, you heard, how that bastard Knoecher manipulated and charmed our friends at supper last night, backing them into politically damaging corners, wheedling virtual admissions of guilt out of them."

Lehmann nodded back, glumly.

"Well," Charteris said, "if I *had* told one of them, and right now I told you who—what good would it do?"

With another backward glance, Lehmann said, "If a murder has been committed on this ship, we'd have a suspect—we'd have a starting place."

"I disagree. I think whoever I might have warned—

whoever *you* might have warned—would most certainly
have warned others. It would be the humane thing to do,
wouldn't it?"

Lehmann drew in a breath, nodding again, resignedly.
Then he paused on the narrow catwalk, turning to touch
Charteris's arm, holding on to a cable with his other
hand. His eyes were pleading. "Don't betray us, Leslie.
Help me contain this. The future of my company, the
future of zeppelin travel, may well depend upon the out-
come."

"You have my word."

"Good."

They walked, the slightly springy catwalk beneath
their feet reminding Charteris of an endless pirate's plank
they'd been forced to walk.

"Ernst—do you think this could be connected to that
bomb scare?"

Without looking back, but shaking his head, Lehmann
said, "I doubt it. There is no bomb on this ship—the
search, the precautions, were too thorough. Besides,
Knoecher wasn't part of that effort."

"I don't understand."

"Sabotage is Colonel Erdmann's bailiwick. The S.D.
officers who went over this ship, stem to stern, with the
finest of fine-tooth combs, were especially trained for
antisabotage duty. Knoecher is not in that field."

"Ah. He was in the business of looking for traitors,
not bombers."

"Yes."

"But, Ernst, those are hardly exclusive categories. Suppose your Mr. Knoecher discovered that there was indeed
a bomb aboard this airship—and discovered, as well,
who'd brought it aboard."

Lehmann's head tilted to one side as he walked along,

considering that. "You have a point. . . . All the more reason to allow us to contain this volatile situation ourselves."

"Fine. And, Ernst, should you need my help in the
inquiry, say the word."

"Help in what way?"

"I studied criminology at Cambridge, and I worked for
a time as a police constable. Mystery writers don't just
drop from the sky, you know . . . sorry—unfortunate image."

Pausing on the catwalk again, Lehmann turned and
smiled warmly. "I appreciate the offer, but I rather think
Colonel Erdmann will handle any inquiry, should this go
more public."

"Erdmann will be informed of this."

"Certainly." Lehmann pressed on. "He will be my next
stop."

"Do you want me to come along, and fill him in?"

"No. That won't be necessary. Please go about the
business of being just another passenger. . . ."

"Another satisfied customer, you mean?"

They had reached the door to B deck.

Lehmann arched an eyebrow, smiled a little. "More
satisfied than Eric Knoecher, I venture to say."

Then the former captain of the *Hindenburg* reached for
the handle, slid the door open and gestured for Charteris
to step on through.

SIX

How the Hindenburg's Doctor Prescribed Slippers, and Leslie Charteris Was Summoned

As they had agreed last night, Charteris knocked at Hilda's door promptly at nine A.M. The lovely braided blonde appeared at the author's first tentative rap, almost startling him.

"Do I seem overanxious?" she asked, her smile slightly embarrassed. Her impressive topography was well served by the simple but stylish navy-blue short-sleeved linen dress with white piqué piping, made quietly elegant by white gloves.

"I'm not complaining, my dear—particularly if you're anxious to see me."

"The truth is," she said, sliding the cabin door closed behind her, "I am simply famished—have you been up long?"

"Awhile." He gave her no particulars regarding the already-busy morning's events.

Walking arm in arm, the couple paused in the foyer where the A deck corridor came out near the stairs; on one side of the shelf-perched bust of Marshal von Hindenburg was a map of the Atlantic where a steward was moving the tiny red flag marking the airship's westward progress. Then the white-jacketed lad pinned a note on the bulletin board, on the other side of the glowering bust, adding to various postings of news, activities and regulations.

"They have canceled this morning's tour of the ship!" Hilda said, a finger touching the offending notice on the bulletin board. "I was so looking forward to that!"

"Just postponed till this afternoon, my dear," Charteris said, reading over her shoulder.

"Why do you suppose they did that?"

"Probably to annoy you. Word has no doubt gotten around how beautiful you look when you wrinkle your nose."

She smirked at him. "Do you think mocking me is the way to my heart?"

"Possibly, but first I think we should take care of your stomach."

In the dining room, which was doing a lively business, a steward ushered them to a table for two along the wall. The breakfast smells were appetizing, to say the least, an olfactory promise the fare delivered on: eggs, sausage, ham, salami, cheese, fresh rolls and breads, butter, honey, jams, choice of coffee, tea or cocoa. Much as on an ocean liner, there was no shortage of food, and good food at that; but unlike an ocean liner, no one was avoiding it, for fear of seasickness.

The airship seemed to have passed effortlessly through

the worst of the weather; the ship's outer fabric had withstood rain and wind and even hail while the passengers within sensed only a murmur reminiscent of surf lapping against shore. The windows of the promenade looked out on a gray, indistinct world, while the bright, lively inner domain of the *Hindenburg,* as evidenced by its dining room, seemed untouched by the passing storm, passengers chatting gaily, new friends being made, old ones reaffirmed, amid the bustle of stewards and the clink of china and clank of silverware.

"I am glad we are seated alone," Hilda said, slathering honey on a biscuit—a healthy girl with a healthy appetite. "I don't mean to be unsociable, but all that political talk bores me."

Actually, Charteris thought "bored" was probably not the word—"disturbed" was more like it. But he let it go.

"Where is your cabin mate, this morning?" she asked.

"He's taken cold. Keeping himself to bed. I doubt we'll be seeing much of him."

"My cabin was a little chilly. I rang for the steward, and was brought an electric heater—perhaps you could order one up for Mr. Knoecher."

"He can fend for himself."

She nibbled her biscuit. "Do I sense you don't care much for him, Leslie?"

"I would prefer a different cabin mate, and the next time you get chilly, don't send for a heater."

Her lips pursed into that kiss of a smile. "You make me hesitate to ask my next question."

"And what would that be?"

"I was wondering what we might do with ourselves, this morning, now that the ship tour has been canceled."

"Postponed. Well, assuming making mad, passionate love in your cabin—with the heater off—is not presently an option, how about a friendly game of cards? Do you happen to play bridge?"

"Why, yes I do. And I love it."

A busboy was removing their empty plates.

Charteris touched a linen napkin to his lips. "Then let's seek some victims."

The deep blue eyes twinkled, the smile lines around them crinkled. "Why, are you good at it?"

Tossing his napkin on the table before him, he said, "Among the ways I took money from people, prior to bilking the public for my published lies, was playing bridge. I was, for a time, a professional at a London club."

Her eyes flared with interest. "You were a gambler?"

"Gambling as a pure sport doesn't appeal to me. The only games worth playing are those matching your wits against another's. Like in a good game of poker, backgammon or even gin rummy."

"Or bridge."

"Bridge best of all."

"You fascinate me, Leslie."

"Well, hell—I'm trying to."

Elbows propped on the table, she gazed with quiet amusement at him over clasped hands. "What were some of your other jobs?"

He shrugged, sipped his coffee. "I prospected for gold and fished for pearls, in Malaysia. Worked in a tin mine and on a rubber plantation. Seaman on a freighter. This is all required training for writers, you know."

"How exotic. How romantic." She only seemed to be half kidding.

"Oh, terribly exotic, very romantic, all of my jobs— like driving a bus, for instance. Or working as a bartender. I even blew up balloons for a game booth in a traveling fair—but if this balloon springs a leak, don't expect me to repair it."

"Why? Don't you think you have enough hot air?"

He laughed at that. "What a relief!"

"What is?"

"That you have a sense of humor. So many Germans don't, these days, it would seem."

"That is all too true, Leslie."

He reached across the table and took her hand, gently. "I don't mean to condescend. I'm rather fond of Germany, or at least I have fond memories of it."

"You spent time in my country?"

"Oh yes. Back in, when was it? Thirty-one, I went open-air hiking all over the fatherland."

She nodded. "We are big on rucksacking through the countryside, on foot, or bicycle."

"I remember singing along the roadsides and in country inns with German boys and girls."

"More often girls, I would guess."

"Boys or girls, they were so much more charming than their hot-rodding and jitterbugging American counterparts. I have to admit, my dear, that I came away thinking there was a new spirit at large among the youth of your country."

"You were right—unfortunately."

"Well, back in thirty-one, ol' Schickelgruber was just a housepainter turned beerhall politician. I think, without him, that youthful spirit I saw might have developed into something very fine indeed. . . . But now I've gone and done it."

"What?"

"Dragged politics back in."

"Are you political, Leslie?"

"Heavens no! The idea of accepting any prefabricated

platform is to me the antithesis of sound thinking."

They strolled to the reading and writing room on the starboard side (passing the window where Charteris had found the necktie fragment). With its comfy chairs at tiny tables and wall-attached desk trays, this cozy nook, just beyond the lounge, was a retreat for letter writing or curling up with a book or magazine. The linen wall panels were a soothing gray decorated with pastel paintings delineating the development of the worldwide postal service, which struck Charteris as perhaps the dullest subject ever chosen for artistic interpretation.

A white-jacketed steward was on hand to unlock the bookcase and provide periodicals and novels, at no cost, or to sell *Hindenburg* stationery and stamps (letters could be posted to the ship's mailroom by a pneumatic tube); also free was the loan of chess sets, Chinese checkers and playing cards.

Charteris was gathering two decks of the latter when he noticed Leonhard Adelt at one of the wall desks, typing; Adelt's wife, Gertrude, was at one of the round little tables, thumbing through an issue of the American fashion magazine *Vogue*.

"That looks too much like work," Charteris said to Leonhard, when the handsome journalist paused to change sheets of typing paper.

"Good morning, Leslie," Adelt said cheerily, looking up from his typewriter. He was wearing glasses, and the same dark suit as last night at dinner.

"I don't type, myself, of course—strictly a dictation man."

"Really, Leslie? How long does it take you to do a book?"

"Two years."

"So much dictation!"

"Oh, no—I think about it for two years. The dictation takes two days."

Adelt rolled his eyes and laughed, then gestured toward the typewriter. "Yes, well, I'm just earning my keep. Frankly, Ernst booked us free passage in return for my writing a magazine article about the joys of zeppelin travel."

Hilda had joined Gertrude at her table and the two were chatting over the magazine, admiring some fashions and making fun of others. Adelt's wife wore a pink high-collared frock with a blue floral pattern, short, puffy sleeves and heart-shaped buttons; her blonde hair was up, and a pink leghorn-style straw hat perched there. Though Gertrude was slightly older than the braided beauty, and had a certain sad tiredness in her pretty face, she was the only woman on the airship whose comeliness rivaled Hilda's.

"Little early in the voyage to find much to write about," Charteris said to the journalist.

Adelt half smiled and replied, in that perfect but heavily accented English of his, "I should probably hire you to ghost this piece—it would seem to require a fiction writer. So far this is the most uneventful journey I ever undertook in an airship."

"Not counting the presence of our friend Eric Knoecher, of course."

Adelt smirked humorlessly. "I don't think Ernst would appreciate my mentioning undercover S.D. spies being aboard. But I must thank you again, for the warning."

"Think nothing of it."

"Though, to tell the truth, I haven't yet had to watch what I say around him. Haven't even seen the son of a bitch today."

Charteris shrugged. "He's sick in our cabin—fighting a cold."

"Wouldn't it be sad if he lost."

"It's a nasty cold, all right, but I doubt it'll prove fatal. . . . Do you and your wife play bridge, by any chance?"

Charteris and Hilda spent a lively morning playing bridge with the Adelts in the lounge, the author and his pretty partner taking two rubbers in a row, including a grand slam, Charteris finessing the queen. Luck had been involved, and the Adelts played well themselves, but Charteris was pleased to be able to demonstrate to Hilda that his claims of bridge proficiency had not been entirely "baloney."

At eleven, Chief Steward Kubis served bouillon (in the fashion of the best ocean liners), and the couples rose from the lounge's canvas-and-aluminum chairs to stretch and sip the soup.

"You and the lovely Miss Friederich make a good team," Adelt said to the author.

They were standing at the promenade windows. Though the sky remained overcast, the ship was no longer traveling through gray clouds.

"We had the right cards," Charteris said.

"I think she had the right partner."

"I don't think you should complain about yours. You're a very lucky man, Leonhard."

"Oh, I know. I know."

They were looking down upon an ocean liner that was dwarfed by, and lost within, the huge shadow of the dirigible, making its distinct black stain on the gray-blue sea.

"I haven't seen Ernst all morning," Adelt said, as the

foursome reassembled at the table. "Where do you suppose he could be?"

"I wonder," Gertrude said, shuffling cards. "And I
don't believe Captain Pruss took breakfast in the dining
room, either."

"Perhaps that storm was trickier to manage than we
might imagine," Charteris put in lightly. "I believe it's
my deal. . . ."

Charteris and Hilda took a third rubber, and Gertrude
commented that she was glad they weren't playing for
money; then the two couples had lunch in the dining
room, a sumptuous feast of Rhine salmon, roast gosling
meunière, mixed salad and applesauce, and pears condé
with chocolate sauce.

Fortunately the rescheduled ship's tour gave them a
way to walk off the wonderful but heavy meal. Gathering
in the starboard lounge, the Adelts joined Charteris and
Hilda, as did Margaret Mather, with Joe Spah tagging
along as well. Normally Captain Lehmann conducted the
airship tours personally; but it seemed today he was otherwise occupied. The ship's doctor, Kurt Ruediger, slender, youthful, blond, was standing in for Lehmann, this
afternoon.

Charteris had met the young doctor on the maiden voyage, and found him pleasant enough, if somewhat callow.
Ruediger—the first doctor ever to regularly serve aboard
a commercial aircraft—was just a year out of his intern-
ship at Bremen, and had snagged this plum position due
to a sailing-club friendship with Lehmann.

Speaking in German, Dr. Ruediger informed the tour
group that everyone would have to don special slippers—
crepe-soled canvas sneakers with laces whose grommets
were of reinforced cloth.

"You will be walking on the metal gangways and mov-

ing up and down the aluminum shafts of our ship," Ruediger said, his voice an uncertain second tenor. "A spark
struck by a hobnail or static caused by the friction of
steel or wool might have an adverse effect."

"He means the ship could blow up," Charteris whispered
in English to Hilda, whose big blue eyes grew bigger.

A steward had deposited a large box of the slippers on
a table, and Dr. Ruediger said, "Please find something in
your size."

This proved a task easier said than done, as the shoes
were unmarked, and nobody seemed able to find a pair
that fit properly. The slippers were floppy and oversize,
and to Charteris it seemed a scene from a circus—clown
shoes all around.

In his sweater vest, bow tie and gabardine slacks, Joe
Spah, the smallest participant, proved the biggest clown,
immediately falling into a soft-shoe routine, a buck-and-
wing evolving into a ballerina's pirouette. Then he placed
two fingers under his nose as a makeshift mustache and
did a Charlie Chaplin walk right up to Ruediger, and
gave the Nazi salute.

"Seig heil, Herr Doctor! Ready when you are!"

Ruediger smiled politely, as did the entire group, a few
of them even laughing a little; but this feeble comedy did
not provide a light moment, rather cast something of a
pall.

As the group trooped down to B deck, Margaret
Mather—in an aqua-blue crepe dress with a bow at the
waist (too young for her by twenty years)—sidled up to
Charteris.

"I do hope I can take you up on your offer to read my
poetry," she said, almost giddily.

Charteris, who didn't exactly ever remember making
such an offer, said, "Ah."

"I have a notebook filled with them. I think some publisher could do nicely putting out a complete volume of my work."

"Have any of them been published?"

"Not yet."

It seemed to Charteris that everyone he met had the notion that he or she could write a book; and of course one of the troubles of the literary world was that so many of them did.

The spacious, gleaming metal kitchen was the first stop, with its ultramodern aluminum electric stove, baking and roasting ovens and refrigerator; delicious smells vouched for another fine evening meal ahead. Dark-haired, bucket-headed Chief Cook Xavier Maier—properly outfitted in white apron and high cap—took time out to welcome the little group, while an assistant tended the steaming pots and sizzling pans, and a teenaged cabin boy peeled potatoes.

The chef demonstrated the dumbwaiter that conveyed dishes to the dining room above, saying, "We will go through four hundred forty pounds of fresh meat and poultry on this crossing, eight hundred eggs and two hundred twenty pounds of butter."

The expected ooohs and ahhhs greeted these statistics, and a few questions about storage were asked and answered. Then, as the group was filing out, the affable chef came over to the author, Hilda on his arm, and said, "Mr. Charteris, welcome back to the *Hindenburg*."

Charteris knew the man from the Ritz in Paris, where Maier had been head chef.

"Pleasure to be back, Xavier, with you providing the cuisine."

The chef's face dimpled in a smile. "Are you still threatening to write your own cookbook?"

"It's not an idle threat, Xavier. There's no better reading than a cookbook—no complex psychology, no dreary
dialogue, no phony messages."

"Well, I am still willing to contribute a few recipes."

"I'll be taking you up on that."

As they moved aft down the keel corridor, Hilda asked
Charteris, "So do I gather you're a gourmet cook, on top
of everything else?"

"Learning that was simply self-defense, dear."

"Oh?"

"The odds of finding a woman as beautiful and charming as you who can also cook are long indeed. And I
told you, I don't like to gamble."

Hilda smirked at him. "Have I just been insulted? Or
complimented?"

"Yes."

Soon they had left the passenger area, passing a handful of new larger cabins (the only ones on B deck), into
the belly of the beast. Moving single file down the narrow, blue-rubberized *Unterlaufgang*—lower catwalk—
the passengers (ship's doctor in the lead) were craning
their necks, eyes wide, mouths open but not speaking, as
the enormity of the airship made itself known to them.

The journey in the dark, last night, to the stern of the
ship where Spah's dog was in its wicker basket, had not
prepared Charteris for this staggering sight. On the
maiden voyage he and Pauline had not taken the tour, as
his wife suffered from vertigo. So he was as much a
virgin as the rest of the group.

They were tiny worshipers in a vast cathedral of wires
and arches and rings and girders and struts and yawning
open space. Awestruck, they wended their way, sur-
rounded by catwalks, rubber-treaded ladders, crisscross-
ings of bracing wires, steel-and-wire netting, and—

strangest of all—the huge billowing gas cells that were
the lungs of the ship. Light filtered in through the ship's
linen skin, providing an eerie grayish illumination that
created a sense of unreality.

Dr. Ruediger pointed out fuel and water tanks border-
ing the gangway, saying, "We start with 137,500 pounds
of diesel fuel for our four Daimler-Benz V-8 engines. As
the fuel is consumed, the ship becomes lighter. . . . In
fact, as you consume and use food for energy, the ship
loses weight, and the captain compensates by valving off
hydrogen."

His voice echoing, the doctor rattled off more facts and
figures, about maintaining the ship's trim, the collecting
and discarding of water ballast, and other matters. But
the passengers weren't really paying much attention—
they were Jonahs wandering through a whale, and were
busy being awestruck.

The postponing of the morning tour had, quite obviously (Charteris knew), been to allow a search for the
absent Knoecher. But despite its cavernlike interior, and
the plentiful pleats and crevices and overlaps of fabric,
as well as the shafts designed to allow leaking gas to
escape, and the network of girders and ladders and the
framework skeleton itself, the *Hindenburg* provided few
if any hiding places for a human.

On the other hand, concealing a small bomb would be
child's play.

As they traveled the narrow walkway to the stern, the
engines—so barely noticeable on the passenger decks—
built to a roar; other sounds fought for attention, including
the whir of ventilation units. Now and then a gray cover-
alled crew member would be spied on a ladder or perched
above them, attending to a valve or other controls.

For the most part, these crew members ignored the

intruders threading through their domain. But one of them—a tall, pale, baby-faced young man—was staring down. Charteris couldn't shake the feeling that the young crew member was staring down at him, in particular.

"There's Ulla!" Spah cried, pointing. He was just in front of Charteris.

"Who's Ulla?" Hilda asked Charteris; she was following his lead.

"His dog."

"Doctor," Spah was saying, "I want to stop and say hello!"

"I'm sorry, Mr. Spah, but our group needs to stay together. Those are my instructions."

"Well, that's fine—then we can all visit my Ulla. But do keep in mind she's young and excitable."

"Joe," Charteris said, "your Ulla almost knocked you into the ocean last night. Let's just move on, shall we?"

"Leslie! Don't tell me you don't like my dog!"

"I have nothing against dogs except that they are dirty, parasitic and only too happy to lick any hand that feeds them."

Spah grinned back. "Oh, Saint—you're joking again!"

Actually, he wasn't.

The group was stopped on the gangway, now.

With a strained smile, the doctor said, "Mr. Spah, you can come back later with a steward as your escort. We're on a strict schedule, so that I may take another group out at three o'clock. Please come along, sir."

But Spah was breaking off to climb a ladder up to the freight platform, saying, "Then go on ahead without me— I'll catch up."

"Mr. Spah, I can't allow—"

Spah paused on the ladder and sneered over at the young doctor. "So the Germans are even running their zeppelins like concentration camps these days, huh?"

The young doctor looked stricken. Then he said, "All right, Mr. Spah. Please be careful."

The group pressed on, descending two flights of stairs into the tail, where Ruediger—his voice weary—explained the emergency steering controls under the massive rudders. From here they could look out the tail fin's windows at the Atlantic, eight hundred feet below, milky white in the afternoon mist.

By the time the doctor had led them back up the stairs, Joe Spah was waiting. The acrobat fell back into line, in front of Charteris, to whom he said, "I'm going to report that doctor for cruelty to animals."

Ruediger either didn't hear that or chose to ignore it as he led the group up a ladder to a higher gangway, where they headed back, walking single file through a jungle of lines and wires, the immense tan gas cells billowing like loose, sagging flesh. Shortly they came to a lateral crosswalk that led out to an engine gondola.

"Would anyone like to visit gondola number three?" the doctor asked over considerable engine noise. "Mr. Spah, perhaps?"

A gangway with a thin guide rail stretched over the sea to the small gondola, where a single mechanic tended one of the ship's diesel engines.

"No thank you. I am an acrobat but not a fool."

The doctor paused, as if tempted to disagree.

Margaret Mather, clasping her hands like a schoolgirl, said, "How I wish I had the temerity to try."

Brightly, Gertrude Adelt said, "I'd like to give it a go!"

"Dear, are you sure?" her husband asked.

And indeed it was a treacherous proposition—Charteris was rather surprised the doctor had suggested it. The wind had to be barreling by at something like eighty knots.

Gertrude unpinned her leghorn hat and handed it to her husband; then she scrambled across the gangway, whipped by wind, and was gathered inside at the gondola's door by a gray-uniformed mechanic.

Hilda said, "She is braver than I."

"Or maybe just more foolish," Charteris said.

Perhaps a minute later, Gertrude made her way quickly back, taking her husband's hand, clearly shaken, saying, "The view was spectacular, but the noise! The noise was like the hammers of hell!"

As they resumed their Indian file way down the gangway, someone was moving up toward them: Chief Steward Kubis.

"Sorry to interrupt," the steward said, "but Captains Pruss and Lehmann have requested Mr. Charteris's presence."

"You stay with the group," Charteris told Hilda, touching her arm. "And I'll see you at supper."

She nodded but looked less than thrilled at being left behind.

Then Charteris went with the steward while the tour headed toward the bow, for a look at the control gondola, which the author had, after all, already visited earlier this morning, when he had met with the two captains to tell them of their missing passenger.

And somehow Charteris didn't think the captains were summoning him now to inform him Eric Knoecher had been found.

SEVEN

How the Hindenburg *Lost Contact with Home, and Leslie Charteris Was Recruited*

The chief steward delivered Charteris to the officers' mess, forward on portside B deck. The cozy room, decorated by a few framed nautical prints, was divided into two oversized booths, and Captain Pruss, Captain Lehmann and Luftwaffe undercover man Fritz Erdmann were seated in the slightly smaller of these, by the wall of slanting windows (a continuation of the promenade deck), through which the gray overcast day filtered in. The other booth was empty.

Charteris took the single chair at the round table the L of the booth encompassed. By the window sat the crisply uniformed if blandly handsome Captain Pruss, his cap on the table before him, crown down, like a soup bowl waiting to be filled. Next to him (and directly across from the author) was the *Hindenburg*'s previous captain, stocky and unprepossessing in his rumpled brown suit; beside him slumped the glum Erdmann, graying blond hair slicked back, an unconvincing tourist in his tan sport jacket over a yellow sweater with a gold-and-yellow tie.

No one rose but they all nodded to Charteris.

"Thank you for joining us, Mr. Charteris," Lehmann said, in English, forcing a smile out of the melancholy mask that had once seemed so genial. He was tamping tobacco into a meerschaum pipe—Charteris knew the *Reederei* director was an inveterate pipe smoker, to the point of holding its unlighted bowl in his palm, and clasping its cold stem in his teeth.

But Erdmann, apparently not realizing the pipe was a sort of prop to the captain, said, "Is it safe to smoke in here?"

"Oh yes, yes, certainly." Lehmann dug into his pocket and tossed a book of Frankfurter Hof matches onto the table. "Go ahead, gentlemen—I think we could all use a smoke about now, and the smoking room would not provide the privacy we need."

Charteris—his suspicions now confirmed that the officers on an airship were held to less stringent precautions than its passengers—withdrew his silver cigarette case from his sport-jacket pocket and offered a Gauloise to Captain Pruss, who waved it off, and to Erdmann, who accepted. Lehmann was lighting his pipe, getting it going on a single match; Erdmann fired up the French cigarette and shared a match with Charteris. The sweet fragrance of the pipe smoke mingled with the harsher blend of the cigarette's, forming another gray cloud, like those outside the slanting windows.

A steward poured coffee for all of them and disappeared.

"I'm going to make a wild guess," Charteris said, "and say Eric Knoecher hasn't turned up."

Erdmann twitched a weary smile, and Lehmann said, "The entire ship has been searched—every cabin inspected. There is no sign of him."

"I assume you've questioned the stewards who might have been on duty, in the wee morning hours."

Lehmann nodded. "No one was seen on either promenade deck after around three-thirty A.M. The few hearty souls still up, at that hour, had helped close down the smoking room, and stumbled out to the lounge to finish their last drink. Then off to bed."

Erdmann's gaze was unblinking as he said, "I understand, Mr. Charteris, that you agreed to tell anyone who asked that your cabin mate has a cold, and has confined himself to the cabin."

"Yes. And a few people have asked about him, and I've passed that tale along. No one's questioned its veracity. No one much misses Mr. Knoecher, it would seem."

"That surprises me," Erdmann said. "He had a certain charm."

"A cultivated charm that he used to obtain information from his victims. From your use of the past tense, Colonel, I assume you agree with me that Mr. Knoecher has become a victim himself."

"A murder victim," Erdmann said, exhaling smoke through his nostrils, dragon fashion, "yes. And this presents certain . . . difficulties."

"Such as the S.D. not being keen on having their agents bumped off."

Captain Pruss frowned. " 'Bumped off'?"

Charteris grinned. "Sorry, Captain . . . that's the Americans' rather colorful vernacular for homicide."

Lehmann, pipe in hand, leaned forward, saying, "All politics aside, the Zeppelin Company isn't keen on having murders committed aboard our ships, either."

"Admirable policy."

Lehmann's expression seemed somewhat exasperated. "Mr. Charteris ... Leslie ... you know that public relations are a major concern of ours. We are with this flight inaugurating our second season of round-trip travel to the United States. The damage this incident could do to the future of zeppelin travel is ... well, it's distressing even to contemplate."

Charteris shrugged, saying, "You're always going to have difficulties, Ernst, convincing Americans that you're a friendly, cuddly bunch under that goose-stepping regime."

"Be that as it may," Lehmann said, "there remains the possibility that the ... disappearance of Eric Knoecher will not be made public."

"Because if it does, zep travel gets a black eye." Charteris cast a glance at the Luftwaffe colonel. "And so does your government, if it becomes public knowledge that special police are traveling your ships as undercover spies."

Erdmann said nothing, but Lehmann said, "That's a rather harsh assessment, Leslie."

"But an accurate one, Ernst. So what do the boys back home have to say? What's the good word from Marshal Goering? Am I being enlisted to help cover up?"

Erdmann flicked ash onto the saucer where his coffee cup rested. "Neither Captain Lehmann nor myself will make the decision as to whether or not this apparent murder is revealed to the world at large."

"Hasn't someone back at Nazi Central made that decision already?"

Captain Pruss shifted in his seat, gesturing toward the grayness out the windows. "Mr. Charteris, we are currently in an electromagnetic storm. These conditions have created a complete radio blackout."

"How long will that last?"

"As long as the storm. Possibly many hours."

"Until we have a decision," Erdmann said, "until we have our orders, from the Air Ministry, we would . . . appreciate your help."

"In keeping Eric Knoecher alive and well and sick with a cold in my cabin, you mean?"

"Yes." The Luftwaffe colonel glanced at Lehmann; there was something pained about it. "That, and something more."

"What, gentlemen?"

Lehmann sighed pipe smoke. "I have discussed your offer with Captain Pruss and Colonel Erdmann."

"What offer, Ernst?"

"To help in our . . . investigation."

"Isn't that Colonel Erdmann's job?"

Erdmann said, "I understand you worked as a police constable."

"Yes—briefly. Didn't handle any murder cases, to speak of."

"And that you studied criminology at school. And obviously, as a writer of mystery novels—"

Charteris interrupted with a laugh. "It might be dangerous assuming Zane Grey can punch cattle, my friends, or H. G. Wells pilot a spaceship. But if there is some manner in which I can help—certainly I'm at your service."

Lehmann nodded, smiling a little. "Thank you, Leslie."

"But I don't offer this to help the brownshirt boys. I feel it's obviously an unsettling thing that we may have a murderer among us—however aptly chosen his victim may have been. Still, this seems more appropriate for the colonel, here—"

"The colonel," Lehmann said, with a wag of the head toward Erdmann, "cannot risk exposing the true nature of his presence here—which is to say, security."

"We're back to the bomb threat, again."

Lehmann nodded gravely. "Yes. Furthermore, if the colonel actively investigates, the disappearance of Knoecher will become known. What we need, from you, Leslie, is something more along the lines of a . . . sub-rosa investigation."

"A sort of discreet poking around, you mean."

"Precisely. Asking 'innocent' questions, assessing reactions, without letting anyone know about Mr. Knoecher's apparent dire fate."

"Understood."

"For example, Leslie, this morning, when you mentioned Knoecher's cold, and confinement, to your cabin— did anyone react to this in any way that might be considered suspicious?"

"No. And I have to admit, I had that thought in mind. After all, the murderer would know I'm lying."

"What I would suggest," Erdmann said, shifting in his seat, "is striking up friendships with the handful of passengers we consider our most likely suspects."

Charteris frowned. "You have thirty-some passengers, and at least as many crew members, plus stewards and officers . . . how can you narrow that group to a handful?"

Erdmann swallowed, his glum expression taking on a glazed cast. Finally he said, "I believe the names are all you need. How we arrived at them are irrelevant."

"No."

Erdmann looked up sharply. "What do you mean by that?"

"Actually, Fritz, 'no' is a word that requires precious little parsing. However, I'll gladly explain my meaning: I won't cooperate with you unless you're forthcoming. And if you refuse to answer the first question I have for you, well, then—I suggest you comb the passenger list for some other former-police-constable-trained-in-criminology-turned-mystery-writer."

And Charteris gave them a big smile, stubbed out his cigarette on his saucer, and rose.

"Please sit, Leslie," Lehmann said, motioning with his pipe in hand. "Sit, please!"

"Before I do, let's hear what the colonel has to say."

Erdmann sucked on the cigarette, which was presently about an inch and a half long. "First of all, could I beg another cigarette from you, Mr. Charteris?"

"All right." Still standing, he dug out his silver case and passed it over to Erdmann.

"When I knew we had an S.D. man aboard," Erdmann said, tamping the tip of the smoke on the case, "I took him aside and made him tell me who his . . . subjects . . . were to be."

Nodding, Charteris sat. Taking back his cigarette case, lighting Erdmann up with a match, and then doing the same for himself with another Gauloise, the author said, "Was Mr. Knoecher . . . forthcoming?"

"Yes. He didn't like it, but I was a ranking officer, with a problem rather larger than his."

"Sabotage."

"Yes. We'd had a bomb scare."

"And you wanted to know who your potential bombers were."

Erdmann nodded, once.

"What are the particulars of this bomb scare, Colonel?"

Erdmann glanced at Lehmann, who said, "Before you stand and threaten to leave again, Leslie, let me answer that. . . . It is what I consider to be a crank letter from a woman in Milwaukee."

"Milwaukee!"

"Yes. We know precious little about this woman at present, other than that she is friendly to the German cause—a member of a local Bund group."

"What did her letter state?"

Lehmann grinned nervously, drew smoke from his pipe, which drifted out of his mouth lazily as he said, "That this airship, on this passage, would be destroyed by a time bomb."

Charteris frowned, gesturing with the cigarette in hand, making smoke trails. "*Could* we have a time bomb aboard this ship? I find the prospect very credible, personally, having seen all the possible hiding places on my little tour."

The *Reederei* director shook his head. "Thanks to those precautions in Frankfurt that so offended you, Leslie, the presence of a bomb on the *Hindenburg* is a virtual impossibility. Every lighter, flashbulb, flashlight, every matchbook was confiscated."

Charteris pointed to Lehmann's own book of hotel matches in the middle of the table like a tiny centerpiece. "Not every matchbook."

"Let's not be absurd. As Colonel Erdmann will attest, the S.D. team that went over this ship did a painstaking, rigorous job of it. The mail and cargo has been examined with special equipment, the passengers' baggage thoroughly checked, even the crew was subject to stringent searches. No one had the opportunity to smuggle a bomb aboard this ship."

Charteris turned to Erdmann. "Do you agree, Colonel?"

"I do. There is no bomb aboard the LZ-129. Our security is far too comprehensive."

"Is it? Let me ask you—on Eric Knoecher's list of 'subjects,' which is now your list of likely murder suspects . . . was Joseph Spah by any chance included?"

Erdmann shrugged with his eyebrows. "Yes. Spah travels as an American, with a French passport, though he was born a German. As an artist, a performer, he frequently travels throughout Germany, and is known to spend time in the company of antiparty people."

"People in your anti-Hitler resistance movement."

"Mr. Charteris . . ."

"Oh, I forgot. There is no resistance movement in Germany. Please go on, Colonel."

Erdmann gestured with an open hand. "That's all the information I have on Mr. Spah, other than I understand he is considered potentially a dangerous spy by the S.D.—and that he has been a troublemaker on this flight."

Charteris exhaled smoke. "Well, I can add to your information—of course, with your excellent security, on this ship-that-could-not-possibly-have-a-bomb-aboard-it, you probably already know."

Erdmann blinked. "Know what, Mr. Charteris?"

"That Spah left our tour group—when was this, perhaps half an hour ago? He was allowed by Dr. Ruediger to leave the group, unattended, presumably to visit his dog."

"Unattended," Lehmann said, hollowly.

"Quite unattended—unless you consider his dog to have provided adequate supervision. He had plenty of time, alone, Ernst, to plant a bomb somewhere in the folds and flaps of your baby's tummy."

"We will have that area searched," Captain Pruss said.

"Splendid idea. Personally, I think Joe Spah is merely a clown—clever or obnoxious, depending on your tastes. Who else is on your list, Colonel?"

Erdmann dug a small notebook from inside his sport jacket. Flipping it open, thumbing to a certain page, he said, "Let us begin with the obvious—one of our Jewish passengers, a Moritz Feibusch, a broker of canned goods from San Francisco."

"An American?"

"Naturalized—German-born, with many relatives in his native land. While Mr. Feibusch has a commendable reputation as a businessman, he has spent an unusual amount of time in Germany this year—he had been there since January—and may be attempting to arrange expatriation of a number of friends and relatives to the United States."

Charteris laughed dryly. "Why would Uncle Adolf care about that? Fewer Jews in Germany would seem to be a felicitous state of affairs from the Nazi point of view."

The Luftwaffe colonel was shaking his head. "Not when officials have been bribed and corrupted to do so. At any rate, this explains Mr. Feibusch's presence on Knoecher's list. Interestingly, Mr. Feibusch's rather constant companion on this trip—a Leuchtenberg, William G., of Larchmont, New York—is *not* one of your missing cabin mate's 'subjects,' though he too is an American Jew, an executive with Alpha Lux, a manufacturer of gas filters."

Lehmann interjected, "The two men are not traveling

together—they were *thrown* together as a result of a seating arrangement."

"Seating arrangement?" Charteris asked.

Nodding, the *Reederei* director said, "We were instructed to seat the two American Jews together—it's a common practice, such segregation. From what I've observed, Mr. Leuchtenberg has spent the entire trip inebriated. If he's a spy or a murderer, he's an extremely adept actor."

"It's Joe Spah who plays a drunk in vaudeville," Charteris said. "I believe Leuchtenberg must be the fellow who was singing German folk songs in the back of our bus."

Lehmann nodded. "Most likely. He would seem harmless."

"You apparently haven't heard him sing," Charteris said, flicking ash onto his saucer. "Though considering Leuchtenberg's line of work, he'd have knowledge of the dangers and capacities of hydrogen." Charteris glanced Erdmann's way. "Who's next, Colonel?"

Flipping a page, Erdmann said, "A cotton broker from Bremen named Hirschfeld. George W. Very successful, and on the surface his credentials would seem impeccable."

"Now, Fritz, don't tell me he made the mistake of being born Jewish, too."

"No. Despite his name, he is not a Jew; but his mother was American, a Texan. He is thought to have dangerous connections. He spends much of his time in America, New York particularly."

"He spends time in New York! He does sound like a dangerous character."

Erdmann ignored the author's sarcasm and pressed on.

"The wealthiest man on this airship, no doubt, is Nelson Morris, of Chicago, Illinois."

"I've met him. Meatpacking magnate."

"Yes—and Jewish. With his enormous financial resources, he is in a position to help those of his persuasion back in Germany."

"Actually, I don't think they're persuaded into being Jewish, exactly—but do go on."

Erdmann glanced down at his little notebook. "Morris is traveling with a friend named Edward Douglas."

"I met him, as well. Advertising man."

"Knoecher didn't give me much background on Douglas, other than to say the S.D. has him pegged as a spy. He was a naval officer in the Great War and has remained in Europe ever since."

"All right." Charteris blew a smoke ring. "I can approach him easily enough. What about the third man in their party? The perfume king—Dolan?"

"J. Burtis Dolan. Strong French connections, but not considered a major risk."

"Who else?"

"Well, there's a woman named Mather—"

"Not Margaret Mather! What possible harm could that spinster do?"

"She travels widely in Europe and America. She is precisely the sort of 'innocent' who makes an ideal courier. In addition, she has Jewish friends in Massachusetts."

"I'm sure she'll prove to be a regular Mata Hari."

"I take it you've met her as well."

"Yes, Fritz, it's a small world on an airship. We held hands on the bus."

"To each his own." Erdmann thumbed to the next page, but didn't bother looking at it. "The final pair of names on the list I know will be familiar to you—I saw you dine with them last night."

"What, the Adelts, I suppose? Jew-loving journalists— the worst kind!"

"Mr. Charteris, these two are being considered for reeducation."

This seemed to alarm Lehmann; his eyes flared, nostrils. "Good God, man! Where?"

"Dachau."

Lehmann turned pale.

Erdmann added, "Knoecher was making an evaluation."

"It's, it's, it's absurd," Lehmann said. "Leonhard Adelt is my biographer! I've known him for many, many years—and Gertrude, too! Certainly they've had their difficulties with the current regime, but that is hardly uncommon, these days."

"*I* did not place them on the list, Captain," Erdmann said, rather solemnly. "These are names Knoecher gathered. Whether they deserve reeducation is for someone else to judge."

"What is Dachau?" Charteris asked.

"A concentration camp," Lehmann said, his voice hushed, his eyes hooded.

"I would call that a motive for murder," Erdmann said.

Charteris said nothing, but silently agreed.

"Keep in mind the Adelts are Catholics," Erdmann continued, "and are understandably upset about the recent arrest of over one thousand monks and nuns on sex-crime charges. In addition, the Adelts are both known to have Jewish and leftist international connections."

Lehmann's pipe had gone out. He didn't bother to re-light it.

Charteris flicked ash onto his saucer. "Anyone else on the list?"

"No," Erdmann said.

"No crew members?"

"Certainly not," Lehmann said. "We're a family, the *Reederei*."

"Is he right?" Charteris asked Erdmann.

"Knoecher said nothing of suspecting any crew member—who of course have passed S.S. and S.D. scrutiny. So, Mr. Charteris—you will help us?"

Charteris stood. "I'll poke around—discreetly. But I think we both know that there was at least one more name on that list of Knoecher's."

Lehmann lowered his gaze and Erdmann smiled, faintly; but Captain Pruss, confused, said, "Who, Mr. Charteris?"

"Me," Charteris said, and went out.

EIGHT

How the Hindenburg *Conserved Water, and Leslie Charteris Found a Cabin Mate*

Charteris stopped at the bar outside the smoking room, to collect a double Scotch and water. He sipped it, finding it to his liking—he appreciated good solid drinks, as opposed to samples of pale faintly tinted water—then ordered a second one.

Once inside the sealed smoking room, it was rather a bother to deal with that turnstile contraption you entered through, and of course you had to leave any burning cigar or cigarette behind upon returning for more libation.

Its air pressure regulated somewhat higher to keep out any stray wisps of hydrogen, the smoking room was a veritable chapel of combustion precaution: that single electric lighter on a cord, which smokers were clumsily sharing, the peachwood flooring in place of the more easily burning carpet found elsewhere on the ship, those automatically self-sealing ashtrays that swallowed tapped-in ashes. Charteris, resting his drinks on a table, could only grin as he matched a Gauloise, thinking of the director of the *Reederei*—within a few yards of this airtight chamber—puffing away at his pipe and inviting his cohorts to light up.

Douglas and his friends Morris and Dolan were seated in one corner, lost in conversation, wreathed in smoke. This was apparently a male preserve, though Charteris knew of no rule against women joining in the tobacco idolatry. The air was as filled with masculine braggadocio as it was with cigarette, cigar and pipe fumes. English seemed to be the language of choice, as various world problems were tackled—sit-down strikes, Japan's intrusion into Manchuria, Stalin exterminating "enemies of the working class," the war in Ethiopia, the war in Spain.

What a relief it was to have these problems resolved.

These discussions were in part prompted by a news broadcast piped in, first in German, then in English. One of the more mundane reports had to do with the price of cotton rising both in Europe and the U.S.A., up from nine to twelve.

A tall-dark-and-handsome brute in his mid-thirties, impeccable in his gray three-piece Brooks Brothers, responded to this pedestrian report thusly: "Yippee!"

So it was that Leslie Charteris, boy detective, made his first deduction: the rangy character who'd howled like a cowpoke was George W. Hirschfeld, cotton broker, son of a Texas mother.

As the news report concluded, Charteris ambled over to where the *Hindenburg*'s answer to Gene Autry stood at the railing beyond which the floor-set windows revealed an atmosphere almost as gray and smoky as the one in here. The man Charteris took for Hirschfeld was holding a big glass of beer, a man's man's drink, in a well-manicured hand.

"If you don't mind my saying so," Charteris said in English, cigarette drooping from his lips, a Scotch in either hand, "that was an enthusiastic response to a pretty dull piece of news."

"Depends on your point of view, son." His mellow baritone bore a peculiar distinction: the man had, simultaneously, German and Texas accents. The author had never heard anything quite like it.

"Again, I don't mean to stick my nose in," Charteris said, "but exactly what point of view might that be?"

"Let's just say a man has to have the ability to separate the wheat from the chaff." He waved dismissively toward their fellow smokers with a hand bedecked by several gold-and-precious-jeweled rings. "For instance, these poor fools around us listen to war news, to politics . . . the Pope wants the Reich to leave the Church alone, the Reich is up in arms about being accused of that Guernica bombing . . ."

"Yes. Important enough topics."

"Not in this man's opinion. I'm more impressed with hearin' that *Gone with the Wind* won the Pulitzer, or that General Motors declared a dollar a share. The technicians in Hollywood are out on strike, did you know that?"

"I missed that one."

He narrowed his eyes and shook a finger at Charteris. "Did you know there's an effort afoot to close down the burlesque houses in New York?"

"Perish the thought."

"Perish the goddamn thought is right." The big man snorted, threw back some of the beer. "Now *that's* important—like the Kentucky Derby's important, or the affair between the King and Mrs. Simpson is important. . . . Let these other poor boobs eat up that slop about war and politics and religion. Give me show business and business business, every damn time."

Charteris tasted his Scotch. "Are you an American?"

"Technically I'm a German. But I got a Texas momma, and I grew up in the U.S. of A., for the most part. Name's George Hirschfeld, of Lentz & Hirschfeld, Bremen—hell, you can't shake my hand with those drinks in it. You must be one two-fisted drinker!"

"Under these conditions I am."

"Hey, a table's opened up over there—care to join me?"

Hirschfeld settled into the booth side and Charteris took a chair with a small round table between them. They were seated near the railing and the windows. Charteris set down his drinks, and extended his hand.

The author was in the midst of a too-firm grip with the German Texan, and was starting to introduce himself, when Hirschfeld said, "I know who you are, Mr. Charteris." He mispronounced it Char-*teer*-us. "You're the mystery writer. Your detective's the Saint, right?"

"It's *Chart*-eris, actually. Are you a reader of mine?"

"No." Hirschfeld was firing up a Pall Mall—Charteris's favorite American brand, coincidentally. "No offense, but I gotta read too much, in my work—reports, newspapers, charts and God knows what all. For relaxation, I'm more a movie man, myself."

"Well, they're probably going to make my stuff into films, pretty soon. RKO just picked up the rights."

This seemed to impress the cotton broker. "Yeah? Who's gonna play your detective?"

"I'm lobbying for Cary Grant. I presume I'll get Grant Withers."

Hirschfeld laughed at that, a deep, raspy sound. "Broadway and Hollywood—that's what America's really about."

"You may have seen a picture or two I wrote."

"Really? You wrote movies?"

"Until the producers and George Raft rewrote them. I ended up telling Hollywood where it could get off."

"No kiddin'?"

"Yes, and Hollywood reciprocated by telling me what train I could get on."

Hirschfeld chuckled, flicked ash into a hungry ashtray, and gulped some beer. "Yeah, but now they've come crawlin' back to you. You got bestsellers to your credit, and so they wanna do business—that's the biggest part of show business, after all, that second word."

"Well," Charteris said, exhaling smoke through a tight smile, "I wouldn't say they've come crawling; but I am doing business with them, yes. How is it you know so much about me, if you don't read me?"

The businessman sighed. "I asked around about you, got to admit. I was interested in who beat me to the punch."

"Beat you to the punch?"

"There are two unattached females of the species on this big fat flying cigar, Mr. Char-teer-us . . . Charteris."

"Leslie."

"Leslie—and I'm George. Anyway, the only two girls aboard who aren't married to some other passenger are that dried-up spinach leaf the college boys are fighting over, and that good-looking blonde you cornered the market on. . . ." He lifted his beer glass, shook his head, smiling ruefully. "More power to you."

"I must admit when I first saw Miss Friederich, I felt

time was of the essence. You have an affinity for the well-turned ankle?"

"That's one of the parts I'm fond of—wouldn't say it was number one on my personal list. You see, my hobby is collecting showgirls, Mr. Charteris—Leslie. I make no apologies, and I get no complaints."

"Now I understand your appreciation for Broadway."

"You spend much time in America, Leslie?"

Funny thing was, "German" George Hirschfeld was the crystallization of Charteris's cock-eyed, clichéd one-time expectations about America. As a youth he'd sat in Singapore, learning of the U.S.A. from books and magazines, discovering a land largely peopled by Indians and characters in fringed buckskin jackets, a purple sage-covered landscape through which cowboys in chaps and sombreros galloped in endless chases, either part of, or one jump ahead of, a posse.

"More and more, these days," the author admitted. "America's where the money is—and impending war isn't."

"Don't listen to the doomsayers. Politics always takes a backseat to money. You probably don't realize you're talkin' to a card-carryin' Nazi."

"Really?"

"Joined May first three, no, four years ago. Party card number 3075295."

Charteris had finished his first Scotch; it was clearly time to begin his second. "If you don't mind my saying so, George, you don't seem the, uh, Nazi type."

Hirschfeld lifted his glass to Charteris. "And I take that as a compliment. See, back in thirty-three these little men in the Nazi party demanded seats on the Cotton Exchange and on the Board of Trade. You know the expression—if you can't beat 'em?"

"Join them."

Hirschfeld grinned and nodded. "I outfoxed the bas-
tards—protected my seat by signin' up."

"I see."

"Do you? Let me ask you this—do you know what a
bale of cotton is?"

"You mean what it sells for?"

"Hell, price is always in a state of flux. What I mean
is, ask any showgirl and she'll tell ya: cotton and money,
they're the same damn thing. Interchangeable. A few
bales of cotton—a Mercedes, a box at Longchamps, a
gold ring the size of an onion. And that's an exchange
that can be made regardless of who holds political power,
irrespective of political ideas and economic theories."

"Well, no matter one's politics, one does need cotton."

"Damn tootin'. You wear it, pants, shirt, underwear,
ties, socks, your wife even serves the evening meal on
it, and as for war? You know what war means to me?
Tents and uniforms and parachutes and rags to clean your
goddamn guns with."

"And to sop up blood."

"Now, now, Leslie, you think I'm coldhearted, cold-
blooded? No. I'm a businessman. What the fools of the
world want to do with themselves is their concern—I just
know, whatever they do, whatever they decide, they'll
still need me."

"Is cotton trading so difficult a business to master?"

"Cotton trading isn't just a business, Leslie—it's an
art. You see, my poppa was a cotton broker, and when I
was twenty-three, he put me to work on our cotton plantation on the Brazos River. This was born and bred into
me."

"Ah."

"A true trader can tell between good cotton and poor

cotton, between rain in Mississippi and Minnesota. Right now I'm in the middle of the biggest cotton deal of my career—fifty thousand tons in one fell swoop."

"This is American cotton?"

"That's right. Last deal like this that came along, Washington wouldn't sell cotton to Germany without us takin' some surplus U.S. lard. Imagine that? Cotton dunked in lard! Not this ol' boy. Because I talk their language. Because they know I'm an American at heart."

An American Nazi.

"I take it you're not Jewish, George?"

"No. My partner is."

"And you're not worried for him?"

"No. Economics will prevail over petty prejudices."

"For your partner's sake, I hope you're right."

"Have I offended you, Leslie?"

"No. Not at all."

"I'm a party member because those are the waters I have to swim in."

That was becoming a familiar refrain.

"That's fine, George—as long as you know to keep a keen eye out for sharks." Speaking of which. "Have you by any chance met my cabin mate, Eric Knoecher?"

"Why, yes! Charming man. I haven't seen him today."

If Hirschfeld was lying, he was very smooth; Charteris saw nothing in the man's eyes, heard not a hesitation or quaver in the man's voice, to indicate a murderer hiding his tracks. On the other hand, this was a man big enough to pitch another man out a window.

"Poor Eric's picked up a cold," Charteris said. "I suggested he stay in our cabin, under the sheets, and apparently he's taken my advice."

"Good advice. You give him one of your books to read, Leslie, to pass the time?"

"No, but perhaps I should. I've sometimes been told that my immortal works have brought cheer and comfort to the bedridden—but I have to admit that certain other readers have indicated I make them sick."

Hirschfeld chuckled, draining the last of his beer. "I don't know Knoecher very well—your cabin mate? He just came up and introduced himself to me, here in the smoking room."

"Really? When was that?"

"Fairly late last night. Maybe one, two in the morning. Wasn't keeping any closer track of time than I was the number of beers I was putting away. . . . And you know, I could use another right now, and you seem to have drained both your drinks. Shall we risk havin' our ears pop to go out and order up some more?"

"No thank you, George." Charteris stood. "I'm afraid I have an appointment to keep before supper."

"It is getting about that time." Hirschfeld half rose. "Perhaps we'll talk some more, later on—and I promise I won't bore you with cotton talk."

The men shook hands again.

"You haven't bored me at all, George. I never thought of cotton in quite this light, before."

Charteris had two appointments, actually. The second was with Hilda, at her cabin, to fetch her for an eight o'clock supper; and the first was with a shower.

The shower, to be precise, as this was the only one on the airship (or for that matter on any airship, this being a true first), and Charteris had signed up for 7:15 P.M. Morning reservations for this choice B-deck convenience were well nigh impossible, but at least freshening up before supper—a late supper, anyway—was an achievable goal.

He waited politely for the previous occupant to exit,

then he went in, used the toilet in the adjacent changing room, hanging his clothes up on the hooks, leaving his monocle on a shelf, and headed into a cubicle where he stood naked and cold awaiting an unseen steward to turn on the *wasser*. Above him was a nozzle that seemed big enough to bathe everyone on the ship in one blast.

But he had been warned by Chief Steward Kubis to "be quick about it," because the spray cut off automatically after three minutes, in an effort to conserve water, and if you were all soaped up at the moment, that was your problem.

"Airships must ration everything by weight," Kubis had told him. "Even the shower water is gathered and stored as ballast in dirty-water tanks."

Despite the shower's rather limp-wristed water pressure, he had managed to soap up and rinse off by the time the nozzle dribbled to its preordained stop.

When, half an hour later, Charteris left his cabin to fetch the lovely Hilda, he was bathed, shaved, trimmed and waxed (mustache only), cologned, pomaded and clothed in his white jacket and black tie, black shoes shiny as mirrors, looking at least like a million bucks.

Hilda, of course, looked like two million. She, too, had managed to book a shower, and smelled of lilacs, her blonde hair flowing to her shoulders now, shoulders that were beautifully bare thanks to a slim sheath of a dress that was all pleated black romaine, ruffled with pink and green satin ribbon.

"We are a pair," Charteris said, as he walked her to the dining room, where a table for two along the wall awaited.

"I never saw a more handsome man," she told him, as they waited for their Beaume Cuvée de l'Abbaye 1926, a fine red wine from the airship's "cellar."

"It would take a better writer than yours truly," he said to her, "to do your beauty justice."

Pretty corny stuff, he knew, but it felt very good, and even very real. They were holding hands and the look in her deep blue eyes promised a memorable evening.

They ate lightly if thoroughly of mixed green salad, cheese, fresh fruit, pâtés à la reine, and roast filet of beef, medium rare. Both declined dessert and sat drinking coffee, listening to the rain beat its insistent but trivial tattoo on the ship's skin, watching lightning-flecked charcoal clouds roll by.

The storm had kicked up again, the ship on a wild ride into pelting rain and torturous head winds—if they were doing fifty knots now, Charteris figured, they were lucky—but the mood it lent to the romantic evening could not have been better conjured by Merlin himself.

"I love the rain," he said.

"So do I," she said.

"I love it in Malaya—the tropical storms sheet down like a waterfall, they beat the roof like a drum, stream from the eaves in a hundred miniature Niagaras. I'd sit at an open veranda and watch it come down, with great dewdrops condensing on the glass of wine I held . . . the air suddenly cool, fresh, temporary relief from a steaming heat."

She squeezed his hand.

He went on: "I love it in Corsica, too—spluttering on the taut cloth of a tent top, peering out from that precarious shelter to watch the drops dancing on the rocks, running down to drench a parched ravine."

Now she was holding his hand with both of hers.

"I've watched thunderheads," he said, "building over the mountains in Tirol, bursting over the green valley where I didn't even have a tent, just a ground sheet to pull over my sleeping bag and hope that not too much of it would creep in . . . which it invariably did."

"I love the rain," she said.

"Ah, but you live in the city. Rain is just a nuisance in the city. To feel the excitement of the rain, you have to be where the rain belongs—out in the open, where you can see it falling all around you, separated from it by the least possible protection necessary to keep you dry—and sometimes not even that."

"I love it, too," she said.

"I've always been a sucker for rain—but, you know, I never loved the rain more than I love it right now. Right this moment."

"I love it."

They made love in her cabin, twice that night, and then they slept snuggled together in the lower bunk—the sound of rain nowhere near them, but they imagined they heard it.

They imagined they heard it clearly and well, though the only real thunder was the muffled sound of snoring from the cabin next door, leaching through the linen-covered foam panels of the wall.

DAY THREE:

Wednesday, May 5, 1937

NINE

How the Hindenburg *Provided a Puzzle, and Leslie Charteris Posted Cards*

Well out over the Atlantic, the *Hindenburg* loped along, stoically battling forty-five-knot head winds. Severe electrical disturbances continued to create a radio blackout, though occasional messages did get in and out—at six A.M., thirteen kilometers east of St. Johns, Newfoundland, one thousand kilometers southeast of Cape Farewell, the airship sent a message reporting continued electromagnetic storms and requesting weather information. Two and a half hours later, a transmission made its way through from Canada, informing the *Hindenburg* radio operator that lighter rains waited ahead.

Outside the slanting promenade windows, a cold, gray morning glided by even as Chef Xavier Maier's fabled fresh rolls warmed the tummies of the airship's pampered passengers.

Leslie Charteris and Hilda Friederich were latecomers to breakfast, barely beating the ten A.M. cutoff. They had slept in, cuddled in the lower bunk of her cabin, Charteris in his T-shirt and boxers, Hilda in a lacy slip. She had sent him off, a little after nine, to his own quarters, mortified by a knock at her door.

Charteris had slept through it, but apparently a steward had come by to make up the cabin—seemed Hilda had neglected to hang the little "Do Not Disturb" placard on the door handle—and she was suddenly embarrassed.

"Who cares what some steward thinks?" he said to her, pulling his trousers on. "If they have the poor manners and lack of sense to come around at such an ungodly hour, they can—"

But he hadn't finished his thought, and had barely buckled his belt, when she jostled him out into the hallway. Shoes and socks in hand, he told the door, in a firm voice, that he'd return in half an hour, to escort her to breakfast. A noncommittal, nonverbal response from behind the door was just ambiguous enough for him to take as a "yes."

Barefoot, he had returned to his cabin, washed up, shaved, slipped into fresh underthings over which he slung studiously casual attire, chiefly an open-neck light blue sport shirt, gray flannel trousers, and blue plaid sport jacket. Staring at himself in the small mirror, brushing his mustache with a thumbnail, he frowned at his reflection, thinking, *What's missing from this picture of perfection?*

Then he gave himself half a grin, shook his head: his monocle.

Sometimes he thought he should abandon the silly prop, but the simple truth was he either had to wear the thing or accept the indignity of reading glasses. And, of course, he was too goddamn vain for that, at such a tender age. Thirty, in just seven days, a single week left of his twenties . . .

He'd forgotten the damn chunk of glass in her cabin, of course, and when he stopped by to pick her up, she almost blushed as she smiled and handed the little round object to him, delicately, holding it between her thumb and forefinger like an entomological specimen.

He tucked the monocle into place, and gave her his most charming smile. "You look lovely to me, my dear, with or without this chunk of glass in."

And she did look lovely, of course, in a dark yellow crepe dress and jacket ensemble with a white cravat, her hair back up in braids. Did the latter signal that, though she'd let her hair down last night, today was another day?

"I feel a little foolish," she said.

"Whatever for?"

"For rushing you out like that. I apologize."

"Well, I won't accept your apology."

Eyelashes batted over her deep blues. "No?"

"Because it's unnecessary. I should have had the proper decorum to slip out before dawn like any good philanderer."

She drew in a breath, then let it out in that rough-edged laugh he so adored. "You are shameless."

"Thoroughly."

Breakfast was typically *Hindenburg* opulent: oranges, bananas, scrambled eggs with cheese, two kinds of sausage, and those luscious warm pastries and rolls with honey and a rainbow array of jellies and jams.

In between nibbles of grape-jellied roll, she said, "You are not a philanderer, Leslie. After all, I am not a married woman, and you are not a married man."

"To tell you truth," he said, applying strawberry jam

to his own roll, "technically I am. My divorce isn't final for several months."

"Still, you are unattached. As am I—I too am divorced."

"You've been married?" He knew she had spoken of a boyfriend who died in the Spanish Civil War, but marriage hadn't come up before.

"Twice," she said. "That should not surprise you, considering last night."

"When flying above the world, a worldly woman would seem an apt companion."

A one-sided smile twitched her cheek; her eyes were fixed on him. "You remind me so of my first husband—he was an artist, too."

"I'm glad to be thought of in that way—but I take it you mean he worked in oils on canvas."

"Yes, and in watercolor. He really was not a wonderful artist by any standard, or even a successful one—but he was a beautiful man, with a big well-shaped head and strong round shoulders."

"He does sound like me."

She laughed a little. "I was only nineteen, and he was at least forty. We were together a long time."

"How long is a long time?"

"Six years. Then, one day, he just left. He was gone for over a month, two months I think. My bad luck was that when he did come home, he found me with someone else. He beat the poor boy to a pulp, then stormed out again. That was the last I saw of him—the divorce was handled in the mails."

Charteris sipped his black coffee. "He does sound like an artist. Was your second husband any improvement?"

"Not really. He owned a bar in Frankfurt. I am afraid I was attracted to him for more practical reasons, though he was fine to look at, too. I met my boyfriend—the patriot—and then my second marriage was over. Not after six years, that time—just six months."

"Why are you sharing this with me, Hilda? Do you expect me to be shocked?"

"No. I expect you to understand that there have been many men in my life—you owe me nothing but these days, these wonderful days. And nights."

"That's a very modern outlook."

"Thank you, Leslie."

"But what if I develop old-fashioned ideas?"

A tiny smile flickered on the full lips, glistening with lipstick and just a little jam, in one corner. "I like you, Leslie."

"I had assumed as much." He reached across and gently thumbed away the jam.

Her chin crinkled in another smile, and then she said, "You see, I like men. Most women do not. Oh, they say they do—but what they are after, most women, is house and home and security. They do not see what I see in a man—or at least, some men."

"Which is?"

Her eyes narrowed and glittered. "An opportunity to live a larger life. Without a man there is no way for a woman to get beyond a limited sphere of influence, of experience."

Somehow he didn't think this meant she was a gold digger: he took her at her word. It was adventure she wanted; a life worth living, not dishwater dull.

Nonetheless, the only adventure awaiting Hilda, after breakfast, was a shared puzzle with Gertrude Adelt in the starboard side's reading and writing room.

"A thousand little gray-and-blue pieces," Gertrude said, as the two attractive women drew up around a small round table, "and, properly assembled, we'll have a magnificent picture of this very airship."

"Sounds like a perfectly dreadful way to waste a morning," Charteris said, eyeing a certain individual across the room, "but I won't stand in your way."

Nodding to Leonhard Adelt, who was pecking away at a typewriter at one of the wall desks, still earning his keep via that article on zep travel, Charteris headed over to a small table where a stocky man in his mid-fifties sat with a stack of postcards as thick as a Manhattan phone book.

The man—who wore a rumpled brown suit about the same color as his thinning hair, with pleasant if rather lumpy features—was Moritz Feibusch. Charteris had never met the man, nor had Feibusch been pointed out to him. But Charteris—newly minted amateur detective that he was—had deduced the identity of the fellow who sat addressing the cards, imprinting the back of them with an inkpad's rubber stamp, referring to a small black notebook as he did.

Feibusch had been sitting with William Leuchtenburg at a table for two along the wall in the dining room at every meal thus far. The other tables had invariably been taken by romantic couples—this singular instance of two men sitting together, Charteris surmised, represented the pair of American Jews who had been segregated together.

Also, he had recognized Leuchtenburg as the singing drunk from the bus, and knew as well that the Jews would not be seated at a table larger than one of the two-seaters—wouldn't be practical, and Germans were, if anything, creatures of efficiency.

Pulling up a chair, Charteris said to Feibusch, "That's quite a stack of cards you've got there. Do you really have that many friends?"

The lumpy features were pleasant enough, particularly with the man's ready smile. "I have my share of friends—but there's always room for one more. I'm Moritz Feibusch, from San Francisco." He extended a hand that had seen its share of work.

Charteris took it, introducing himself.

"I heard about you!" Feibusch said, brightening even further. "You're our ship's celebrity!"

"Just goes to show you that it isn't always cream that rises to the top."

Feibusch let out a single hearty laugh. "Well, Mr. Charteris, I must admit, not everybody in this little black book is a dear friend. In fact, most of them are business accounts."

"And it doesn't hurt to treat business acquaintances like dear friends."

"Surely doesn't. I figure just about anybody would get a kick out of getting one of these. . . ."

And Feibusch handed Charteris a pre-postage-affixed picture postcard with an airbrushed pastel painting of the *Hindenburg* in full flight against a blue sky, a tiny ocean liner looking insignificant and lost in the blue ocean below. Turning it over, Charteris saw that Feibusch had written the address in by hand, but the space for a message was stamped: "Greetings from the maiden voyage of the *Hindenburg*," also hand-signed by Feibusch.

"Very nice," the author said. "Of course, this isn't the maiden voyage. . . ."

Feibusch shrugged. "It is for me. Anyway, when I bought these cards from Steward Kubis—two hundred and some!—I noticed the rubber stamp and asked what it was, and he told me, and I asked if I could use it. It was left over from last year. He didn't see why not. And neither did I."

"What business are you in, Mr. Feibusch?"

"Moritz, please, make it Moritz. And may I call you Lester?"

"It's Leslie, and of course you can."

"I'm in tuna fish." Feibusch paused in processing the postcards, turning toward Charteris. "Broker of canned tuna fish and other canned goods, *and* fancy goods." He beamed, shaking his head. "Now, fancy goods, that's what's took off like a rocket ship."

"Fancy goods?"

His eyes went wide with enthusiasm. "Packages of preserves—sugared oranges and lemons, raisins, dried prunes, peanuts, cashews—all done up in pretty gift boxes with cellophane wrapping. Like a hatbox you can look down into, and see all the delicious candied fruits and nuts. All tied up with a pink ribbon, and set off like so with apple blossoms—much better than flowers! Perfect for weddings, ship sailings, especially Christmas. The Germans, Viennese, Hungarians, they all love my gift boxes."

"You're quite a salesman, Moritz. I'd buy one of the damn things, if you had one with you."

Feibusch leaned close to the author, conspiratorially. "If I had one of the damn things along, trust me—I'd sell it to you."

They both laughed, then Charteris said, "Say, don't let me interfere with your efforts, there."

"Thanks," Feibusch said, and resumed his addressing, stamping and signing, a one-man assembly line. "Please do keep me company, if you like. It's rather a relief to"— he glanced about—"sit with someone who's sober."

"I noticed your friend does like to keep lubricated."

"He's in the bar now. Before lunch, and, oy, he's already putting it away like Prohibition's going to start up

again any second. He's a nice enough man—Leuchtenburg is his name—prominent sort, president of his own
company. But he's been pickled since day one."

"Why? Other than he likes it, of course."

Now Feibusch's eyes narrowed. "I think he's resentful
of these Germans."

"He's German himself, isn't he? A German-American,
anyway."

"German-American Jew. That's something else alto-
gether. Why do you think we're stuck together, him and
me? If you don't have a concentration camp handy, at
least herd the Jews around one table, right?"

"It has gotten unpleasant."

"Unpleasant! These Germans, they've gone mad. I sell
to groceries, butcher shops, bakeries, dairies—and do
you know I have to go in the back door, do business in
the back room? Because out front, in the window, it says,
'Jews Not Admitted.' "

"If it were me, I don't think I'd do business there anymore."

"In my business, I have to travel, and I have to do
business with all kinds; hell, Lester, my partner is Irish!"

"You are open-minded."

Feibusch sighed. "What is a man to do? Business in
Germany remains good. What would the Christians of
Europe do without Jews to sell them Christmas and
Easter goodies? Ah, but the hotels in Germany, many of
them won't give lodgings to someone like me, anymore.
I come to towns and the sign that used to say, 'Welcome
To,' says, 'Jews Strictly Forbidden,' now—or worse,
'Jews Enter at Your Own Risk.' "

"I've seen it myself. Do you know I saw a sign outside
Cologne that said, 'Drive Carefully! Sharp Curve! Jews
75 Miles an Hour.' "

"I believe it, I believe it. The radio, they don't play Mendelssohn anymore!"

Charteris nodded. "The best film directors in Germany are going to Hollywood, you know—Max Reinhardt, Fritz Lang. . . ."

"The owners of the *Frankfurter Zeitung* were forced to sell! The result? A dull paper, unreadable."

Charteris shook his head. "Bad movies."

"Wagner on the radio, all day, all night."

"Not exactly music to fall asleep by, is it?"

Feibusch sighed. "So my friend Leuchtenburg chooses to stay drunk."

"What do you do, Moritz? Besides fill out postcards?"

"I enjoy life, Lester. So this is a German ship? Does that mean Chef Maier's food is any less tasty? Make the best of life, I say."

"I guess that's possible, when you can go back to San Francisco, at the end of the day."

Feibusch paused in his postcard assembly. "You make a good point." In a hushed voice, he said, "I still have many relatives in Germany. I help as I can."

"How?"

"I'm bringing my two nephews over, to work in a canning plant. My mother, in October, when I come for the Easter selling, I will bring home with me. My wife and I have no children; Mama will be no burden."

"Aren't there restrictions . . . ?"

"The papers are difficult to come by, yes." Feibusch looked side to side. Very quietly, he said, "A little money here, a little money there. German palms grease up like anybody's. My biggest problem is Mama herself."

"How so?"

"She doesn't want to leave 'her Germany'—even though it has not been *her* Germany for a long time. Did you know that there was a law passed recently, in the glorious fatherland? No Jewish old people allowed in German old folks' homes; no Jewish orphans in the orphanages, either. Takes up too much valuable space."

"Criminal."

Feibusch shrugged elaborately, and returned to his postcards. "It will be Germany's loss, America's gain. The Nazis deprive Jews of their very citizenship—they cannot hold public office or enter the civil service, many fields are closed to them, teaching, farming, journalism, radio, even the stock exchange. Next it will be medicine, law. . . ."

"It's difficult to imagine where it will end."

"Difficult and terrible, Lester. The real tragedy is, the German people themselves, they are not bad. It's these leaders, these mad leaders."

"But a people are only as good as their leaders."

"I know, I know. Still, as individuals—I've met so many nice people on this trip. Like you, Mr. Charteris. What, if I may ask, is your heritage?"

"British subject—my mother was English, my father Chinese, a surgeon. I spend more time in America, these days. I plan to naturalize."

"Good. Nothing against Britain, but America—that's the place."

A wry smile tickled Charteris's lips. "No prejudice there?"

"Plenty. A Jew like me—a man of mixed blood like you, we will always meet stupidity, in a free land like America. Just, thank God, not this madness."

Charteris nodded. "Well, as you say, on an individual basis, the Germans are a fine people. My cabin mate is German—poor blighter's under the weather, though. Cooped up in our cabin with shakes and sniffles."

"Too bad. Even with this rain, this voyage is a delight."

"Well, Eric's in no condition to enjoy. Eric Knoecher is his name, my cabin mate."

"Oh, I've met him! The importer."

"Yes, that's right."

Feibusch paused again, at his postcards. "He looked me up, first night. He seemed healthy enough, then. Compared notes, tricks of the trade. We're in the same business, right?"

"Right."

"Fine fellow, friendly fellow. Do give him my best, my sympathy. You see, there's an example for you. Like you said."

"Pardon?"

"Your cabin mate! As individuals, the Germans can be wonderful people."

"Yes." Charteris rose. "Eric would seem to be a shining example, at that. . . . If you'll excuse me."

"Certainly, Lester. Pleasure meeting you, nice chatting with you."

"Likewise, Moritz. Can I post those for you?"

"Please!" Feibusch handed a batch of cards to Charteris, who dropped them down the pneumatic tube to the ship's post office, while the seller of fancy goods returned his full attention to his stamping and signing.

TEN

How the Hindenburg *Shadowed the* Titanic, *and Leslie Charteris Met a Fan*

Summoned by the ship's gong, Charteris and Hilda had a delicious if uneventful lunch with the Adelts. Several casual mentions of his bedridden cabin mate created no reaction whatever from either husband or wife, though Gertrude made an interesting observation about the undercover Luftwaffe colonel.

"That man whose wife came aboard to see him off," she said, "Colonel Erdmann . . . what do you suppose he's a colonel of?"

"Beats me," Charteris said.

"Military of some kind," her husband said dismissively, dipping a spoon into his soup.

"He has such a sad face." Gertrude's pretty face was sad, itself. "So often he just sits near one of the obser-

vation windows, staring out at nothing with such a . . .
profound look of sadness. Have you noticed, Leslie?"

"No," he lied.

"It all but makes me cry."

Her husband patted Gertrude's hand. "You're just
tired. There's nothing like boredom to wear a person
out."

Gertrude could only agree, and, after dessert, the man
and wife disappeared for a postluncheon nap—such
snoozes having become *de rigueur* on this voyage,
which—though so much quicker than travel by steamer—
seemed every bit as leisurely.

"You wouldn't like to go to your cabin for a nap, dear,
would you?" Charteris asked Hilda, as they strolled over
toward the starboard lounge.

She almost smiled, her eyes wide and amused. "Alone
or together?"

"I was thinking, together." He yawned, not very convincingly.

"Do you think the Adelts are . . . napping?"

"If I had a wife that beautiful, I wouldn't be."

She nudged him with an elbow, but the faint amusement on her lips had fully blossomed into that wonderful
kiss of a smile.

At the starboard promenade, he and Hilda saw more
evidence of passengers lost in ocean-liner mode—an old
couple sat in the lounge, blankets covering their legs,
staring out at the grayness, as if on a steamer deck. (It
was chilly today, and the stewards were rushing around
closing the fresh-air vents.) Those two little boys were
on the floor of the lounge, playing dominoes while at the
adjacent table their mother wrote a letter and their father
read a book—reading and letter writing not being re-
stricted to the library. Around the lounge, and on the

upholstered benches by the windows, other passengers were similarly occupied, jotting messages to friends or engrossed in some novel, unfortunately none of them having the courtesy of being wrapped up in anything of Charteris's.

Margaret Mather, in a powder-blue frock with lacy collar and cuffs, appropriate for a woman perhaps half her age, sat alone on one of the padded benches, looking rather expectantly out the slanting windows. In her lap, a hand clutching it, was a spiral pad.

"Hello, Miss Mather," he said. "May we join you?"

The sparrowlike spinster beamed at him, smiled rather coolly at Hilda, and said, "Oh most certainly," patting the bench next to her, her eyes locked on his.

The three of them squeezed onto the banquette.

"Do you know something we don't know?" Charteris asked Miss Mather, as she continued to watch the gray overcast sky, an endless blue-gray sea below, about as boring a tonal study as he could imagine.

"Chief Steward Kubis came by a few moments ago," Miss Mather said brightly, "and said we'd be coming to Newfoundland, shortly."

Hilda rose and leaned against the shelflike sill. "I do not see land yet, Miss Mather."

"Patience, dear." Miss Mather smiled over at the author, perhaps pleased that he had not moved away, even though now there was more room on the bench. She almost whispered, "Your friend must not be an experienced traveler."

"How often do you get to America, Miss Mather?"

"I try to get home at least once a year, to visit my brother—he teaches art and architecture at Princeton University. Or did I mention that already?"

"Is your brother as political as many professors are, these days?"

"I suppose so." Again, she spoke sotto voce: "He's certainly unhappy with the Germans for stifling the arts."

"Well, it's mostly the Jewish artists they're stifling."

"I hope that's not all right with you, Mr. Charteris!"

He gave her an easy smile. "No. No, it isn't. But what can one do?"

"One must try. What would you say if . . . I shouldn't say."

But she wanted him to ask, so he did. "What would I say if what, Margaret? . . . May I call you Margaret?"

"Certainly, Leslie."

"You were saying. . . ."

"Oh. Well, you may recall my extra luggage. Perhaps you thought that was just feminine vanity."

"Never."

"You see . . ." She curled a finger to bring his face closer to hers. "I carry certain items home with me, to sell for friends of mine."

"Jewish friends?"

She reared away. "I didn't say that. But it is true that there's a terrible need for money for these poor people to buy their freedom. Isn't it a shame?"

"Yes."

Hilda almost squealed. "I see it! I see land!"

Charteris and Miss Mather joined Hilda at the windows and watched as Cape Race grew from a smudge on the horizon into a lighthouse-dotted shoreline giving way to vast green foothills. But even more exciting were the white dots along the coast.

"What are those?" Hilda asked, rather breathlessly.

"You'll see soon enough," Charteris said.

"Why, they're icebergs!" Miss Mather said. Her eyes

were glittering. "Oh, how thrilling! Did you know the
Titanic met its fate in icy waters nearby? Just twenty-five
years ago, that iceberg did its terrible deed. . . ."

"I doubt we'll crash into one," Charteris said.

But there was no denying their ghostly beauty. The
ship *was* flying low, the captain giving the passengers an
eyeful of their first scenery, dipping to steer over a huge
'berg that might have been an abstraction in marble, set
afloat by an eccentric artist.

"O iceberg shining white against the stone-gray sea,"
Miss Mather said, regally, "with pools of vivid green
whose forms spread greener still beneath the pale waters. . . ."

Quickly, the spinster scampered back to the bench,
snatched up her notebook, sat, withdrew the pencil from
its wire spiral spine, and jotted down her immortal words.

"She's a poet," Charteris whispered to Hilda. "Muse
struck her, apparently."

Smirking, Hilda nodded and turned away, smothering
a little laugh with a hand.

"Don't be cruel, dear," he whispered to her.

Miss Mather slapped her notebook shut and returned
to the author's side, saying, "I'll complete it later. One
must capture magic when one can—don't you agree?"

"Oh yes."

"I'll let you see it, when I've finished."

"Ah."

Hilda said, "Look *now!*"

The sun had come out to lay a double rainbow around
the airship, the mammoth iceberg sparkling as if
diamond-studded.

"O rainbow, spring from everywhere," Miss Mather
proclaimed, "and I will watch you grow and grow, until
beneath our floating galleon you form a circle complete."

Then, pleased with herself, she scurried back to her notebook and preserved these magical words in pencil.

The coastline soon receded into the distance as the ship swung southward; before long, they were lost in gray fog over an invisible sea—familiar territory for this ship on this trip.

Charteris returned to Miss Mather's side, on the bench. Hilda remained at the sill, watching the fog slither by like a giant's cigar smoke.

Blessedly self-satisfied, Miss Mather closed her notebook, and then—as he was searching for a way to bring up Eric Knoecher—she did it for him, saying, "You know, that nice young gentleman I saw at your table, the first night?"

"Yes?"

"What's become of him? He seemed like such a lovely boy."

"He did? That is, he did. You spoke to him?"

"Yes." She gazed contentedly into the memory of the encounter. "Very sweet—he sought me out, to . . . it embarrasses me to say so."

"Please. You're among friends."

"He said I dressed beautifully. He said with my slender figure I might well be a . . . you'll laugh."

"No."

". . . a fashion model."

Hilda laughed, but managed to turn it into a cough.

"His name is Eric, isn't it?" Miss Mather went on.

"Yes," Charteris said, "Eric Knoecher. He's my cabin mate, actually."

"Really? Well, where is he keeping himself?"

"*In* the cabin, I'm afraid. He's come down with a terrible cold."

"Oh dear! Such a nice-looking young man. Perhaps I could take him some soup."

Charteris shook his head. "No, he's specifically requested I keep everyone away from him—he's afraid he's contagious."

"Oh!" Miss Mather glanced suspiciously at Hilda, then back to Charteris. "Well, uh, where are *you* staying, then?"

"With him. I seem to be immune."

She sighed and sat back, notebook in her lap, held by both hands. "Well, please do give him my best."

"We'll do that," Charteris said, and rose, and he and Hilda wandered over to the lounge. A steward was taking drink orders from the bar and Charteris asked for a double Scotch and water and Hilda requested a Frosted Cocktail.

They sat and chatted and then their drinks came and they sat and drank and chatted—all the while Charteris wondering if Miss Mather had been so easily forthcoming about her aid to German Jews with that nice-looking young Eric Knoecher.

"Excuse me, sir?" piped up a voice just to his left, a male voice, rather high-pitched, almost as if it had not quite changed yet. The English words were precise if heavily German-accented.

Looking up, swiveling slightly, Charteris saw respectfully standing there, in gray coveralls and crepe-soled slippers, a young crew member—the boy couldn't be older than twenty-five—fresh-faced, blue-eyed (weren't they all?), a tall, pale lad whose wholesome good looks were offset by ears that stuck out slightly from the elongated oval of his head, features somewhat embryonic, his lips puffily feminine, his jaw a bit weak.

"Excuse me for interrupting, sir."

Suddenly Charteris realized this was the baby-faced crew member who had stared down at him from the rafters of the ship, on yesterday afternoon's tour.

"Not at all. It's rather a treat to see one of the crew invade our sacrosanct little world."

But Hilda seemed annoyed by this intrusion, openly frowning, and Charteris gave her a quick sharp look, and she softened.

"I was hoping you might sign my book." From behind his back the boy withdrew a well-read-looking copy of *The Saint Overboard,* the Hodder & Stoughton British edition, its dust jacket protected in the manner of a lending library, one of whose cast-off copies this apparently was.

"Well, it would be my pleasure," the author said. "Everyone on board seems to know who I am, and some even claim to read me, but you're the only one with proof. Do you have a pen?"

"I came prepared, sir." The boy rather stiffly handed forward both the book and a fountain pen.

"This particular work has been translated into German," Charteris said, as he thumbed to the title page. "But you have an English copy, I see."

"I prefer to read American and British books in the tongue they were written in, sir."

"You speak very well. What's your name, son? So I can it inscribe in the book?"

"Eric," he said. "Eric Spehl."

Another Eric. Another blue-eyed Eric, at that.

"No joke intended, Eric, but could you spell Spehl?"

The boy didn't smile; well, it hadn't been much of a joke and he'd probably heard it a thousand times.

"S-P-E-H-L," he said.

Charteris signed it—"To Eric Spehl, with Saintly best

wishes"—and added the stick figure with halo that was the "sign of the Saint," a logo that had risen out of Charteris's own limited artistic ability but which had added enormously to the success and recognizability of his swashbuckling creation.

He handed the book back to the lad, who held it open, letting the glistening black ink dry. Strangely, Spehl's expression remained blank, with little of the die-hard fan's glowing-eyed pleasure. Obviously a shy one.

Hilda was frowning again, tapping her finger on the table. Embarrassed, Charteris made conversation with the young crew member.

"Do you like mystery fiction in general, Eric? Or are you strictly a Saint fan?"

The boy seemed to brighten a little. "Oh yes, I like detective stories and Wild West novels. Biographies, too."

"That's an interesting combination—escape fiction and biographies."

"Well, sir, in both cases they represent lives more interesting than mine."

"What could be more interesting than working on a zeppelin? What's your job, by the way?"

"Rigger."

"That sounds more like duty on a sailboat."

"I use a sailmaker's needle, sir, and heavy thread that can stand up to weather like we've been having."

"You work mostly with your hands, then."

He nodded. "I was an upholsterer's apprentice before I came to work for the *Reederei*. But I am no seamstress."

This last seemed vaguely defensive.

"I'm sure you aren't, Eric."

"I have to climb high up into the ship to patch a gasbag tear, or repair the linen skin over the frames."

"Exacting work. Dangerous. And of course you get to travel."

Spehl nodded. "I like that very much. I'm just a farm boy, and now my world is so much bigger."

"Where were you raised?"

Hilda sighed heavily. Charteris glanced at her again, trying to convey his unhappiness with her rude behavior. She glanced away.

"Goschweiler, sir—a little village in the upland meadows of the Black Forest. Beautiful there. But just one small corner of the big world."

"Still, home always has its special place in our hearts, doesn't it? Well, thank you, Eric, and do keep reading me."

Charteris held out his hand and the boy blinked, then accepted the handshake, and Spehl's grip was firm, powerful, more than you might expect of a slender lad like this, if you didn't know the good and taxing work he did with his hands.

The inscription dry, Spehl closed the cover on the Saint book, nodded, muttered another thanks, and moved quickly off. Another jumpsuited crew member—whose presence Charteris hadn't noticed before—rose from a bench by the slanting windows, where he had apparently been waiting for his friend. A shorter, more burly fellow, he fell in at Spehl's side, and they made a quick exit.

"Why were you so ill-mannered with that boy?" he asked the braided beauty, mildly aggravated with her.

Her chin was high; she sniffed. "He was intruding. We were having a quiet moment. Why did you keep him here, talking to him, for such a long time?"

He sipped his Scotch. "First, my dear, that young man is a reader of mine. That means he's a customer. And callow youths all around the world, like that one, keep

me in business, and allow me to maintain the high style
of living to which I've become so accustomed, including
the ability to flit about the skies with lovely mysterious
women."

She couldn't help herself: she laughed at that. Shaking
her head, sipping her Frosted Cocktail, she said, "I was
boorish. Accept my apologies."

"No. You'll have to find some way to make it up to
me."

"What do you have in mind?"

"I'm sure you'll think of something."

"You mean a late-afternoon nap in my cabin?"

He yawned again, no more convincingly than before.
"I could use a quick one. Snooze, I mean."

"You are an outrageous, impudent man," she said.

And stood, and held her hand out to him, and walked
with him from the lounge, on the way to her cabin. As
they headed for the stairs down to B deck, Miss Mather,
seated on the window bench, glanced up from her poetry
in progress to smile at him, and ignore her.

He nodded at the spinster and they moved on.

Soon the couple were just outside Hilda's cabin door.

"O beautiful Viking," he said to her, "let down thy
golden braids and unleash thy Valkyrie spirit upon me,
and lift my undeserving soul to the skies."

And Hilda, bosom heaving with her full-bodied laugh,
dragged him inside.

ELEVEN

How the Hindenburg's *Erstwhile Captain Entertained, and Leslie Charteris Had a Caller*

After the usual sumptuous dinner, as stewards moved in to clear the tables, word spread that Captain Lehmann was going to entertain in the lounge. Most of the passengers gathered there, or along the adjacent promenade, as the fatherly former captain of the airship stood like an itinerant street musician with the accordion slung before him. Charteris (in his white dinner jacket), Hilda (in a low-cut green gown) and the Adelts were seated at a table along the waist-high partition between lounge and promenade. It was fair to say that, with the exception of the die-hard chimneys in the smoking room on B deck below, the *Hindenburg*'s passengers were gathered nearly en masse.

"Many of you who have sailed with us before," Lehmann said in German (Charteris finding the word choice of "sailed" rather than "flown" an interesting one), "have inquired about the absence of our celebrated aluminum piano."

Gertrude Adelt called out gaily, "Oh yes! We enjoyed it so, when you played for us!"

Lehmann smiled, with mixed embarrassment and pride, and said, "And I enjoyed it so when you, Mrs. Adelt, and other passengers sang along. But commerce rules even the skies—the piano weighed more than you, my dear . . . and we are fully booked on our return voyage with, as you know, so many travelers set to attend the English coronation."

Heads nodded all around the lounge.

"So," Lehmann continued, "rather than leave a pretty lady behind—we unloaded the piano."

Gentle laughter blossomed around the room, and now it was lovely Gertrude Adelt's turn to react in embarrassment, and perhaps pride.

Hoisting his accordion, Lehmann continued, "This portable 'piano' will have to do for the evening. If our German passengers will bear with me, I'll repeat some of that for our American and English guests."

Lehmann gave a condensed English version of his spiel, and then—first in English, then in German—assured everyone that he would give equal time to German and American folk songs and English ballads . . . but said he would keep things neutral by beginning with an instrumental rendition of something by Straus.

The evening evolved into a rather merry sing-along, and Charteris joined in lustily. The author had a pleasant second tenor and liked to sing, though he felt more than a pang or two for the absence of his wife, Pauline, who sang *very* well, and had been his duet partner in this same lounge just a year before.

Hilda had a pleasant, relatively on-key alto that reminded Charteris enough of Marlene Dietrich to stoke the fires of his infatuation, and relegate his soon-to-be ex-wife to a distant compartment of his mind. Since he would sing the English and American tunes, and she the German ones, they were trading off, and singing to each other, and it was very romantic and not a little sexy.

He was most disappointed when a finger tapped him on his shoulder and Chief Steward Kubis leaned in across the partition to whisper, "You are wanted in the officers' mess, sir."

Sighing, nodding reluctantly, he patted Hilda's hand, said, "You'll have to excuse me, dear," exchanging disappointed glances with his braided amour of the moment.

The officers' mess was cleared but for the blandly handsome Captain Pruss and the doleful Colonel Fritz Erdmann, seated again by the windows, the grayness of the day replaced by the ebony of the night. A small conical lamp on the booth's table gave off a yellowish cast, to match Charteris's own jaundiced reaction.

"You know, Captain," Charteris said in English, pointedly, not sitting, "I am a paying passenger. I have a right to enjoy myself like any other customer of the *Reederei*. If you've pulled me away from the side of that magnificent blonde countrywoman of yours, just for me to give you a report of my amateur detective findings to date . . . then might I suggest we reschedule for a more propitious time?"

"Please sit," the crisply uniformed captain said, with a respectful nod.

Erdmann said, "We apologize for the intrusion into your evening. There are developments we need to share

with you—and we need your help, your . . ." Erdmann
searched for the English words. ". . . expert opinion."

"For God's sake, I write blood and thunder. I'm not
an 'expert' on real crime and espionage. Have you people
gone mad?"

The melancholy mask of Erdmann's oblong face
twitched a smile. He leaned forward, hands folded almost
prayerfully. "There is much madness at large in our
world today, would you not agree?"

"Yes, but you may wish to speak to your boy Adolf
about that. I've had little to do with causing it, personally.
In fact I'll go on record right now by saying that insanity
in world leaders is in my view a less than desirable qual-
ity."

Pruss shifted uncomfortably in his seat, and Erdmann
sighed heavily.

Then the undercover Luftwaffe colonel said, "A bomb
exploded today on the Paris-Marseilles Express. One
death, twenty injuries—it could have been worse. Probably should have been worse—the train was at its max-
imum speed of sixty miles per hour and passengers were
showered with shards of glass. The dead passenger could
not be identified, so badly mangled was his corpse."

Charteris sat.

"Apparently the bomb was smuggled aboard the train,"
Erdmann continued, "tied to the coupling between passenger coaches. Investigators are convinced it was caused
by a . . . how do you say *Hollenmaschine*?"

"An infernal machine," Charteris said.

"Yes. A combination explosive and incendiary device.
The Reich's Ministry of Information cites this incident
as further proof that the threat of anarchy hangs over us
all."

"A threat hangs over the world, all right," Charteris muttered.

"Do I have to remind you," Erdmann asked dryly, "that a bomb on this ship would do considerably more damage?"

"That Parisian train wasn't filled with hydrogen, you mean?"

Captain Pruss said, firmly, "Because of your concerns about Joseph Spah's unsupervised visit to his dog, Mr. Charteris, I have had the ship inspected again—bow to stern. No bomb was found."

"How reassuring," Charteris said.

"I believe the time has come to take Joseph Spah into custody," Erdmann said. "Major Witt and Lieutenant Hinkelbein agree with me."

"Who are they?" Charteris asked. "The other two Luftwaffe men snooping around in mufti?"

Erdmann frowned in confusion. "Mufti?"

"Out of uniform, Fritz. Undercover. Spies."

Swallowing thickly, but not showing any pique, Erdmann said, "Yes—they are my assistants in our security effort."

"Why aren't they here?"

"Because they aren't aware of your role in this affair— your undercover role, that is. Your spying."

"Is that the Nazi way, Fritz? Keep the right hand from knowing what the left is doing?"

Erdmann grinned; it was a sudden, surprising thing. "I didn't think you were naive, Leslie—that's the way of all governments, of all spy agencies."

Charteris could only grin back at him: Erdmann had him.

"All right," the author said. "From what you say, I assume this radio blackout is over—it's foggy and overcast, but the electrical storm isn't snapping around us, anymore."

"That is correct."

"So what are your orders from the fatherland? Or *is* arresting Spah an order from the Ministry of Something or Other?"

Erdmann glanced at Pruss, and both men seemed strangely chagrined.

"What is it?" Charteris asked.

Rather stiffly, Captain Pruss said, "We have decided not to inform the Air Ministry."

"What?" Charteris leaned forward. "Surely you're joking, gentlemen. A murder on board the *Hindenburg*, and you're keeping it to yourself?"

"It was my decision," Erdmann said.

Another voice from behind them said, "And mine."

They all turned and were rather surprised to see Captain Lehmann standing in the officers'-mess doorway.

"Ernst," Erdmann said, with a nervous flicker of a smile, "I thought you were entertaining the passengers. . . ."

Thoughts raced through Charteris's mind: *Was Lehmann supposed to be keeping the passengers busy while this security/murder-investigation powwow was under way? Or had Erdmann, for some reason, held this meeting during Lehmann's entertainment session to* keep *something from the* Reederei *director, something that would be discussed in this meeting?*

Strolling toward the booth, Lehmann said, "Oh the entertainment continues. Seems one of the passengers, Mr. Doehner, the father of those lovely little boys, also plays the accordion. He knew some American songs that I didn't—so he is relieving me at my post, so to speak, briefly."

"Please join us," Erdmann said, a little too cheerfully.

Lehmann pushed in next to the colonel, looked toward Charteris and said, "Any message to the Air Ministry could be intercepted by non-Germans. This information in American or British hands, for example, could be harmful. The negative publicity could be damaging to both the *Reederei* and Germany herself."

"Knowing our policy makers as I do," Erdmann said, "I believe we would risk serious reprimand should we broadcast this situation. We must contain it ourselves."

"Is that so," Charteris remarked casually. "And you plan to start by arresting this buffoon Spah?"

"What is this?" Lehmann asked, glaring at Erdmann.

Charteris smiled to himself: he thought that might be what Erdmann hoped to conceal from Lehmann, executing the arrest before the *Reederei* director could do anything about it.

"I have just informed Mr. Charteris of the French train bombing," Erdmann said coolly. "And Captain Pruss has recently shared with me a fact of which neither you nor Mr. Charteris is aware."

Eyes now turned upon Captain Pruss, who sighed and said, "Chief Steward Kubis has informed me that Mr. Spah was found wandering through the body of the ship this afternoon, again to visit his animal, he says—again, unaccompanied, and without any permission."

Erdmann's jaw was set; he spoke through his teeth, "That's the second time this 'buffoon,' as you call him, Mr. Charteris, has strayed into forbidden territory. This alone is enough to justify his immediate arrest."

Lehmann, trembling, said in German, "We do not *arrest* passengers for disobeying ship's guidelines."

"Oh, they're guidelines now?" Erdmann said testily, shifting into German as well. "And here I thought these were rules, even laws. Understand, sir, that I had strict, specific orders from Berlin to keep this Spah under watch. To protect your ship from a potentially dangerous spy. Those were my orders, sir—not guidelines."

"May I remind you, Colonel, that you have no authority on this ship other than that which the *Reederei*, in a spirit of cooperation, grants you. This is a privately owned vessel and not under government control."

"Everything in Germany," Erdmann said, "is subject to government control."

"Boys, boys," Charteris said, pulling the conversation back into English, enjoying this. "Don't squabble. Your uncle Adolf wouldn't approve."

Captain Pruss said, "I have ordered another bow-to-stern inspection. Within the hour, we'll have a report. But I would vote for detaining Mr. Spah in his cabin, under house arrest. The manpower and work hours he continues to cost us, checking up after him, are inexcusable."

"What is inexcusable, gentlemen," Lehmann said, coldly angry, shifting back to German, "is that you would plan the arrest of this man without my knowledge."

"The captain of this ship . . ." Erdmann began, with a nod toward Pruss.

"Reports to the director of the *Reederei*," Lehmann said. "Which happens to be me. All decisions related to this matter are henceforth to be screened and approved by me. . . . Understood, gentlemen?"

"Understood," Pruss said sheepishly.

Erdmann only nodded.

Charteris's mood had improved; this was vastly more entertaining than the sing-along in the lounge.

"When we arrive in New York," Lehmann said, still in German though his voice had taken on his more usual, avuncular tone, "we face numerous responsibilities, both

technical and diplomatic. Our corporation—with the government's full backing—is attempting to form a transatlantic service in partnership with the Americans. This
joint venture will not be jeopardized by our arrival in the
States with an American in custody as an accused mur-
derer/saboteur."

"He's not an American," Erdmann said defensively.
"He is a Strassburger, a German!"

"Technically, perhaps. But he carries a French passport
and lives in America."

Charteris asked, in English, "May I inject the foreign
viewpoint, gentlemen?"

"By all means," Lehmann said.

"Spah is one of the few names on the list of Eric
Knoecher's 'subjects' that I haven't got 'round to inter-
viewing yet. No one's asked, but I can report with a clear
mind and a cool head that those I've spoken to have
given me no reason to suspect them of Knoecher's murder."

"Who have you spoken to?" Erdmann asked.

Charteris gave them a brief rundown.

"All of them have valid reasons for being on
Knoecher's list," Charteris said, wrapping up, "but nothing worth killing him over. Not right here on the spot,
anyway."

"No one reacted to your lie about Knoecher being sick
in bed in your cabin?" Erdmann asked. "Not a suspicious
eye movement, or nervousness of speech, or—"

"Nothing. But I would suggest, before you arrest Spah,
you allow me to continue my informal investigating. He's
a talkative little bastard—I'll get something out of him."

"You would talk to him this evening?" Erdmann
asked.

"Yes. He was in the lounge, right in the swing of

things. Decent voice; not off-key, anyway."

Lehmann nodded. "Yes, he's not setting any bombs at the moment, that's for certain."

Charteris gazed at Erdmann, keeping his expression soft but his eyes hard. "I believe our esteemed Captain Lehmann is correct in his assumption about the negative response to Spah's arrest. This man is scheduled to appear at a very famous theater in New York City—his arrest would make front-page news all over America."

"Yes, yes," Lehmann said, nodding, nodding.

"And, as I'm sure you've all noticed, this is a little man with a very big mouth. He would spout off to the papers, the radio, the newsreels, getting himself all the ink, all the publicity, he could squeeze out. He'd seize upon it to make himself a martyr—a famous one."

"Not if we keep him in custody," Erdmann said, "and he never sets foot off the ship."

"He's in America, once we land," Lehmann said. "Their laws pertain. We could not legally detain him on the ship—we would risk igniting an international incident of major proportions."

"I'm not sure the Air Ministry would agree with your assessment," Erdmann said.

"Perhaps not—but you agree with mine that discussing this over the airwaves is a far greater risk."

Erdmann drew in a deep breath, let it out. "Then I suppose arresting this American 'advertising executive,' Edward Douglas, is out of the question."

"Douglas?" Lehmann asked, frowning, puzzled.

"Why Douglas?" Charteris asked.

"You may recall I mentioned that the S.D. believed Douglas to be a spy."

"But you didn't say why."

Erdmann hesitated, apparently deciding how much to

reveal. Then he continued, saying, "Douglas works for General Motors, or at least he works for their advertising agency. General Motors owns Opel, makers of probably the most popular auto in Germany."

When Erdmann didn't continue, Charteris said, "So?"

". . . So—the Opel company also manufactures many other engineering-related products in Germany, from spark plugs to aircraft engines. The S.D. believes Douglas has sent information on German steel production, aircraft assembly, ball-bearing plants and much more to America."

Charteris shook his head, not getting it. "If he works for General Motors, and General Motors owns the company, why wouldn't he?"

Erdmann's eyes tensed. "It's believed he's sharing this information with United States naval intelligence. He was attached to them during the war."

"If you don't want Americans to share your secrets, don't go into business with them. This strikes me as rather thin."

"No, Mr. Charteris, the evidence is quite fat. You see, I have one of my assistants, Lieutenant Hinkelbein, keeping his eye on all cablegrams that go through the ship's radio room."

Erdmann paused and withdrew from inside his suitcoat pocket a folded slip of paper.

"I believe Douglas has clearly shown himself to be a spy," Erdmann went on. "He is brazenly sending and receiving code messages like this one."

The colonel handed the *Reederei* director the cablegram carbon copy.

Lehmann studied it. "This would certainly seem to be a coded message," he said softly, gravely.

"May I see it?" Charteris asked.

Lehmann handed it to the author, who read it, then began to lightly laugh.

"What amuses you?" Erdmann asked tightly.

"He received this, I take it."

"Yes."

"Well, it's a childishly simple code. It's baseball references."

Erdmann frowned. "What?"

"Baseball. You know—the American bastardization of cricket. This appears to have come from his home office, in New York—'AFTER YOU LEFT FIRST BASE' . . . first base would be Frankfurt . . . 'LOCAL UMPIRES SEARCHED YOUR DUGOUT' . . . 'umpires' are game officials, 'dugout' is where the team gathers during the—"

"I don't need to understand this stupid American sport," Erdmann said testily. "What does the cablegram mean?"

"It means that your police searched his apartment or his house in Frankfurt, 'FOUND NO FOUL BALLS STOP' . . . that means your gestapo didn't find anything incriminating at his home . . . 'YOU'LL HAVE TO HOLD UP AT SECOND STOP WELCOME HOME REILLY.' Second base would be New York—he's to wait there before going to his home in, where did you say? New Jersey?"

Erdmann thought about this, while Lehmann leaped in. "Then if he's a spy, he's finished his work, and going home?"

"That's a reasonable interpretation," Charteris said. "Or it could just be the boss saying welcome back. Remember, I haven't had a crack at Douglas yet—and we have already met, so he'll be simple enough to approach."

Erdmann exchanged a glance with Lehmann.

"Why don't you, then?" Lehmann said to Charteris.

"Perhaps if he's a spy headed home, he's no longer a danger to anyone."

"Can we be sure?" Erdmann posed. "This may be what Knoecher confronted Douglas with—and Douglas may have murdered him."

"If so," Charteris said, with a shrug, "it's a military action, isn't it? It's not as though Douglas were some madman, some Jack the Ripper at large on the ship."

"Jack who?" Lehmann asked.

"Suffice to say your passengers would not be endangered by the man's presence. But I will talk to him. And to Spah."

And he did. Douglas, first. In the smoking lounge.

Coming directly from the officers' mess, Charteris stopped by the smoke-filled cubicle, and pulled up a chair, coming in on the middle of what the Americans called a "bull session" between the perfume magnate Dolan and stockyard king Morris.

The two men were developing a strategy for the U.S.A. in the Pacific, hinging on the need for a two-ocean navy to protect both coasts from the ambitious Japan and a volatile Europe.

"With Japan such a threat to the Philippines," Dolan was saying, "the whole Pacific basin is in peril."

"That's to put it mildly!" Morris bellowed. "Why, the Japs could destroy the Panama Canal in a day, by air!"

It was easy enough to develop a side conversation with the advertising man, Douglas, who reached for the lighter on the wall and yanked it over to get Charteris's Gauloise going.

"I'll leave it to the colonel and the major," Douglas said to Charteris, "to settle the Pacific."

Testing the waters, Charteris asked, "No military background, Ed?"

"Oh, I was in the navy in the war. Petty officer. But I'll gladly leave the big picture to the armchair admirals."

Morris and Dolan weren't hearing any of this, both caught up in their own bombast.

"So tell me, Les," the handsome mustached advertising man said, swirling bourbon in a glass, "how did you manage to rustle a filly like that little blonde? Only she's not so little."

"It comes from not spending all your time down here in this den of iniquity." Charteris sipped his Scotch. "Why, do you wish you'd given me some competition?"

"No. I'm afraid, just as with these military maneuvers, I'm on leave. Out of the game."

"You sound like a man who's been burned."

Douglas chuckled wryly; he had a cigarette of his own going. "You write romances, right?"

"Of a sort."

"I guess you could say I'm carrying a torch."

"Not with all the hydrogen on this ship, I hope."

"No." Douglas chuckled again, but his eyes were woeful. "I just closed my office in Frankfurt and had to leave somebody behind."

"Some female body?"

"Yes indeed. Very female. As female as that braided specimen of yours, Les."

"Why didn't you bring her with you?"

Douglas sighed, sipped, smoked. "I hope, one day soon, to bring her to America. But it's not as easily done as said."

"Why?"

". . . She's Jewish."

"Ah."

"She was my secretary. That's how we began, anyway. I'm divorced; have a daughter."

"Me, too. On both counts."

"Really? Do you miss her, Les?"

"My daughter or my wife?"

Douglas laughed, smoke curling out his nostrils. "Let's not get into that, either of us. . . . Well, I've had my share of flings since my marriage dissolved, but this is different. Marta may be a little young for me, but she's such a fine, smart woman, and what a beauty. Dark brown hair, eyes the same, figure like . . . well, like your blonde."

"You have money. You can buy her way out, can't you?"

"I hope so. It's just . . . I know they have their eye on her."

Charteris drank a little Scotch, kept his tone casual. "Whose eye? The Nazis?"

"Yes. You see, I have . . . had . . . an office at a building on Neue Mainzer Strasse; trouble is, so does a guy named Goebbels."

Charteris's eyes opened so wide, his monocle fell out; catching it, he said, "The Propaganda Ministry has an office in your building? And you had a Jewish secretary?"

"Yeah, and it went over swell. Whenever they saw her, it rubbed 'em the wrong way, those fanatic sons of bitches. I was advised to dispense with her services. When I told 'em to go to hell, they started shadowing me. Shadowing us."

"It's like something out of Kafka."

"No, it's far worse than that. You can close the covers on a book; but when they're tapping your phones, searching your desk and file cabinets every other Tuesday—well. Time to go home."

"And you couldn't find a way to bring her with you?"

Douglas grinned half a wry grin. Shook his head. "She wouldn't come. You're right, I got the dough to make that happen, too. But she has family. Germany's home to her. I'm praying to God she comes to her senses before it's too late, while I can still get her out. Maybe if she misses me, half as much as I miss her . . ."

Douglas swallowed, smiled embarrassedly, and gulped at his drink.

"I'm behaving like a lovesick schoolboy," he said. "Spilling to you like this. You're the second guy on this trip who's stood still for this mush."

"Really?"

"Yeah, first night aboard, I sat and talked with this nice fella in the import business. You know, most of these Germans, if they're not party members, if they're just regular people, they're not bad at all. He was real friendly. Outgoing. I liked him. Funny thing, I haven't seen hide nor hair of him since that first night."

Neck tingling, Charteris said, "Sounds like you're talking about my cabin mate."

"Yeah?"

"Eric Knoecher."

Douglas snapped his fingers. "That's it. That's the guy."

"Poor bloke's been sick ever since that first night."

"No kiddin'?"

"Yes. You probably noticed him coughing and sneezing."

"No, I can't say I did."

"Well, anyway, Eric's been sick in bed, stuck in the cabin, since he woke up Tuesday morning."

"Oh, well by all means give him my regards, and a get-well-soon. He was the kind of sounding board a lovesick goon like me needed, just about then."

Soon after, Charteris excused himself, thinking that either he was a terrible detective or Ed Douglas was a terrific actor—because there had not been the slightest sign that Douglas was stringing him along, that the advertising man might know that Eric Knoecher was dead.

In fact, Charteris didn't think Douglas did know. Nor was he convinced the man was a spy for General Motors or Admiral America, either. This was simply a middle-aged man who had fallen for a good-looking young woman. It just happened that the middle-aged man was an American working in Nazi Germany and the good-looking young woman was a Jewess.

When Charteris returned to the lounge, Lehmann was again at his accordion, and the Americans, Brits and even a few Germans were managing a rousing "Home on the Range." He stopped to whisper in Hilda's ear that he'd rejoin her soon, but needed to do something first. She nodded, smiled prettily and returned with gusto to one of the few American songs she knew.

Charteris went over to where Spah was seated with Margaret Mather and her college boys. Margaret fluttered her eyelashes at him, and he somehow resisted the urge to flutter his back at her.

Leaning in, he said to Spah, "Can I have a word with you, Joe?"

"Sure!"

Spah scampered after Charteris like a puppy, following him around to the dining room, where the tables were already set for tomorrow's breakfast. Not a soul was on this side of the ship, and Charteris sat on one of the benches by the slanting windows and Spah sat next to him, gazing up at the taller man with a curious expression.

"You're in danger," Charteris said.

Spah beamed, as if delighted. "I am?"

"Listen to me, and take this seriously. Quit clowning."

"All right." But he was still grinning.

"You're walking that narrow line."

"What narrow line?"

"Between clown and jackass."

Spah wasn't smiling now. "What are you talking about?"

"Steward Kubis is a friend of mine. I got to know him last year, on the maiden voyage. He confided in me that you are on the brink of arrest."

Spah's eyes popped open; it was comic but not, for a change, intentionally so. "Arrest? What the hell for?"

"For these continued unscheduled trips to see your flea-bitten mangy hound."

Spah grinned again but this time it was glazed. "I'm going to be arrested for seeing my dog?"

"You're going to be arrested for breaking the rules on a Nazi ship."

"Such stupid rules!"

"Actually, they're not stupid rules. Are you aware that a passenger train in France blew up today?"

"Yes—it was on the news broadcast they piped in."

"*You* are suspected of planting a bomb, Joe—of hiding it somewhere in the vast framework and skin of this beast."

"A bomb? That is ridiculous!"

"Ridiculous, perhaps. But not funny. You have a history of associating with Communists and other anti-Nazi elements; you live in America; and you've been doing your hilarious Hitler impression for a German audience."

Spah said nothing; the grin had long since faded.

"No more clowning, Joe—understood?"

He swallowed and nodded. "Understood."

"I need to ask you something else."

"Anything. Only a friend would say the things you've said."

"Is there anything else these Germans might have on you? Anything you're hiding?"

"No. My life is an open book."

"The first night aboard, I saw you talking to my cabin mate, Eric Knoecher."

"Yes, that's right. Is he any better? Or still sick in your cabin?"

"Did I tell you that, Joe?"

"Maybe. Or was it Leonhard or maybe Gertrude? Why, is that important?"

"Joe, what did you and Eric Knoecher talk about?"

"Nothing. Fluff!"

"What kind of fluff?"

"He recognized me, like you did, from the stage, and also from the papers, from press I received. That's what we talked about."

"What, you in the press?"

"Yes. He asked me about my 'engagement' to the striptease artist, Mathia Merrifield. He wanted to know all about her—what red-blooded man wouldn't?"

"You're engaged to a stripper?"

"No! It was a publicity stunt—to get Mathia some press. She's an American girl, a close friend."

"How close?"

"That wouldn't be polite; you shouldn't even ask. Anyway, I'm happily married with a wife and three kiddies, you know that, I told you before, didn't I?"

"I believe you did. You just left out the American stripper, is all."

Spah shrugged, made a face. "Anyway, she was going to appear at some theater in Munich, doing what she does best—take off her clothes—and I have some fame there, so we cooked this up. Or her press agent did, I should say."

And Eric Knoecher was interested.

"Joe," Charteris said, "hasn't it occurred to you that this could be used against you? You can be kept out of Germany on moral grounds. Adultery, bigamy . . ."

"Yes, it was big of me to help the girl get some publicity. So what if they ban me? I told you, I'm not going back to Germany. Just to my wife and kids."

"Not your stripper."

"No." He grinned. "Anyway, she's still in Munich."

Charteris waggled a finger in the acrobat's face. "Joe— we have one more day, partial day at that, on this ship. Keep your nose clean. Let the steward feed your mutt."

"She's no mutt! She's—"

"She's a pedigreed bitch, I know. Stay away from her."

That might have been good advice where the stripper was concerned, too; but at least she wasn't in freight on this ship. As far as Charteris knew, anyway.

The community sing was winding down when Charteris and Spah strolled back. They were concluding with "Muss I denn?", the beautiful German folk song that spoke of leaving a "little town," leaving a sweetheart behind. Had Ed Douglas been present—and understood the German words—he might well have broken down and cried.

Charteris walked Hilda back to her cabin. They spent a memorable hour within, and—as she had requested, for the sake of avoiding embarrassment, that he not stay the night—he kissed her at the door and moved across the hall to his own quarters.

Sliding the door open, his hand felt for the light switch; but from the darkness something, someone grabbed him, perhaps emerging from the lower bunk, and yanked him inside, his monocle flying, and he was knocked into the far wall, which gave a little.

Startled, he tried to get his bearings and saw a form, barely identifiable as the back of a gray-jumpsuited crew member, lurch for the door, slide it shut, sealing them into darkness.

Though he could see nothing, Charteris plunged blindly toward where the form had been—as small as the cabin was, there was little chance of missing—and in doing so threw himself into the open arms of his unknown assailant. Powerful arms hugged him, pinning him, crushing him, bones popping, please God not breaking, and Charteris brought a knee up, where it would do the most good.

His intruder howled in the darkness, and—some small night vision coming to him, now—Charteris brought clasped hands down, hard, on the back of the doubled-over figure. Then he grabbed the cloth of the jumpsuit and slammed the bastard into where the washstand should be. And was.

Whimpering with pain from this blow, and the one to his groin, the intruder nonetheless managed to scramble around and tackle Charteris, knocking the author back, his head smacking into the aluminum bunk ladder. Woozy, almost unconscious, Charteris somehow found his way to his feet and swung madly, randomly in the darkness, fists hitting nothing.

Then a fist flew into him, into his stomach, doubling him over, and now he was on the floor of the pitch-dark cubicle, and he was the one being pummeled by clasped hands on his back.

Grabbing in the darkness, grabbing for anything, his hands gripped an ankle, and it was not very dignified, it was not something the Saint might have done, but Charteris bit into the flesh of the man's leg, hard, savagely hard, bare skin between pant leg and sock and Charteris tasted blood. It was a good wound.

Which elicited another howl that signaled to the author a turning point in this close-quarter battle in utter darkness, and he got to his feet and was bringing his fist back when powerful hands gripped his throat and squeezed, squeezed hard and harder and his fist turned into limp fingers and his head began to spin.

But he clearly heard the harsh whisper of a male voice, German-accented English, saying, "Stop this, what you're doing! Stop it!"

Then he felt himself propelled backward, and his head was slammed into the metal of the folded-up-into-the-wall suitcase stand.

And Leslie Charteris, amateur detective, author of the sophisticated Saint tales, retired for the evening.

DAY FOUR:

Thursday, May 6, 1937

TWELVE

How the Hindenburg *Buzzed Boston, and Leslie Charteris Tugged a Pant Leg*

In the drizzly darkness of the predawn morning hours, the *Hindenburg* got its bearings thanks to the tiny twinklings of coastal lighthouses, glimmering up through the gloom below like displaced stars. Trekking along at sixty-three knots, just a few miles from the shore, the great airship swooped so low, her altitude was less than her own length. Rudely wakened fishermen floundered from their shacks, rubbing sleep from their eyes, summoned by the husky rumbling of engines in the sky, only to see the massive ship pass overhead like a mysterious gray cloud.

About the same time those fisherman were stumbling groggily back to their beds, Leslie Charteris was sitting up in his, every bit as groggy as they, if not more so. How he had gotten into the bunk, he was unsure—he assumed sometime in the night he'd woken from the blow, found himself on his cabin floor, and felt his way up to the softer surface of the bedding, flopping there, unconsciousness giving way to sleep.

Now he was awake, but his head was pounding and he was dizzy to boot. The cabin was still shrouded in darkness. He managed to rise to his feet—a task that seemed to him no more difficult than scaling a cliff—and stood there for several long seconds getting his bearings, his balance, then his fingers guided him like a blind man reading Braille to the light switch.

As the light clicked on, its forty watts seemingly flooding the cabin with dazzling light, Charteris closed his eyes tight and groaned with discomfort. He sat down on the edge of his bunk and held his head in his hands; in back, his fingers found a goose egg almost dead center—no clotted-over blood, though.

Breathing easier now, his head still hurting but the dizziness ebbing at least, he returned to his feet, which were steady enough, and lumbered the great distance of a foot or two to the washbasin, where he stood sloshing water on his face for at least a minute.

Studying himself in the mirror, he realized he was still wearing his white dinner jacket—rumpled, to say the least, though his bow tie was perfectly in place. That made him laugh, which made his head throb, so he stopped. Something winked at him from the floor—his monocle. He stooped, picked it up—it was in the corner, where the bunk met the wall—and the round glass eyepiece was undamaged. He snugged it into place.

Soon he was in his underwear, slippers and a robe. His wristwatch said the time was 4:30 A.M.; most of the *Hindenburg* was still asleep, the passenger decks anyway. He was unaware that the ship was a mere four-hundred-some miles from Lakehurst, New Jersey, her destination.

But he did realize that time was slipping away. He could not roll back into his bunk, however his head might throb, however tired he might still be. So in his robe he made his way down to B deck, where the shower was free; in fact, not even a steward was in attendance. No reservations, no one to cut off the flow of water for conservation reasons.

He therefore took the longest shower in the history of the *Hindenburg*—perhaps a good fifteen minutes—and while the water pressure was nothing to write home about, the spray was hot enough to relax and soothe him and make him feel human again. Alive.

Back in his cabin, he put on a yellow sport shirt, tan slacks and a brown herringbone drape-style sport coat. The freshly shaven man in the mirror seemed none the worse for wear, so Charteris set about his business.

The first order of which was to knock at Chief Steward Kubis's door. Kubis was up, already in his crisp white jacket and perfectly knotted black tie; but the steward was still surprised to see Charteris so early.

"What is it, sir?"

"Take me to see the two captains."

"Captain Pruss and Mr. Lehmann, sir?"

"That's right. Then fetch Colonel Erdmann and bring him to us. And that's all the discussion we're going to have about it, Heinrich."

Kubis nodded, and within five minutes Charteris was once again in Ernst Lehmann's cabin, in the forward officers' quarters section of the ship. The small window let in the light of early morning; the former *Hindenburg* captain's accordion again sat on the floor, resting against the bulkhead as if tuckered out from last night's sing-along.

Lehmann, in a gray suit and blue bow tie, sat with his

back to his aluminum desk, facing Charteris, who again sat on the single bunk. Captain Pruss, in his impeccable blue uniform, stood at the door, hands clasped behind him. Kubis, God bless him, had gone after coffee and a metal pot on a metal tray rested on the desktop and all of the men were sipping at steaming hot cups, savoring the brew as if it were a lifesaving elixir.

Both captains listened with quiet alarm lengthening their expressions as the author informed them of his midnight intruder, apparently a crew member.

Lehmann, teeth clasped on the stem of his unlighted pipe, posed the first question, not to Charteris but to Captain Pruss. "Do you think this has to be a crew member? Could someone else have acquired a uniform?"

Pruss frowned, shrugged. "Uniforms are plentiful enough on this ship, but I'm not sure how—"

"It has to be a crew member," Charteris said, interrupting. "Or someone higher up than that, pretending to be one."

Lehmann drew back. "What are you implying?"

"Nothing. Just examining the facts. My cabin door was locked—and my uninvited guest was waiting inside for me."

"So he had a passkey," Pruss said.

"Yes—which means a crew member, a steward, an officer. Not a passenger."

Sighing, shaking his head, nibbling on the prop pipe, Lehmann said, "And here we've been considering only passengers as our suspects."

"What if the murderer—a passenger—had Knoecher's key?" Pruss asked. "Your cabin mate, after all?"

"I've considered that. But that key almost certainly went out the window with Knoecher, tucked away in his pocket—and now in some shark's belly."

A knock at the cabin door announced Erdmann, who looked alert and businesslike in a well-pressed three-piece brown suit. The Luftwaffe colonel nodded his good mornings, helped himself to a cup of coffee, sat next to Charteris, who filled him in.

"I could not have anticipated this," Erdmann said, eyes glazed. "There were no crew members on Knoecher's subject list at all."

"Mr. Charteris," Captain Pruss said, exasperation coloring his voice, "we have sixty-one crewmen on this ship. How do you suggest, in the short time left on this voyage, we narrow that number to one?"

Charteris sipped his coffee. "Oh, I already have a suspect for you—that is, if you're interested, gentlemen."

"Don't be coy," Erdmann growled.

"You have a rigger named Eric Spehl."

Everyone frowned, but particularly Captain Pruss, who said, "Why, yes—how is it that you know one of our crewmen, Mr. Charteris?"

"He went out of his way to come meet me on A deck—broke a regulation doing so, for all I know."

Lehmann looked up from his coffee cup to say, "He did. Crew members are strictly segregated from passengers."

Charteris shrugged. "In any event, he sought me out, said he was a fan—even had a book for me to autograph."

Colonel Erdmann shrugged, too. "Why take that at anything but face value? You're a famous man, Mr. Charteris. Is it surprising you have a reader among our crew?"

"Something about his manner seemed . . . off-kilter. His words were admiring, but now, upon reflection, his manner seemed something else again. I believe I was being sized up."

Eyes narrowing, Lehmann leaned forward. "For a midnight beating, you mean?"

"Yes. I'm somewhat bigger than he is, and he might have wanted a look at me. He's rather slight, young Spehl, but he has powerful hands."

And Charteris touched his throat, twitching a smile as he recalled the stranglehold.

Erdmann shifted on the bunk, saying, "And his purpose was to warn you off your investigation?"

"The voice in the dark said I was to stop what I was doing, that's right."

Lehmann was shaking his head, chewing on the pipe stem. "Just because this boy asked you for an autograph . . . that isn't very much to base a case on, Leslie."

"We have much more than that. It, uh, may not seem very sporting to you, gentlemen, but I took a bite out of this particular assailant."

Erdmann blinked. "A bite?"

"Not having a guard dog handy, or Spah's bitch Ulla, I had to do it myself. I bit him on the ankle—good and deep. I drew blood." He sipped his coffee, as if to banish the taste.

Lehmann's eyes were wide. "So if Eric Spehl has a human bite mark on his ankle . . ."

"More or less human," Charteris said. "Why don't you fetch the lad?"

The two captains and the Luftwaffe colonel all exchanged glances, as if waiting for someone to make a decision.

Oddly enough, considering the influence of the *Reederei* director and the Luftwaffe undercover agent, it was Captain Pruss who stepped forward.

"I'll have him summoned. I believe the boy is on duty right now."

Pruss stepped out, and Charteris said, "I think it was his right ankle, but I can't be sure. It was, after all, pitch-black in there."

Pruss, having dispatched an underling to bring the rigger, stepped back inside the cabin.

"What do you suggest we do," Erdmann said, "if the boy does have the impression of your teeth on his ankle?"

Charteris grinned. "Well, hell, Fritz—you've been dying to pinch somebody. Here's your chance. Put him under house arrest and haul his Aryan behind back home and turn him over to one of your goon squads. Put all that nasty gestapo energy to some proper use, for a change."

Half of Erdmann's face smiled but there was no mirth in it. "Sometimes you test my patience, Mr. Charteris."

"My apologies. I get cranky when I'm attacked in the night."

Before long, a steward delivered the seemingly bewildered, baby-faced Spehl to the cabin. Holding his cap in his hands, the tall, slender rigger—in his gray uniform and matching slippers—already looked like a prisoner.

"Mr. Spehl," Captain Pruss said in German, "lift your trouser leg."

"The right one," Charteris said, also in German.

The pale, blue-eyed boy frowned in blinking confusion, turning to Pruss. "Sir?"

"Just obey the order, Rigger."

"Yes, sir."

And the wide-eyed, apparently perplexed young crew member tugged up his gray pant leg.

No bite mark was readily apparent.

Charteris knelt before the lad, and had a closer look:

nothing. Just pale flesh, and an innocent blond down, as if Eric Spehl had barely entered puberty.

Irritated, Charteris lifted the rigger's left pant leg himself—and the result was the same.

Nothing. No bite mark. Pink downy flesh.

The author pulled the boy's right sock down, yanked the trouser leg higher, thinking perhaps his bite had been higher or lower than his memory, and his perception in the darkened cabin, had led him to believe.

"Captain Pruss," Spehl said, voice cracking with embarrassment, "with all due respect, sir, what is he doing?"

"Just stand fast, Rigger."

Charteris did the same with left sock and pant leg.

Nothing.

Chagrined, his head still pounding, Charteris rose, and found himself staring into the blank face of Eric Spehl, and the clear blue eyes of Eric Spehl—eyes that somehow, somewhere, conveyed to Charteris laughter.

This boy was guilty—in one fashion, one way, or another. But Charteris could not prove it—nor could he even say, at this moment, why he was so convinced.

"That will be all, Rigger," Pruss said.

"Yes, sir," Spehl said, with a respectful nod to his captain, and darted out.

Charteris sat back down on the bunk, heavily. "Could I possibly have a goddamn cigarette?"

Lehmann nodded, and took a book of matches from a desk drawer. Charteris fired up a Gauloise, and provided the Luftwaffe colonel with one, as well.

Getting his pipe going, Lehmann said, "So much for your suspect."

"He's the one," Charteris said.

"How do you know?" Pruss asked.

"I know." *His eyes were laughing at me,* he thought, but didn't say it.

Wreathed by his own sweet-smelling tobacco smoke, Lehmann said, "Perhaps you didn't bite as hard as you thought. . . ."

"I drew blood. I broke skin."

Erdmann said, "Then that young man has remarkable recuperative powers."

Charteris snapped his fingers. "Damn! That's it."

"What is 'it'?" Erdmann asked, sighing smoke.

"He *sent* the message, but he didn't deliver it."

"What?"

"He sent some crony of his, some other crew member to thrash me."

Lehmann was shaking his head. "Now, please, there's simply no basis to this. . . . You're just being stubborn, Leslie."

"Oh, I'm stubborn all right, but there's a basis, too. Spehl had another crew member with him—who accompanied Spehl when he came to see me, to have his book autographed."

Now Lehmann leaned forward, keenly interested. "*What* other crew member?"

"I didn't get much of a look at him. Just a burly bloke, huskier than Spehl. He didn't approach me, this other fellow. Sat on a window bench while Spehl talked to me. *He* got a good look at *me*—I barely noticed him."

Erdmann laughed hollowly. "That's not much of an identification."

"One of your crew members has a bite mark on his leg. Find him and you've found our man."

Pruss stepped forward, shaking his head. "If you're suggesting we repeat this farce, sixty more times—"

"You have a murderer on this airship," Charteris said. "Or perhaps two murderers—accomplices. If you don't care to pursue it, so be it. I, however, will be talking to the New York police and the American press, to everyone who will listen in fact, who might be interested in hearing of my delightful voyage on the *Hindenburg*."

"Please, Leslie," Lehmann began, his expression grave. "Be reasonable—"

"Do you know what a *real* murder, widely reported in the press, could do for my book sales? I can see the royalties now. . . ."

Silence filled the cabin, touched barely by the distant thrum of diesels and raindrops dancing lightly on the ship's sheath.

Finally, abruptly, Erdmann stood. "My men and I will handle this. Discreetly."

Lehmann looked up, narrow-eyed, at the Luftwaffe colonel. "I believe that's a wise course of action."

"When we have your bitten assailant in custody," Erdmann said, "we'll inform you. Perhaps you'd like to confront him yourself."

"Perhaps I would," Charteris said. "I believe he'll give up his friend Spehl, and you'll have Eric Knoecher's murderer in custody—and no publicity problems whatsoever."

"We're in agreement, then," Lehmann said, looking toward Pruss. "Colonel Erdmann and his men will handle this inquiry."

The captain nodded. "I have to get back to the control gondola. Gentlemen."

And Pruss slipped out.

Charteris got to his feet. Yawned. "I believe I'll have breakfast. Getting the hell knocked out of me has worked up an appetite."

Erdmann said, "Thank you for your cooperation."

"You know, one thing apparently has not occurred to you yet, Fritz."

"And what would that be . . . Leslie?"

"The unanswered question."

"Which is?"

"If Spehl is our man—and I believe he is—what was his motive for dumping Knoecher overboard?"

Lehmann jack-in-the-boxed to his feet, asking, "What are you saying?"

"If Spehl is a saboteur, then never mind comical ol' Joe Spah taking the occasional unsupervised stroll, aft. Who better than a rigger to tuck a bomb away somewhere in the skin of this airborne monster?"

And Lehmann, his expression more grave than ever, sat back down.

Erdmann merely nodded, in affirmation of Charteris's assessment, as the author made his way out of the cabin, and down the planklike gangway to the entry to B deck.

Because this would be a short day—landing at Lakehurst was expected for around four P.M.—Charteris and Hilda had agreed to take an earlier breakfast than usual. But it was still a good hour before he was due to knock at her door. Before going back to his cabin, he strolled to the portside promenade, to view another gray, rainy dawn.

The dining room was already doing a brisk business. Some of the passengers, convening for the trip's final breakfast, were casually attired in pajamas and bathrobes. Others were already spiffily done up in their arrival outfits. Miss Mather, in a blue dress trimmed lacy white, was seated with her college boys, flirting, laughing. The trio of businessmen—Douglas, Morris and Dolan—were having a rather silent breakfast, wearing seemingly slept-in suits, and looked hungover, which was not surprising, considering how much time they spent in the smoking room/bar area.

"Lester!"

Moritz Feibusch, seated alone at a table for two against the linen-paneled wall, was waving at him. Charteris strolled over and sat for a few moments with the pleasant, lumpy-faced tuna-fish man.

"Just so you know," Feibusch said, "I'm giving up."

"Giving up?"

"I'm at a hundred and fifty and who-knows-how-many postcards and, oy, my poor hand is swollen from signing my name. How do you famous people stand it, all the autographs?"

"Endorsing checks from publishers makes up for it. You have the whole day in front of you, Moritz. You can still make your quota."

"No. This is my birthday trip, Lester, remember? For once, I'm going to sightsee. We'll be flying over Boston and New York and I wouldn't miss it."

"Where's your friend—Leuchtenberg?"

"I think the drinking finally caught up with him. He should have a *Hindenburg*-size head about now."

A steward brought a cup of coffee to Charteris, who chatted with his friend in fancy goods for a few minutes, then returned to his cabin.

It was still too early to knock at Hilda's door, so he used the time to prepare his papers for customs and pack his things. He left the shaving kit out, in case he should decide to freshen up before landing in New Jersey; but otherwise he was ready for arrival. Then he left the cabin and angled across the hall to Hilda's door.

He gave her a good-morning peck. "You look even more beautiful than usual, my dear."

Which of course she did. Today, for the first time, her braids were tucked under a stylish, raffishly angled hat—a shallow-crowned, wide-brimmed straw hat, a vivid rose color matching the rose-and-pink-and-black floral design of her white crepe dress with attached cape and long tight sleeves. It was a slinky affair that made her look tall and slender without downplaying her curves.

"Did you sleep well?" she asked, her arm tucked in his, as they moved down the cramped corridor.

"Sound and deep. I couldn't have slept sounder if a building had fallen on me."

She laughed. "You are so funny."

A laugh riot, he thought inside his throbbing head.

In the dining room, they sat nibbling fresh rolls, saying little. Charteris was distracted by the knowledge of the behind-the-scenes investigation in progress; but there was also a certain sense of loss, knowing his comely companion on this journey would soon be exiting his life. As he was usually the one who drove the conversation, the couple settled into silence broken only by the occasional comment about how good something tasted, the clink of dishes and silverware, and the patter of rain gently pelting the skin of the ship.

"You are quiet today," she said, buttering a biscuit.

"It's always sad, when a pleasant journey ends."

"Has it been pleasant for you?"

"You've made it so. Hilda ... I hesitate to ask this, since you made it clear that ours is a ... temporary friendship."

She reached across the table and touched his hand. "What is it, Leslie?"

"It's just that I know a shipboard romance in most instances should be tucked away in one's memory book, each party moving his or her own separate way."

A wonderful smile blossomed. "Are you saying you would like to see me again, Leslie? After we land?"

"The thought has crossed my mind. You're visiting your sister in New Jersey, and I'm heading to Florida, to see my daughter . . . but I'll be back in that part of the world next week, to meet with New York book and magazine editors."

"I would love to see you again."

He raised his coffee cup in salute. "Just for old times' sake. That's what this will all be by next week, you know—memories, old times."

Suddenly passengers were crowding around the promenade windows. Charteris and Hilda rose from their table to join them, finding a place along the slanting Plexiglas, where they discovered the sun was finally out, the fog burning off, the vast blue shimmer of Boston Harbor revealing itself below, ship whistles blowing them a robust welcome to America.

Holding hands, he and Hilda watched as the airship—at an altitude of merely five hundred feet—coasted over suburbs, people tinted blue in the ship's shadow as they would run out of houses to gaze up and point and wave, cars pulling over along roadsides as drivers got out to get a better look, dogs barking wildly, and, in rural stretches, barnyards where stirred-up pigs and fluttering chickens reacted in apparent terror, which for some reason elicited giddy laughter from the high-flying sightseers.

Miss Mather flitted to his side, beaming, saying, "Is it ridiculous for me to feel so happy?"

"Not at all," he told her. "I feel the same."

"Did you see the flower gardens? Yellow forsythia in bloom, and other flowers trailing pink, grass plots so vivid green, apple trees in blossom, woods full of dogwood and young green leaves—"

"Shouldn't you be writing this down?"

"I can't steal myself away!"

Then, like a hummingbird, she flew off. Hilda was amused, and so was he.

They were wandering back to their table to finish their coffee when Chief Steward Kubis approached Charteris and again delivered a whispered message.

"There's something I need to do," Charteris told her.

"That's all right. I have to go to my cabin to pack my things and collect my papers for passport examination."

"If I haven't stopped by for you within an hour, my dear, I'll meet you as soon as I can here at the promenade."

"Fine."

He took a moment to watch her walk away—that was always worth finding time to do—and then he fell in with Kubis, who ushered Charteris down to B deck, forward through the keel corridor, back to Lehmann's cabin.

Erdmann, Pruss and Lehmann were all waiting; and no one was seated—they were standing in the relatively small space like men at a graveside.

"What the hell is it?" Charteris asked.

"Our inquiry into your midnight caller," Erdmann said, "has turned something up—something very disturbing."

Lehmann looked gray and stricken.

"You found him?" Charteris asked, brightening. "The man with my bite marks on his leg?"

"All of the crewmen have been checked," Erdmann said, "and none have such a wound."

Frowning, Charteris demanded, "What in God's name is it, then?"

"One of our crew members is missing," Pruss said.

THIRTEEN

How the Hindenburg Toured New York City, and Leslie Charteris Spent His Marks

The missing crewman was a mechanic, Willy Scheef. Lehmann explained that a mechanic on a zeppelin faced one of the ship's hardest, most demanding jobs—and by all accounts the noisiest, stuck inside a cramped engine gondola (there were four), keeping an eye on oil pressure, water temperature and engine revolutions. And the diesel din ("the hammers of hell!" Gertrude Adelt had called it) was rivaled by intense engine heat.

"But mechanics also work the shortest hours," Lehmann said in English. "Rotating shifts of two hours in the day, and three at night."

"Plenty of time," Charteris said, "to work a midnight visit in."

"We can't be certain it was Scheef who attacked you," Erdmann put in sharply.

The four men were seated now, Lehmann on the edge of his desk, Pruss in the desk chair swiveled to face Charteris and Erdmann on the bunk. The foggy forenoon was filtering its way through the cabin's small sloping window.

"It's a simple process of elimination," Charteris said. "If none of the sixty men you inspected has a bite on his ankle, Colonel, then the missing crew member is the man I bit."

The Germans took a few moments to digest that tongue twister, then Captain Pruss said, somberly, "So we do have a murderer aboard." His face was the color of pie dough.

"Perhaps not," Lehmann said, wincing in thought. "Perhaps Mechanic Scheef had an accident and fell from his post; it's happened before. The guardrail is rather insubstantial, and no doubt slippery in the rain."

Hands on his knees, Charteris laughed, once. "Now that stretches coincidence and convenience a little far, doesn't it?"

"Or," Lehmann continued, as if the author hadn't spoken, "Scheef may have panicked when he realized a Luftwaffe inquiry had been launched, and hastily committed suicide, rather than face Nazi justice."

"It's even possible," Pruss said, "he might have parachuted. We're close enough to shore."

Charteris's eyes widened, his monocle popping out; he caught it and said, "And no one saw?"

Pruss winced, as if embarrassed by his own argument. "He would not necessarily be noticed, if he jumped far enough aft."

Erdmann was shaking his head. "If this Willy Scheef is our guilty party, he didn't know my inquiry had to do with him. My two assistants and I went through the ship inspecting footwear, making sure the new regulation canvas-topped crepe-soled shoes were in proper use. It seemed the easiest way to check ankles for Mr. Charteris's tooth marks."

His unlit pipe in hand, Lehmann smirked humorlessly, saying, "A spy might easily have seen through such a simple ruse."

"And I thought I wrote fantastic plots," Charteris said, shaking his head, monocle back in place. "Gentlemen—a few hours ago, in this very cabin, we confronted the man who sent Willy Scheef to scare me off—one Rigger Eric Spehl—after which the man who sent the message scurried to push his messenger overboard."

"Incredible," Lehmann huffed.

"Well, it's not as entertaining as slippery catwalks and suicidal murderers and parachuting spies. In a mystery novel, we call it 'tying off loose ends.' Something we picked up from real-life experts in murder . . . like Eric Spehl."

"What evidence do you have that Spehl did this?" Lehmann almost demanded. "Even circumstantial—please share it with us."

Charteris waved dismissively. "What more do you need? After we accused Spehl, he rushed to remove his accomplice!"

"We didn't accuse him—we looked at his ankles."

"Doing that may have been enough to inspire Spehl to confront Scheef, and then Spehl would have seen the bite, and, as the Americans say, push would have come to shove."

"You're spinning fiction again, Leslie," Lehmann said, eyelids at half-mast, prop pipe in his teeth.

"I don't understand you, Ernst. You have a murderer aboard. What are you going to do about it?"

Lehmann gestured with the pipe. "You haven't answered *my* question, yet: what evidence, even circumstantial evidence, have you against Spehl?"

That stopped him. Charteris drew in a breath, held it, released it. "Nothing, really. Just what you already know."

"That he sought you out for an autograph."

Charteris's forehead tensed. "I have the unsettling feeling you're about to tell me that you intend doing nothing."

"We will be landing this afternoon," Lehmann said.

"Approximately four o'clock," Pruss put in.

"It is my feeling," the *Reederei* director continued, "that our best course of action is to land, allow our passengers to debark, bring new passengers aboard, and head home. Once home, a few days from now, the matter will be turned over to the S.D., and if Eric Spehl or any other crew member is guilty of murder, the S.D. will find it out, and prosecute and punish. We will not deal with this matter in the air, or on American soil."

"Good Lord, man, he's killed twice!"

Lehmann shrugged grandly. "Who has killed twice? We have gone over that. We don't know what in fact happened to our missing passenger and our missing crew member. We will turn it over to the proper German authorities for investigation—in Germany."

"Ernst, this is madness—"

Erdmann, who'd been strangely silent, said, "Mr. Charteris, while I am more in your camp in this matter than Captain Lehmann's, I would have to agree with him that it is unlikely Spehl—or whoever our assailant might be—would kill again."

"Fritz! What is your reasoning?"

"Let's assume you're right about Spehl—or substitute

any other crew member, for that matter, including Scheef himself. Obviously, Eric Knoecher had something on whoever murdered him. So Knoecher was disposed of. Then Spehl . . . or whoever . . . became aware of the story you were spreading that Knoecher was still alive and un-well in your mutual cabin. This told him you were up to something, that you knew something. And of course you were asking questions, around the ship—*discreetly* investigating . . . but investigating."

"Yes."

"So you were 'warned.' By an accomplice, apparently. And now that accomplice has been removed. This is all according to your own version of the events, Mr. Charteris."

"That's right."

"Well, if no further investigation takes place, and you debark this afternoon—why would Spehl . . . or whoever . . . kill again?"

"And if *Scheef* alone was the murderer," Lehmann said, "he's either dead, by his own hand or God's, or has escaped."

"In either event," Erdmann said, "the safety of the passengers and the rest of the crew would seem assured."

Charteris threw up his hands. "By Nazi standards, maybe. But by any other, this is insanity." He looked to Lehmann. "How far will you go to protect yourself from damaging publicity in America, Ernst?"

"This far."

"I am still capable of blowing the whistle to the police and the press, you know."

"We do know." Lehmann's voice was at its gentlest, its most fatherly. "I would ask you, Leslie, as a friend, to allow us to handle this ourselves. In a few hours, this voyage will be over. You'll be off the ship. What is it to you what a bunch of Nazis do to each other?"

Charteris laughed humorlessly. "That's the best argument you've come up with, I'll give you that. But you'll have to do better."

"What would you suggest?"

"Put Eric Spehl into custody."

Erdmann frowned. "On what charge?"

"Jesus Christ, man! You're a Nazi! Who *cares* what charge?" Then he again turned to Lehmann. "Ernst, if we *are* friends, at all, to the slightest degree, for God's sake listen to me: that boy is guilty. I saw it in his eyes."

"His eyes," Lehmann said quietly.

"Put that boy in custody and keep him there at least until you lift back off from Lakehurst. And I would suggest keeping him in custody until you turn this business over to your authorities in the fatherland."

Lehmann's eyes narrowed. "And that will buy your cooperation?"

"Yes."

The *Reederei* director looked to Erdmann. "Colonel?"

Erdmann was already nodding. "I agree with Mr. Charteris. And I will take Rigger Spehl into custody myself, and keep him in my cabin."

Lehmann glanced to Captain Pruss. "Is that acceptable, Captain?"

"Yes. We can cover for Rigger Spehl's duties. Perhaps this is the prudent thing, at that."

"My only other concern," Charteris said, "is Spehl's access until this very moment to every nook and cranny of this ship. If he is, in addition to a murderer, a saboteur . . ."

Captain Pruss held up a hand, palm out. "The ship has been thoroughly checked. Our chief rigger has inspected gas cells and shafts, every bracing wire, every catwalk.

And I will instruct him to do so once again, after Colonel Lehmann has secured Spehl in custody."

Relieved, heaving a huge sigh, Charteris stood. "Thank you, gentlemen. I appreciate this."

They shook hands all around. Comrades again. The author was thanked for his cooperation and his investigative efforts. Lehmann assured him the promise of unlimited future passage on the *Reederei* line would be kept.

"You must be relieved," Lehmann said, as Charteris was leaving the cabin, "to have your amateur-detective duties behind you."

But as he walked the plank once more, moving through the sliding door into B deck, sauntering down the keel corridor, Charteris was nagged by feelings, by thoughts, that he simply could neither shake nor fully identify. Even with Spehl in Erdmann's custody, the mystery writer in him—the amateur detective he'd become—felt something remained to be done. This first case of his, minus the Saint, seemed unfinished, somehow.

The trip was certainly coming to a close. Coming up the stairs to A deck, he found Kubis and other stewards piling baggage under the bust of Marshal von Hindenburg. Down the corridor, other stewards could be glimpsed with armloads of dirty bedclothes, making a pile at the far end.

Charteris called out to the chief steward. "Heinrich!"

The chief steward looked up from his work; Charteris's own suitcase was in the pile Kubis was erecting. "Yes, sir?"

"A word?"

If Kubis was impatient with yet another demand from the author, it did not show in the man's bright-eyed, cheerful countenance.

Apologizing for taking the steward away from his work, Charteris walked him around to the dining room, which was otherwise empty at the moment.

"Do you know Eric Spehl?" Charteris asked him.

"Yes. He seems a nice boy. Farm stock."

"How well do you know him?"

"Just to drink with."

"What about Willy Scheef?"

"He's a mechanic on the ship. I know him, too."

"To drink with."

"Yes. We all drank together in Frankfurt, the night before we sailed, just about the whole crew. Where we always go—to the Heldenkeller."

"What's that, a weinstube? A rathskeller?"

"Yes. Yes, of course."

Charteris put a hand on the steward's shoulder. "Heinrich, if I wanted to talk to a mutual friend of theirs, could you arrange that?"

"What mutual friend?"

"I don't know. That's part of your role—to suggest someone who I could talk to, who I could . . . question about Spehl and Scheef."

"What questions about them? And why?"

Charteris waggled a finger. "Now, that's *not* part of your role. What would be part of it, however, would be keeping this between us. . . . Heinrich, you know how they have passengers pay thirty reich marks a day in advance, into an account, to cover daily shipboard expenses?"

The bright blue eyes blinked. "Yes, certainly."

"Well, since tips and full board are included in the cost of my ticket, I must have sixty or seventy marks left in that silly account. What good are marks to me, Heinrich?

You wouldn't know a good German I could bequeath them to?"

Fifteen minutes later, Kubis delivered a stocky gray-jumpsuited crewman named Walter Barnholzer—dark blond, chipmunk-cheeked, in his late twenties—to the author's cabin, which looked sparse indeed, stripped of its bedclothes, and no fresh flower in the wall vase.

Kubis, who made a quick discreet departure, had also delivered (as Charteris had further directed) a bottle of bourbon and two water glasses.

"It's all right if I have a little," Barnholzer said in German, and licked his lips. "I've served my last rotation in the gondola—I'm in number four."

Barnholzer, like the (apparently) late Willy Scheef, was a mechanic.

Gesturing for his guest to have a seat on the lower bunk, Charteris poured Barnholzer some bourbon, added some tap water, and did the same for himself (if less generously, where the liquor was concerned).

"I know that you are a famous writer," Barnholzer said, after a long satisfying sip from the water glass. He had an earnest smile highlighted by crooked front teeth. "Heinrich said you were writing an article."

"Yes," Charteris said, leaning against the wall by the little sink, "talking to passengers, to crew members. Getting the human side of the *Hindenburg*. Tell me about yourself, Walter."

The crooked-tooth smile flashed. "Well, I am a proud party member. I think I believed in the party from the very beginning, though I didn't join till thirty-two."

"Ah."

Barnholzer frowned a little. "Are you going to take notes, Mr. Charters?"

"*Chart*-er-is. No. I have a photographic memory, Walter. Do go on."

"You see, we've had to pull ourselves up by our bootstraps from the poverty the Jews and the socialists plunged us into. And the Führer's plan *is* working—there are jobs now for everyone, and Germany has taken its rightful place among the nations of the world." He gestured expansively with his free hand. "Look at this great airship—it tells you what Germany can do . . . could I have another?"

"My pleasure, Walter." And Charteris made the friendly Nazi an even stronger mix of bourbon and water, having barely touched his own first drink. "Tell me something about your background, why don't you?"

"Well, I was born in Tettnang, near the Bodensee. My father was a foreman in the Daimler works and that's where I first went to work. . . ."

Charteris stopped listening, though the pudgy-cheeked mechanic could never have guessed. Barnholzer's was a story the author didn't feel the need to hear—after all, he knew it already.

This was a man, like so many of his countrymen, who had been born at exactly the right moment to receive the worst education possible, to endure postwar Soviet government, inflation, and depression. To men like Barnholzer—who didn't seem such a bad sort—the National German Socialist Workers Party must have seemed like the greatest thing since sliced bread. After the perfidy of Versailles, the perceived greed of Jewish bankers, the ineptitude and anarchy of Catholic and Communist "democracy," a weak boy like this could only inevitably embrace the strength of Hitler.

It was already an old story, and it sickened Charteris, whose smile did not betray that fact.

"I don't know if this is what you are looking for, for your article, Mr. Chartreuse."

"Oh yes, very interesting, very interesting indeed . . . can I freshen that for you?"

"Please."

Charteris did so, then said, "Tell me about some of your friends. Steward Kubis mentioned one of the riggers—Eric Spehl?"

"Yes. Yes, Eric is a friend. Maybe not a close friend. Kind of odd, Eric—quiet, reserved. He even likes to read books."

"Imagine. Is he in the party?"

Barnholzer laughed. "Eric? No, no . . . You understand I am not S.S., I don't feel the need to inform. If it were my duty, of course, I would. . . ."

"Of course."

"But Eric, he's a Catholic, you know. Very religious. Wears a blessed Virgin Mary medal on a chain on his neck. He's been complaining about the arrests of these perverted priests, and sex-crazed nuns."

"Oh, they're the worst kind. So he has some contro-versial ideas, this Eric Spehl?"

"He walks a dangerous path. The woman he lives with, Beatrice Schmidt, is on the dangerous citizens' list. Older woman, dark-haired, a tramp and a leftist. He frequents coffeehouses, cafés, bars, where these black-shirted Com-munists talk against the state."

"Do you think Spehl could be aligned with the resis-tance?"

Three glasses of bourbon or not, Barnholzer saw the danger in that question. The plump crewman's eyes raced with the knowledge that he'd been too free with his words.

"There is no resistance in Germany," he said softly.

"Oh. I forgot. Is your fellow engineer, Willy Scheef, also a friend of Eric's?"

Barnholzer nodded, grinning crookedly, glad to be back on safer ground. "Willy's a good man. Everybody's pal. Fun. Do anything for a friend. Maybe drinks too much."

"Not in Communist bars, I hope."

"Willy! No. No, no. He's not a party member but he is loyal. . . . I may have misspoken about Eric. I didn't say he was disloyal. Sometimes a man will do foolish things to get into a woman's . . . well, into a woman."

"Walter," Charteris said, taking the empty water glass from the mechanic, "you've been most helpful to me."

Barnholzer looked like he was trying to decide whether to frown or cry. "Please don't put my name in your article."

"Oh, wouldn't it be all right to write up your fervent views about the party you love?"

And the crooked-tooth smile blossomed. "That, yes . . . please don't say I told you what I did, about Eric Spehl."

"You will remain an unnamed, reliable source, Walter. . . . Here—take the bottle with you."

"Thank you, Mr. Chartiss."

Before long, feeling every bit the proficient amateur detective, Charteris was heading to the portside promenade, thinking how right he'd been about Spehl. So Willy Scheef was the kind of fellow who'd do anything for a friend? Well that would seem to include attacking someone in the night.

Most troubling were the indications that Spehl was a leftist zealot, an active member of that supposedly non-existent resistance. Much as he might sympathize with Spehl's anti-Nazi sentiments, much as he tended to agree that Eric Knoecher had made a prime candidate for cast-

ing overboard, Charteris could only wonder if somewhere, tucked in the folds of fabric holding together this
ship, a bomb ticked away, waiting to make a great big
point about the fallibility of Hitler's Germany.

He found Hilda saving a seat for him in the dining
room at a table for four, shared with the Adelts. The
handsome middle-aged journalist wore the same dark suit
he'd come aboard in, and his blonde young wife looked
typically pretty in a yellow-and-white frock.

"Luncheon's a bit premature, isn't it?" Charteris said,
pulling up a chair, joining them.

"They're serving it early," Gertrude said, "so we'll all
be able to take in the view."

"We will pass over New York shortly," Hilda said.

"Ah," Charteris said.

"Yes," Leonard said, "and we'll be flying low enough
to get a nice close look. I think after this long, dull
crossing, the captain wants to finally give us our money's
worth."

"I trust that isn't a sentiment expressed in that article
of yours," Charteris said, pouring Hilda and then himself
a glass of Liebfrauenmilch.

"Oh, no," Leonard said. "I assure you I've lied so thoroughly and convincingly that even the Ministry of Propaganda would approve."

"So you've finished it, then? Your article?"

"All but the ending. This brush with the roofs of skyscrapers should provide it."

The view of New York from the promenade's slanting
windows proved no disappointment. With his arm around
Hilda's shoulder, Charteris stared down as the towers of
Manhattan revealed themselves magically, poking up
through the mist.

"We're flying quite high," Leonhard said, at Charteris's left. "The skyline looks like a board of nails. . . ."

"We'll get a closer look. Patience. It'll be worth the wait."

"There's the Statue of Liberty!" Gertrude said.

"Small as a porcelain figure," her husband muttered, as if writing his article aloud.

Hilda said, "So then you like New York, Leslie?"

"It was love at first sight," he said.

As the airship dipped lower, and the skyscrapers seemed to reach for them, he thought of how when he had first arrived in America, on that small steamer, with twenty-five bucks in his pocket, he'd found the buildings of Manhattan even taller and shinier than he'd imagined. He remembered sitting in that cheap hotel room on Lexington Avenue, looking across at the soaring white towers of the Waldorf—so clean and graceful compared with the stodgy, smoke-grimy architecture of home, rising sheer and white against a spotless blue sky the likes of which London seldom saw.

When was that? Thirty-two?

And now, after this very gray trip, the sky was that spotless blue again. The sun was out, and the ship was loping low across Times Square, sightseers pointing to the sky, standing frozen on the west side of Broadway. How he loved the electric nervous urgency down there, scurrying crowds on sidewalks, the press of honking traffic in packed streets. The elemental force of it had spurred him to try to match that pace, dazzling him with the prospect of infinite horizons.

But the Hindenburg had the power to bring this frantic city to a standstill, stopping traffic, and that was a delight, as well. On rooftops and firescapes, from windows and sidewalks, thousands of sophisticated New Yorkers gaped like farmers, craning their necks for a look at the vast airship draping its blue shadow over their city.

Despite the bright sunshine, lurking behind the tall buildings, thick black clouds billowed, like foul factory smoke.

"More rain coming," Charteris said softly.

"Oh dear," Hilda said. "Will our landing be delayed?"

"I don't know. I doubt it."

The sunshine carried them over Brooklyn, where the Dodgers were playing some team or other (the prevailing opinion on the promenade was the Pittsburgh Pirates), a game that halted temporarily as the fans stared upward, cheering and waving. The ship—which had acquired an escort of small planes of press photographers—swung north, crossing crowds on Wall Street.

The ship swooped so low over the Empire State Building, the shouted greetings of sightseers and photographers on the observation platform were easily heard; a passenger could have readily recognized a familiar face in the crowd.

"That was originally designed to be this ship's mooring mast," Charteris said to Hilda, pointing out the Art Moderne structure's tapering silver peak.

"It would be more glamorous than Lakehurst, New Jersey," Leonhard said. "But also less practical."

The good weather lasted as the airship flew over the Hudson River, and as it turned south to the lower bay, toward New Jersey, the boats in the harbor tooting hello as the ship glided over. But to the west, black clouds were conspiring to conjure up a summer thunderstorm.

Charteris felt a hand on his shoulder, and turned to see Lehmann, his expression genial.

"I thought you would like to know," the *Reederei* director whispered, "Mr. Spehl is safely in Colonel Erdmann's custody."

"Were there any problems?"

"None."

Then Lehmann began circulating among the passengers, many of whom stood expectantly, small luggage in hand, as he bid them, "*Auf wiedersehen*." This seemed to be the former captain's way of reassuring them the landing would come off without further delay—original arrival time was to have been six A.M., but the rain and head winds of the voyage had long since changed that.

By the time the airfield at Lakehurst came into view, the storm clouds were closing in, snapping with electricity, though there was no thunder, at least not that could be heard about the ship.

"We will land?" Hilda asked, clutching his arm.

"I don't think so," Charteris said.

No land crew stood assembled on the tarmac. Around the edges of the field, autos were parked and a modest crowd stood, waving. The vast, arched, hungry hangar awaited.

But no crew.

As if on cue, the rain began, pelting the ship, sounding gentle but in the context of the swarming black clouds, alive with lightning, disturbing indeed. Hilda clutched his arm, trembling, as the ship moved on, crossing over the pinewoods, making for the coast, to ride out the storm.

FOURTEEN

How the Hindenburg *Made a Detour, and Leslie Charteris Played a Hunch*

For over three hours the passengers of the *Hindenburg* waited for the storm to clear, many of them shuffling from the starboard promenade adjacent the lounge to the portside windows by the dining room, taking in alternating vistas of seacoast and forest. Some had their cameras out (no flashbulbs, of course) while others just sat with hand luggage in their laps, and the slightly dazed expressions of the delayed traveler. Others expressed pleasure at having their cruise expanded at no extra cost, while the two Doehner boys seemed fairly glazed over with boredom, perfect little bookends in their Buster Brown suits as they sat on either side of their mother on an upholstered window bench, clutching their teddy bears like life preservers.

The view was pleasant enough, as the ship swung southeastward, over Toms River, down the narrow, sandy peninsula that paralleled the coastline, the all-but-deserted beaches of resorts blindingly white in the streaming sunshine. At times they flew over the scrub oak and pine of the coastal plains. Miss Mather pointed out poetically, to anyone who might be interested (or not), pairs and trios of startled deer scurrying through the sparse woods, fleeing the ship's shadow.

To the west, however, the sky looked ugly, boiling with black storm clouds, through which spears of lightning thrust themselves.

Leonhard Adelt, narrowed eyes slowly scanning the dark-cloud-infested sky, said, "They're like a pack of angry wolves."

"It'll let up," Charteris said, not convincing himself let alone Leonhard. Charteris and Hilda were standing with the Adelts at the slanting windows, cool air easing in.

Kubis and other stewards had begun to circulate with silver trays, serving tea and biscuits.

The author nodded toward the lounge. "Why don't we all sit down? It would appear to be teatime, and I for one have had my fill of sand and scrubby trees and storm clouds."

"Hell," Leonhard said, and heaved a sigh. "What a bitter damn disappointment . . ."

Hand in hand with Hilda, Charteris arched an eyebrow in the journalist's direction. "What's your rush anyway?"

Gertrude said, "We're being met by Leonhard's two brothers, who my poor husband hasn't seen in thirty years. Apparently an extra hour or two is simply too much to bear."

"All right, all right, you've made your point," Leonard said, laughing gently, slipping his arm around his pretty wife's waist as the two couples made their way into the lounge and found a table.

Thunder rumbled; the first they'd heard.

"Not at all dangerous," Steward Kubis said, as he served the two couples tea.

"What time will we land?" Hilda asked, her voice cool but anxiety tensing her brow. She had taken off the rose-colored straw hat, which was fine with Charteris, who felt that any woman beautiful enough to wear a fashionable hat without appearing foolish would look more beautiful bareheaded.

"You need not worry, madam," Kubis said, with his practiced charming smile, "a zeppelin can cruise about indefinitely above storms. It is not like a plane that has to come down for fuel."

Charteris nodded. "I understand the *Graf Zeppelin* arrived over some South American country or other, during a revolution, and had to circle around for days."

"I heard that, too," Leonhard said, a biscuit poised for a bite. "They waited until the fighting was over, and then landed!"

With a chuckle, Kubis confirmed this tale, and went on to serve tea, and reassure other passengers.

But Hilda still seemed distressed. He patted her hand. "What's wrong, dear? Are you so anxious to leave my side?"

"I should have wired my sister about the delay. I waited too long."

"And I, as well," Leonhard said. "I'm sure my brothers were standing in that crowd at Lakehurst."

"I'm sure they'll understand," Charteris said, then turning to Hilda, added, "Which reminds me—do you have a number where I can reach you in Trenton?"

"Why don't you call me where I'm staying," she said,

"at the Sterling? I don't know the phone number, but it is a well-known hotel."

"All right. Let me give you my number in Florida."

Leonhard loaned Charteris a fountain pen and the author jotted down his number on a napkin and gave it to Hilda. Then, in the time-honored tradition of travelers at the end of their journey, he traded similar information with the Adelts, who would still be in New York on business when Charteris returned to talk to publishers, everybody passing around scribbled-on napkins like business cards.

"Ironic, isn't it?" Leonhard said, half a wry smile tugging his face. "You know what today is, don't you?"

Charteris sipped his tea. "No, what?"

Hilda said, "Ascension Day."

"Is it forty days after Easter already?" Charteris toasted with his teacup. "Ah, yes, another holy day of obligation. Well, we've ascended, all right."

"Are you Catholic too, Leslie?" Gertrude asked.

"Nominally. This is the day we celebrate Jesus telling the disciples to get off their duffs and spread the Good News."

Hilda blinked twice and smiled at him.

"I'm impressed," Leonhard said.

"Well, don't be," Charteris said, buttering a biscuit. "You see, my brother is a priest. Which, considering the sort of life I lead, would seem to indicate some incredible form of family compensation."

That amused everyone, but soon Hilda was frowning again, drumming her fingers.

"It'll be fine, dear," Charteris told her. "We've swung northward again. Look—they're preparing the table for the customs and immigration men."

Which Kubis and another steward were in the process

of doing, where the promenade emptied into the stairway.

"Have you noticed that sad colonel anywhere?" Gertrude asked them.

"Erdmann?" Charteris said, innocently. "No."

"It's funny he's nowhere to be seen." The pretty blonde shook her head, her cap of curls shimmering, her big blue eyes wide with thought. "You'd think he'd be sitting here, waiting to be first off the ship."

"Why do you say that, darling?" her husband asked.

"Well, when we . . . ascended, to use the word of the day, he seemed so reluctant to be leaving. Remember him sitting just over there, so melancholy? And his wife coming aboard to embrace him so warmly? You'd think they were never going to see each other again."

Before long the stewards were passing among them again, with sandwiches of cold cuts and cheeses piled on their silver trays. Carafes of Liebfrauenmilch were distributed, as well.

A muffled sound—a steam whistle—caused everyone to turn and look.

Leonhard Adelt said, "We will be landing soon—that was the call for the ship's crew to landing stations."

Hilda sighed and smiled, relief dancing in her dark blue eyes.

Charteris touched a napkin to his lips. "If you'll excuse me."

"What is it, Leslie?" Hilda asked, reaching out for him, fingertips brushing his hand.

"Little boys' room. I'll be back before too long. They won't let any of us off without going through customs."

He went up to Kubis, who was supervising the other stewards in their sandwich-serving. "Can you get away for just a few moments?"

"Well, sir, I . . ."

"Can't I wring one last imposition out of those marks I bequeathed you?"

Kubis smiled a little. "Certainly, sir. Anything for the man who wrote *Saint in New York*."

"Take me to Colonel Erdmann's quarters."

Now the steward frowned; he had been made aware of Erdmann's house arrest of Spehl. "But, sir . . ."

"No questions, Heinrich. This is an imposition, remember?"

"Yes, sir."

As he followed Kubis out of the lounge and along the starboard promenade, the slanting rain-flecked windows—cool air rushing in—revealed an early twilight had settled in, though as overcast as it now was, the difference between day and dusk was minimal. They'd be over Lakehurst again, shortly—he wondered if they would land or swing around for another sightseeing jaunt.

As Kubis began down the stairs, Charteris—somewhat surprised by the chief steward's route—asked, "Does Colonel Erdmann have one of the new rooms down on B deck?"

"Yes—they're larger, you know. With windows."

Though the bulk of the *Hindenburg*'s cabins were on A deck, where Charteris had been, a handful had been added to B deck since the ship's successful first season, to increase passenger space. These cabins were aft, taking up space that had originally been tentlike crew quarters.

At the bottom of the stairs, Kubis turned sharply to the left, where the floor itself was the retracted gangway, moving through a newly punched door giving access to the keel corridor. On the *Hindenburg*'s previous season of flights, the keel corridor was closed to passengers; but with the addition of this new wing of cabins, that was no longer the case.

The steward turned to the right, down the narrow corridor, and stopped at a door marked B-1, looking to Charteris with a hesitant expression. "Should I knock, sir?" he whispered.

"Please," Charteris said.

Kubis rapped his knuckles tentatively on the door. Nothing.

The steward glanced at Charteris, who nodded, saying, "Again."

Kubis knocked again, louder. Then said, "Colonel Erdmann! Sorry to disturb you, sir! It's Chief Steward Kubis, sir!"

Nothing.

"Use your passkey," Charteris said.

"But, sir . . . !"

"Use it, Heinrich."

"Yes, sir."

And the steward did, but the cabin—which was in fact half again as large as the A-deck cabins, with a sloping window like the one in Lehmann's quarters—was empty, stripped not only of bedclothes, but of Erdmann and Spehl.

"Where are they, sir?" Kubis asked, looking all around, as if the two men might be stuffed under a bunk.

"That would seem to be the question," Charteris said. "Heinrich, one last imposition—that door at the end of the hall leads into the belly of the ship, doesn't it?"

"Yes it does, sir."

"Unlock that for me."

"Sir, I can't. . . ."

"You can. And when you have, I want you to go to Captain Pruss and tell him that Colonel Erdmann and Spehl are missing."

Kubis seemed astounded by this proposition. "Captain

Pruss is in the process of landing the airship, sir—he can't be disturbed. . . ."

"There may be a bomb on this ship, Heinrich. Do you understand? This ship might not land at all."

Frowning, Kubis somehow managed to digest this notion quickly—but then the steward had been around the periphery of the various disappearances and inquiries afoot over the course of this trip; perhaps Charteris's statement made it all make sense.

At any rate, there was no further discussion: the steward used his passkey on the door at the end of the keel corridor, opening it for Charteris, nodding to the author in a fashion that said the message would be delivered to the captain, come hell or high water.

Then Kubis was gone and Charteris, the door closing behind him, was like a small child in a vast, otherwise unattended and quite bizarre amusement park. He moved gingerly along the rubber-carpeted keel catwalk (no slippers this time, rather his Italian loafers), the diesel drone much louder back here, building to a roar as he approached one of the precarious, skimpily handrailed access gangways out to an engine gondola. The roar settled back to a drone as he moved aft, walking uphill, slightly, the ship heavy aft, the bow high, as he gazed up and around at the complex array of framework and rigging and netting and other catwalks, crisscrossing girders, struts and rings, towering gas shafts and—nestled on either side, here and there—gas and water and fuel tanks, amid arches and ladders and wires, and yet most of all so much empty space.

Sun filtered through the translucent linen skin as he moved along, hazy illumination that gave the interior of the leviathan airship a warm yellowish cast, very different from the tour he'd taken Tuesday, when the day was overcast and the world back here was a grayish blue. That the western sky glowered black with the threat of a thunderstorm could not be discerned back he. e in this unreal mechanical wonderland. There was a strange stillness that might have been reassuring, even soothing, if the huge tan bladderlike gas cells looming left and right hadn't been fluttering, quavering like flabby cheeks, as if the ship itself were nervous.

That was definitely *not* reassuring.

He saw no crewmen—all of them were at their crew stations, many of them way in the stern of the ship, where yaw lines would be dropped and mooring cable let down, or up at the bow, working the main winch line and nose-cone connections. This was a cavernous world of his own, though he felt dwarfed rather than powerful, and he was just starting to wonder if he knew what he was doing when he saw them.

They climbed down a ladder and onto the narrow rubber-matted keel catwalk—a nondescript figure in a brown suit and a crew member in the standard gray jumpsuit: Colonel Erdmann, followed by Eric Spehl.

Who for a man in custody seemed pretty much on his own. No handcuffs or leg irons, and the colonel seemed confident enough in his charge to keep his back to his captive.

"Hello, boys," Charteris said, working his voice up above the diesel drone. He was perhaps twenty feet from them.

"Charteris," Erdmann said, frowning, halting. "What are you doing back here? It's dangerous—we're about to land!"

They could feel the ship slowing, even turning.

Charteris strolled toward them. "I'd ask you and your,

uh, prisoner the same thing, Fritz . . . if I didn't already
know the answer."

Behind Erdmann, who remained calm and collected in
the face of this intrusion, Spehl was openly distressed,
eyes wide, mouth hanging open, arms extended, hands
splayed, as if caught in the lights of an oncoming truck.

"Know what answer?" Erdmann asked calmly. But he
did run a hand over his slicked-back blond hair, a nervous gesture of sorts.

"Well, perhaps 'know' is a bit strong." Charteris was
facing the Luftwaffe colonel now, Spehl moving in closer
behind Erdmann, peeking up over his shoulder, making
a two-headed man of him. "My surmise is that you and
young Eric are on your way back after tucking your
bomb into place."

Neither man, crosshatched by the shadow of ladders
and struts, found a response to this.

So Charteris continued, casually: "If it had already
been planted, you would need to reset the timer, because
of the weather delays. Or, if you were planting it for the
first time, now is of course the ideal time to do it . . .
minutes before mooring, with the crew occupied and at
their landing stations."

"This is quite the most absurd thing I ever heard,"
Erdmann said, managing to put some quiet indignation
into it.

Behind him, Spehl was sweating, trembling, his face
drained of blood.

"I am assuming, of course," Charteris said, "that you
don't wish to blow yourselves or for that matter any of
the passengers to kingdom come. You'd like this great
symbol of Nazi power to blow itself up when it's at the
mooring mast, and no one is aboard, and no one, or hardly anyone, is standing near enough to be harmed. Very

humane, Fritz. Commendable thinking, for a saboteur."

Erdmann sighed. "All right. You are partially correct. Rigger Spehl is a member of the resistance—"

"Ah, so there *is* a resistance. That's nice to know."

"He admitted to me that he had planted a bomb, and we went to retrieve it."

"Well, let's see it, then."

"All right," Erdmann said, and reached in his pocket and withdrew a small black automatic, a Luger.

"Fritz, Fritz . . . do you really want to fire that thing and blow all of us up?"

"No. But I am hoping you will listen to reason."

"Ah! An offer to join the resistance? And I'm not even German! What an honor."

Erdmann chuckled dryly at that; the little black automatic in his fist was like a toy—reminding Charteris of the chief steward taking the Doehner boys' tin toy into custody, for making sparks.

"How in hell did you know?" Erdmann asked.

"Well, I should have known much earlier. But all these delays gave me so much time to ponder. And another passenger made a stray remark about you, just now— Gertrude Adelt—reminding me of that touching scene the first night, when your wife bid you good-bye. You knew better than anyone that this ship had been thoroughly searched, and that every last stitch of baggage would be exhaustively inspected. But in your capacity, you could allow your wife to come aboard for a last-minute good-bye—she had to stand for no security procedure, at all, did she? And I'm sure she wasn't pretending, when she embraced you on deck, I'm sure the tears were very real, because she knew the dangerous journey you were about to begin—that if things went awry, she might never see you again. . . . She passed it to you, didn't she, Fritz? Your wife handed you the bomb, didn't she?"

Erdmann's haggard smile and faint sigh said yes.

"It must be a fairly small and simple device," Charteris said.

The colonel nodded. "Yes. You may have learned in your own . . . investigation . . . that Eric here, is something of a photography buff."

"Actually, it didn't come up."

"I forgot—you're not much of a detective."

"Enough for us to be standing here like this, Fritz. So Eric's an amateur photographer—so what?"

Erdmann shrugged. "One flashbulb added to a small dry-cell battery, with a pocket watch attached."

"Ingenious," Charteris said, rather impressed. "A flashbulb is perfect—a tiny glass sphere filled with pure, dry oxygen, exploding into dazzling light by a split-second combustion of aluminum foil."

Another nod from Erdmann. "Enough to melt steel, let alone ignite hydrogen."

"A simple device, a modest investment, to destroy the Nazis' greatest propaganda weapon."

"Will you join us?"

"Why don't you put that pistol away, Fritz, and we'll talk about it."

With Kubis reporting to the captain, all Charteris had to do was stall—of course, if the captain was too busy, landing this beast, then . . .

Erdmann said, "No. I'll keep my weapon, thank you."

"You're not reckless, Fritz. You won't shoot."

"Don't be too sure. A gunshot wouldn't necessarily ignite the ship's hydrogen, not unless there's a leak we don't know about."

The diesels were grinding as the airship slowed.

"You see, Fritz, that's my problem with you and your young protégé, here. You say you're against the Nazis, but you kill just as ruthlessly as they do. . . . By the way, which of you threw Eric Knoecher overboard? I'm just curious."

"I did," Erdmann said, unhesitatingly.

"Funny, isn't it? I took your word for it that there were no crew members on Knoecher's list. It was you, Fritz, who gave us the names of his 'subjects,' our 'suspects.' You sent silly-ass me off on a half-dozen wild-goose chases, while withholding the one name on his list that mattered: Eric Spehl. The young crewman with Communist leanings and leftist associates. Was your name on his list, too, Fritz?"

Erdmann said nothing.

"Oh well, what does it matter?" Charteris said, stalling. "Eric Knoecher doesn't bother me so much . . . the world will survive without his putrid presence. But what does bother me is poor Willy Scheef. He wasn't part of your plot, was he?"

Erdmann's eyes narrowed and a weariness in the man's expression told Charteris he was on the right track.

Edging his voice up above the engine noise, Charteris said, "Poor Willy was what they call in the movies a day player. Eric here recruited him to deliver me that warning by way of a beating . . . but Willy was just doing Eric a favor. He wasn't part of the resistance, just a thickheaded, good-hearted drinking crony who would do anything for a friend."

Erdmann said, "Give me your decision, Mr. Charteris, or I'm afraid—"

"You should be afraid. You have a partner, Fritz, who is very unreliable. Very emotional. Why don't you tell

him, Eric, why you really involved poor Willy? And why
you killed Willy, to cover your tracks?"

The wild-eyed Spehl spoke for the first time, and his
voice was shrill. "I *did not* kill Willy! And neither did
Colonel Erdmann. It was an accident."

"An accident," Charteris said, almost tasting the word.
"I believe I heard this song-and-dance before. . . ."

Insistently Spehl went on: "Willy was angry with me,
for getting him in trouble, when he found out the Luftwaffe agents were investigating; he knew the wound on
his leg would give him away. He was going to give himself up and tell them what I'd asked him to do and . . ."

"You killed him."

"No! We . . . we *did* struggle. We were talking in his
gondola, screaming at each other over the engine, and
when he went out to that little gangway between the gondola and the ship, to go tell on me, we struggled and . . .
he just slipped. I swear to God and all that's holy, he
slipped!"

"I'm sorry, boys," Charteris said, shaking his head. "I
can't come over to your side. You're just too . . . untidy
a bunch, much as I might sympathize with your goals.
That jerry-rigged bomb of yours could go off while people are still on this ship, and you're endangering untold
numbers of American military and civilians at Lakehurst."

Spehl shook his head, violently. "No! It's set for eight
o'clock. Everyone will be off the ship. Casualties will be
minimal."

"Don't you think it's rather bad taste," Charteris said
pointedly, "to fight a war on another country's soil?
German casualties are one thing: Americans are another."

"Then you've made your decision?" Erdmann asked,

raising the Luger so that it was trained upon the author's heart.

"So what's the plan, boys? Disappear into America? Wait . . . Eric, that's *your* plan. But, you, Colonel, you want to go back to your pretty wife, in Germany, and continue fighting from within, don't you? A noble enough goal . . . but Eric, here, kind of made a mess of it, with his extra killing, didn't he?"

"Be quiet," Erdmann said. "This is your last chance."

"Eric," Charteris said, "what do you want to bet that that automatic in the colonel's pocket wasn't meant for me? After all, Fritz didn't know I was going to show up, did he?"

"Quiet," Erdmann said, teeth clenched.

"Why was he packing the rod, do you suppose? Hmmm, Eric? Do you think he was planning to shoot up random crew members—or maybe he had just one in mind . . . maybe a prisoner who had fled his custody, who could die and with his death seem to answer many, many questions . . . allowing the good colonel to go back to the fatherland, to his wife and his mission."

Spehl's hand clasped onto Erdmann's shoulder. "What *were* you doing with that Luger in your pocket?"

Erdmann's eyes and nostrils flared as the boy reached around. "Eric!"

"Give it here!"

And Spehl spun Erdmann to him, grabbing for the gun, trying to wrest it from the colonel's fingers, the two men tottering on the narrow catwalk. The automatic in hand was high over Erdmann's head now, as if he were trying to keep a toy from a child; and as Spehl wrestled Erdmann for it, Charteris made a hasty exit, running down the rubberized gangway toward the passenger quarters.

He was halfway to the doorway when he heard the gunshot.

FIFTEEN

How the Hindenburg *Alighted at Lakehurst, and Leslie Charteris Debarked*

Charteris had a fraction-of-a-second glimpse of the two men, as they stood frozen, like dance partners startled when the music stopped, the tiny black gun in Erdmann's hand still held high as Spehl clutched the colonel's arm and wrist, the gun up, angled toward the back of the ship, where the weapon had dispensed a wild bullet.

The sound of the gunshot had been a small pop—almost like a cap pistol—harmless sounding; but Erdmann's bullet, a small silver pellet whose shape was not unlike the airship's, had traveled down the hollow body of the dirigible and into a billowing hydrogen-filled gas cell, the center of which flared brilliantly, red and yellow and blue spreading out beneath the fabric like colorful spilled liquid, before the gas cell dissolved in crackling flame.

Then the *whoom* of detonation announced blossoms of orange fireballs that rolled inexorably, hungrily, down the length of the zeppelin, expanding as they came, scattering scraps of white-hot aluminum and raining down scorched fragments of fabric along the way.

Somewhere a voice screamed, "Stay down!" in German, and Spehl abandoned his dance partner, scrambling along the catwalk away from the oncoming conflagration, leaping for the nearest engine-gondola gangway, trying to shimmy out of the path of the surging fire.

Flushed with heat, as if some mammoth oven door had dropped open, Charteris ran, looking back as he did, not wanting to, but—like Lot's wife—unable not to. And the last thing he saw, in the burning belly of the beast, was Erdmann consumed by the typhoon of flames, the sizzling saboteur turning black and orange, but the colonel did not scream, rather stood and stoically received the fiery fate he'd conceived.

Then the author bolted through the door, running pell-mell down the keel corridor, toward the stairs, knowing damn good and well that the flames, and time running out, were nipping at his heels.

In thirty-seven seconds, the *Hindenburg* would be, for all intents and purposes, as dead as Colonel Fritz Erdmann.

Moments before the first blast, Leonhard and Gertrude Adelt were standing with Hilda Friederich, leaning out over the slanting windows on the starboard promenade deck, by the lounge. It was drizzling again, flecks of rain glistening on the windows like tiny jewels. The airship had just swung sharply into the wind, and they were watching with no little interest from their balcony perch the show below: the ground crew—one hundred and fifty feet down—scurrying toward and beneath the ship, a mixture of American civilians and navy men, the latter easy to pick out in their white sailor caps and navy-blue coats. A pair of ropes that had been dropped from the bow and stern were latched onto by two columns of these men, who were tugging the ship toward the mooring mast.

Leonhard noted a remarkable stillness had settled over the deck—no motor drone could be detected, no one spoke, not a command, no cry or call, as if the collective ship were holding its breath.

And the ground crew had suddenly stopped scurrying, were instead looking up with wide eyes and open mouths. Some of them were pointing up—Leonhard could not know it, but the members of the ground crew had spotted the small mushroom-shaped puff of flame, high toward the back of the ship, forward of the upper vertical fin, where a tiny unseen bullet had burst through, disappearing into the mist.

Then a muffled, dull detonation broke the silence, seeming to Leonhard no louder than popping the cap of a beer bottle.

"What was that?" Gertrude asked him, clutching his arm.

Hilda's hands came up and covered her mouth, eyes wide, trembling all over. She was looking out and down.

Leonhard followed her gaze. The crew on the ground were suffused in a rosy glow, as if the sun were rising; the sandy ground itself was basking in the eerie twilight sunrise, spreading from the bow of the ship, banishing its usual blue shadow. And then the men down there were scurrying again—but in a different direction.

Running away from the ship in terror.

"Sweet Jesus," the journalist told the two beauties. "We're aflame."

The second detonation was no mere echo: it overshadowed the first explosion with its force and terrible bellow, as if the airship itself were howling in anguish, and—though no one on the *Hindenburg* could see it—this explosion sent flames erupting through the skin atop the ship, telling everyone on the ground that the previous tiny burst of flame had been only a hint of what was to come.

Charteris had made it to the end of the corridor by the time of the second explosion, which threw him like a rag doll, tossing him rudely, and when he stopped rolling and careening, he found himself facedown on the floor of the retracted gangway.

He scrambled to his feet, grabbing a quick look out the B-deck windows, seeing the ship was still high over the ground; then he was heading up the stairway to A deck, where the Adelts and Hilda and the others awaited. He could hear the hell that A deck had become, the stampedelike sound of passengers panicking, running back and forth, some yelling, others screaming.

That was when the world upended, the ship tipping back on its stern, dramatically, sitting itself down on its tail, beginning to collapse in on itself in so doing. Spectators would say the ship looked like a Japanese lantern, lighting up from within, showing off the ship's aluminum framework even as it consumed itself.

Fortunately he'd been holding on to the stair rail, and now he was holding on with both hands, his ears filled with the sound of tables and chairs and other normally friendly objects making deadly nuisances of themselves to the passengers on A deck above, from which reverberated more screams, and the awful sound of human beings tumbling like so many dice.

Gritting his teeth, sucking in air not yet tainted by smoke, Charteris dangled there, the stairs above him taking quite the opposite tilt proper stairs could take. Dirty bedclothes, piled at the end of the hallway above, plummeted past him, spilling down as the dying dirigible did its topsy-turvy backstand, blankets and sheets fluttering like the wings of dying birds.

Pulling himself up and along, with only the railing to keep him from plunging to injury or death, he yanked himself upward, where he might help his friends.

Moments earlier, before the second explosion, with the knowledge that the ship was in flames—flames that had not yet reached them, though they could hear the fire's deep deadly hissing, like a thousand stirred-up snakes— Leonhard Adelt, on the starboard side, had taken his wife by one arm and Hilda by the other.

"We have to get out through the windows!" he told them. "It's our only chance!"

"It's too high!" Gertrude said, eyes huge with horror.

"We'll go lower, believe me! Wait a bit. . . ."

They were at a distance of perhaps one hundred twenty feet now—the distance to the ground diminishing by the second, but not quickly enough to suit the two women, who looked terrified; and so was Leonhard, but he did his best not to betray that.

"I'll go get some bed linen," he told them confidently, "to soften our fall!"

But he didn't go, because that was when the second explosion shook the ship like a naughty child, sending Adelt and Gertrude and Hilda and every other passenger on the starboard promenade tumbling backward, toward the bulkhead by the stair corridor, slamming into it, even as tables and chairs pitched forward, crashing down on them, barricading them in.

Their world almost upside down, Leonhard quickly acted to ascertain the condition of his little group. Thank God for this lightweight furniture! He brushed aside a chair, pulled a table off the two women, who were stunned but that seemed to be all, merely shaken, clothing torn, but no blood visible.

That could not be said for others around them. Elsewhere on this upended deck, George Hirschfeld was clinging to a bench, hanging down the deck's steep incline, a bloody gash on his forehead, and Ed Douglas had slammed into a wall of the lounge, pinned behind a stack of tables and chairs, unconscious. In the corner, where the bulkhead met the slanting windows, Herman Doehner, father of the two boys, was similarly unconscious, head bloody from banging it on metal railings as he tumbled down the treacherous slide the deck had become; but his wife was awake and the two boys—very wide-eyed but not crying—were fussing over the papa.

And Moritz Feibusch lay unconscious, dying, his head cracked open against a metal railing, with forty-three unaddressed, unsigned postcards in his pocket, the rest still in the mailroom, waiting to be posted, waiting to burn.

The officers in the control gondola, in their forward position, were perhaps the last on the ship to know of the tragedy they were piloting.

Ernst Lehmann, observing in the gondola, had felt an odd tremor, rather like an ocean wave lapping onto shore.

"Is a rope broken?" he asked Captain Pruss.

"No," Pruss said, unconcerned.

"I felt a heavy push, Captain. . . ."

That was when someone on the ground yelled, "Run for your lives!"

And the rudder officer began to moan, "Oh, no, oh, no!"

Somewhere a fire bell was ringing, and a red glow was spreading on the ground, like a rosy rash.

The watch officer said, like a man sleepwalking, "I should get the logbook."

Lehmann barked his first official order of the voyage: "Drop the water ballast!"

The second explosion came just then.

That one they heard, all of them, and it shook them, physically, and otherwise—but they could see or hear no flames, could smell no smoke, not yet. The captains of the *Hindenburg* stood helpless, impotent, the red reflection of unseen flames like a blush of embarrassment on their dazed faces.

On the portside deck, by the dining room, a chaos similar to that on the starboard had ensued. Fewer passengers on this side, though all of the stewards were over here, in part for the sake of distributing weight, but also for Kubis's staff to put away dishes and such, including placing leftover sandwiches in the pantry dumbwaiter.

Margaret Mather had been leaning out an open window, chatting with one of the college boys, who was taking photographs with a Kodak, when mysterious sounds from the engines caused her to grasp his arm and look at him for reassurance.

The second explosion—the first had barely been noticed—rocked the ship and sent many of them, passengers and stewards alike, to their knees.

Chief Steward Kubis picked himself up, saying, "Everything will be all right!"

That was when the ship lurched, sitting back on its stern and began crumpling into itself, and the sudden tilt took the floor out from under them, stewards and passengers toppling and tumbling, furniture cascading after them.

Lightweight Margaret Mather—wrapped up in a navy-and-white herringbone coat due to the cool rainy weather—was hurled twenty feet into the end bulkhead and soon was pinned against the projection of a window bench by a crush of German passengers. She thought she was suffocating, thought she might die from the weight pressing on her, but the passengers clambered to their feet and grabbed onto railings and window ledges, hanging there as the floor canted under them.

Relief flowed through her, and then the fire blew in.

Long tongues of flame, she thought, strangely detached and typically poetic, *bright red and so very beautiful.*

Though it was mere seconds, the trip up the back-tilted stairs seemed to take forever, and strained the formidable muscles of the well-toned author's arms. Charteris had never been more glad that he had never allowed his sedentary calling to keep him from physical activity.

As he reached the top of the stairs, the floor under him seemed to right itself somewhat—the stern disintegrating in flame had allowed the bow to drop. Snatching up a blanket that had draped itself over the stair railing, he moved into the starboard promenade deck, where he came upon a picture of chaos, people and furniture scattered like so much discarded refuse. Some of the people were unconscious, perhaps even dead; others had made their way over and around the furniture and the fallen to get to the windows.

Leonhard and Gertrude were poised to jump, pausing

to look back urgently at Hilda, who stood fear-frozen, hands covering her face. As Charteris neared them, fire swept into the room, right past them, not touching them, as if seeking the helpless unconscious and dying in the lounge. Flames jumped and danced and crackled and the Adelts just jumped. Charteris swept Hilda up in the blanket, bundled her in his arms like a baby; she put up no resistance but her eyes were wild. The hissing of flames was at their back and the screams and yells around them were like dissonant notes standing out from a hellish symphony. He kissed her forehead, gave her a tight reassuring smile, and waited as long as he could, till the ship had lowered to about ten feet.

Then he dropped her, gently as possible, hoping the sandy ground below would greet her the same way.

Like Margaret Mather, Joseph Spah was on the portside, and the acrobat was climbing out a window, following two men who'd gone out before him and dropped to the ground too soon, crashing to earth, one hundred feet or more, bouncing as they hit, and now lay unconscious or dead, flaming linen and molten aluminum raining down on them.

Sitting on the ledgelike sill, Spah waited, waited, waited, seconds that seemed forever, and would be forever, if he couldn't find the right moment; all he could think of was, thank God he swung from a lamppost for a living!

Ravenous flames were seething behind him, and he could wait no longer—forty feet now, he guessed. He could do that. He was an acrobat—just keep his feet under him, knees bent, roll when he landed, feet under, knees bent, roll, under, bent, roll. . . .

"It's too high!" a voice said.

Spah turned.

It was the chief steward, Kubis.

"Too high!" Kubis repeated, his eyes almost crazed.

"No," Spah said. "It's too hot."

And he jumped.

Moments later, so did Kubis.

Leonhard and Gertrude Adelt landed softly in the grassy wet sand, having jumped only fifteen or so feet, collapsing to their knees not in pain but in relief.

Short-lived relief: almost immediately they were enveloped in oily black clouds through which deadly tongues of fire licked and taunted. They got to their feet, found each other's hand, but soon parted company, as no path for two could be found in the dangled maze of crumpled wreckage. It was like making their way through a jungle of dangling hot metal wires and glowing cables and jagged debris, under the continued downpour of burning fabric and dripping metal.

Leonhard felt no pain as he bent apart white-hot aluminum framing, to make a door to dive through, into the sea of fire; in shock, it all registered as an eerie dream to him, his body weightless, floating like a star through space.

Then he saw that Gertrude had fallen and some semblance of reality snapped back. He ran to her, hopping red-hot girders, pulled her up and gave her a push—she tottered off like a mechanical toy. He followed after her, but tripped and found himself sprawled on the oil-soaked ground, and it felt good to him, despite the flames dancing all around him; it gave him such a wonderful sense of well-being, to just stretch out on the soft sand and await death.

"Leonhard!"

His wife's voice.

He pushed himself up, saw her beyond the wreckage, beyond the flames, safe, reaching out to him, calling out to him, and he sprang to his feet and ran for his wife, and life.

Then he was beyond the fire zone, breathing air not smoke, and as Gertrude took his hand, he looked back at the fallen giant, swirling with smoke and flame, cracked in the middle now, forward section reaching for the sky as flames shot out the bow like a monstrous blowtorch.

A husky sailor was shouting, "Navy men stand fast!"

And the same ground crew who had fled the falling, fiery airship were heading back to pull people out of there. And figures were emerging on their own, as well, running like Jesse Owens, fleeing the flames, or just staggering, some of them with the clothes burned off their bodies, others with eyes seared shut.

"We should help," Leonhard said, coughing.

"No," his wife said. "We *need* help."

He looked at her, her blue eyes pleading, her lovely face smudged with soot, burned black in places, her hair smoking, sizzling.

Then he nodded, and they stepped over a smoldering body, and walked away, hand in hand.

The ship was nearly to the ground when Charteris jumped.

He hit on all fours, a soft sandy landing, then bounded to his feet, sparks and embers falling around him like red snow.

"Help us!"

A woman's voice, behind him.

Glancing up, he saw the two terrified little boys, the Doehners, climbing out the sill. Their frantic mother pushed them out, one at a time. Charteris caught the boy, and in one fluid motion flung him with all his force, the child sailing in an arc, landing beyond the fire zone. The other boy landed in the sandy earth, not so near by; another passenger—it was the cotton broker, Hirschfeld!—snatched up the lad by the hand and sprinted with him through the obstacle course of flames and debris.

Charteris had seen Hilda drop like a bundle, get to her feet, gather the blanket around her like an Indian and dash into and through the flames.

Now it was his turn to navigate the gauntlet of flaming framework and burning linen and glowing beams and red-hot wires. Covering his head with his sport jacket, he ran a zigzag path through the wreckage; around him others were doing the same—some falling to the earth screaming, burning.

But Charteris emerged from the smoke and flames fairly unscathed—he'd sucked in smoke, and his hair and mustache were singed, though his monocle was gone.

The Saint might have gone back in, looking for it.

Charteris, a ground-crew member taking him by the arm and leading him away, would let it go.

Margaret Mather had watched the men and women leaping from the promenade windows, but she just remained where she'd fallen against the bench, lapels of her coat shielding her face. Flames were flitting all around her, like butterflies, and occasionally they'd land on her sleeves and she would brush them off with her bare hands. The scene around her seemed out of a medieval picture of hell, and she had remained detached, composed, while all around her gave in to hysteria.

She kept her eyes covered and decided that she agreed with whoever it was who was screaming, *"Es ist das*

Ende!" and quietly waited to die, hoping it would not be too prolonged and painful an experience, waiting for the crash of landing.

Then someone was yelling through the window: "Come out, lady!"

She opened one eye, then another.

Framed there in the window was an American—a sailor boy!

She stood primly, looked around for her handbag, finding it between two corpses; then she did her best to crawl out the window in a ladylike fashion, the sailor helping her down.

And then the nice young man walked her out through the bits and pieces of burning this and that.

All but one of the officers in the control car walked away from the burning wreck. Captain Pruss emerged from the curtain of smoke, hatless, his hair burned away; badly burned, but alive.

Charteris—who was wandering the periphery, looking for Hilda—saw Ernst Lehmann stagger from the black billowing smoke, looking stunned but not seriously harmed. The author ran to the dying ship's former captain, to see if he needed help. Lehmann was walking along as if strolling through a park, or so it might have seemed if his face hadn't been fixed in such glazed confusion.

"Are you all right, Ernst?" Charteris asked.

Lehmann looked right through him, eyes unblinking despite the smoke, saying, "I don't understand. . . . I don't understand. . . ."

Then the director of the *Reederei* moved past Charteris, revealing that the clothes had been burned from the back of him, leaving the naked skin from the top of his head to the heels of his feet a charred black blistered mass.

An American officer ran to Lehmann's side and walked him to the waiting ambulance.

Charteris turned to look at the ship, whose linen skin was almost gone now, fire erasing the Gothic red letters spelling *Hindenburg,* leaving a glowing skeleton trailing white-hot entrails and streaming smoke as black as the coming night.

Somewhere, within that colossal smoldering corpse, were the cremated remains of Colonel Fritz Erdmann. And probably those of Eric Spehl, as well.

Then, coughing, he sought out one of the navy boys, to see if he could hitch a ride to the base hospital.

Maybe Hilda was there.

SIXTEEN

How the Hindenburg *Smoldered, and Leslie Charteris Burned*

At the Lakehurst Naval Air Station's small, single-story hospital, Charteris roamed the corridors like a man in a trance. His sport jacket had been lost en route, and his yellow sport shirt and tan slacks were scorched and torn; he looked like a hobo who'd had a particularly rough night of it.

The scene was one approaching battlefield horror. Doctors, nurses and orderlies swarmed like white blood corpuscles fighting infection, hallways lined with burn victims on stretchers; in small doorless rooms, other casualties slumped in chairs and sat on examining tables, as doctors had a look and nurses dressed wounds. One somewhat larger room had badly burned bodies littering the floor like unearthed mummies.

Some of the victims had "M's" written on their foreheads with grease pencil—an orderly with a syringe the

size of a Roman candle was administering morphine, and
hastily marking those who'd had theirs. Screams and
whimpers and howls and moans resounded, and men with
bloody burns, clothes in charred tatters, wandered vacant-
eyed like zombies, looking for friends and loved ones.
The wounded cried out, in German mostly, for their
mothers, their wives, their husbands, their priests. And a
priest was threading through the carnage, delivering last
rites like a postman does the mail.

The smell of burned human flesh and burned clothing
hung like a foul curtain; odors of alcohol and Lysol
added to the nasty bouquet. Charteris began to cough—
apparently he'd inhaled more smoke than he realized—
and suddenly a gentle hand was on his arm, as a nurse
shuffled the dazed author into an examining room and
onto its white-papered table.

A fleshy, bespectacled, kindly-faced doctor in his thirties gave Charteris a quick exam.

"You're one of the luckiest I've seen," he told Charteris, who was putting his scorched shirt back on. "The
nurse will apply some picric acid to your hands—couple
of nasty little burns."

"Is everyone being brought here?"

"To the first-aid station? Yes, but we immediately
shuttle the worst cases to Paul Kimball Hospital—it's
close by in Lakewood."

"Does anyone have a list?"

"Of who's injured and who's survived?"

"Yes."

A commotion in the hall, accompanied by louder
howls, signaled the arrival of more injured, who were
still being carted over from the crash site by ambulance
and auto.

"No list I'm afraid," the doctor said, already halfway

out the door, "much too early for that . . . if you'll excuse me."

Almost immediately a nurse came in with a small bottle of picric acid and some gauze and wet down his palms. She was a brunette of perhaps twenty-five, with a gentle plain face.

"Nurse, do you remember treating or even just noticing a pretty German girl with braided blonde hair, blue eyes?"

"Why yes—I didn't deal with her personally, but I'm fairly sure she's fine, just minor burns, like yourself. Your wife?"

"Is she still here?"

"I'm not sure. As negligible as her injuries are, she was probably discharged . . . is that better?"

"It's fine. Where did you see her?"

"Down the hall to the left—she was standing next to a boy on a stretcher who was very badly burned, comforting him, sweet girl. He may have been taken to Paul Kimball Hospital, or . . . he may have died."

Then she produced a clipboard and asked Charteris if he could sign his name; either the burns weren't bad or he was in shock, because he had no trouble.

In the hallway he ran into Leonhard and Gertrude Adelt; their clothes were scorched rather worse than his, Leonhard's nearly in tatters. Both of them had severe burns on their arms and faces, and Leonhard's scalp looked to be burned to the bone.

"Thank God you're all right, Leslie!" Leonhard said, over the moans around them.

"Have you seen a doctor yet?"

"No. We're just on our way out—getting out of this madhouse!"

"You two need to see a doctor."

The journalist shook his head. "My brothers are just outside and they'll take care of us."

Gertrude reached out, not touching him—her hand was too burned for that. "We'll be fine, Leslie. Did you see Hilda?"

"No, I was just looking for her."

"She's barely scratched." Smiling wearily, Gertrude gestured with her head. "She's down at the end of the hall. Go to her—I think she's in shock."

As if the Adelts weren't.

He told them good-bye, said, "Get to a doctor!" and made his way down the corridor, lined as it was with burn victims on stretchers, weaving around nurses, doctors, orderlies.

Shoulders slumped, head down, she was standing next to an empty, bloodstained, smoke-grimy stretcher. Her braids had come untangled and blonde locks dangled alongside her soot-smudged heart-shaped face, her white crepe dress torn here and there, new dabs of black added to its red-and-pink-and-black floral pattern.

"So they took him away, huh?" Charteris said.

She glanced up sharply. "Leslie . . . thank God!"

"You've been looking for me, then? Frantically?"

Wincing, she said, "What is it?"

"Good-bye, Hilda."

Soon he was standing in the cool, rain-misted evening, his back to the small hospital, where ambulances and autos were still bringing in more wounded. Across the airfield the wailing sirens of fire trucks and police cars and ambulances had mostly died. The voluminous plumes of black smoke were beginning to get lost in the darkening dusk, and—from this distance at least—the orange flames were little more than a campfire, smoldering in the twisted glowing skeleton of the ship, around which the cops and firefighters could warm themselves. The hook-and-ladder trucks had dispensed their water and were disinterested onlookers, now.

"Leslie . . ."

Hilda's husky voice.

He didn't turn. "My condolences."

Then she was next to him, as he stood staring out at the fuming, smoldering wreckage across the airfield. The sky was a vast emptiness, overcast, no stars.

"What do you mean?"

"Funny." He patted his cigarette case of Gauloises in his shirt pocket. "These things made the trip, and I could use a smoke right now . . . but I haven't got a light."

Wind blew the strands of hair. "Why are you mad at me?"

Not looking at her, Charteris said, "I'm surprised he lived through it long enough even to make it to this first-aid station. I'm surprised there was anything left to identify."

"Who?" Her brow was knit. "Who are you talking about?"

Now he turned to her, looked down into the deep blue eyes in the lovely black-splotched face. "Eric Spehl—your boyfriend."

She frowned—and he realized she was deciding whether or not to continue the masquerade; but the day, the evening, had gone on too long, and they had been through too much, together and apart. And, most of all, they were both just too damned tired. Sighing, her eyelids at half-mast, she all but said, *No games, no more games.*

"How do you know?" she asked.

"I write mystery stories, remember?"

"*How,* Leslie? How do you know?"

He shrugged. "No one big thing—several small things,

Beatrice . . . That *is* your real name, isn't it? Beatrice Schmidt?"

That he knew this much unsettled her, clearly; but she recovered, saying, "Yes . . . but I have rather come to like 'Hilda.' "

"I . . . I'd rather come to like Hilda, myself." He twitched half a smile. "I am a little disappointed. You'd think a German girl, at least, would be a natural blonde. You're the 'older' woman, the dark-haired leftist 'tramp' who turned young Eric Spehl political."

She laughed but no sound came out; then she said, "I should have hidden my leftist beliefs."

"You tried, but you must feel them very deeply—there really was a patriotic lover who died in the Spanish Civil War, wasn't there?"

She nodded. "Our cause is just."

He glared at her. "You killed and hurt a lot of innocent people tonight, trying to make some stupid grandiose point."

But she merely smiled, faintly. "Did we? Or was it you, interfering in a plan that left unmolested would not have taken a single life? And would have struck Nazism a terrible blow?"

Now he laughed, only it turned into a cough; the smoke taste filming his mouth was nasty. "Maybe you're right. But you and Eric'll have to take responsibility for Willy Scheef."

She frowned, puzzled, apparently genuinely so. "Willy . . . ? I know nothing of this."

"You know, that's just possible. You may not even know that Eric threw poor Willy overboard."

The eyes widened; the whites were bloodshot. "He did *what*?"

"As I said, Beatrice . . . Hilda . . . it was a lot of little things—there's the irritation you displayed when Eric paid his little unscheduled visit to A deck, for my autograph. Today, discovering that you, like Eric Spehl, were a devout Catholic . . . you let it slip in our little Ascension Day chat. Then there was the fact you were visiting your sister, to help her with her new baby—yet your address was the Hotel Sterling. That just didn't sit right. . . . And of course you were so frightfully worried about the postponed landing—perhaps knowing that a timer was ticking away on a bomb that had been set without those interminable delays factored in."

Her eyes, still wide, had tightened, now. "Those tiny things told you . . . ?"

"No. One slightly larger thing did. This is how Willy gets involved. You don't know about the midnight beating, do you?"

Again, she seemed utterly bewildered. "Midnight—what are you—"

And he told her about Willy Scheef, at Eric Spehl's bidding, coming to the cabin to deliver a message by way of a beating.

"The message Willy delivered was 'Stop what you're doing,'" Charteris said, "but I made the mistake of thinking the message meant I should back off my investigation. Why should I be warned so late in the game? Less than a day left? How much detective work might I still do, and anyway, nothing I'd done had been very effective, had it? But the warning didn't refer to my investigation . . . did it, Hilda?"

"I do not know."

"Oh, well, perhaps—but I think you can figure it out. When I spent the night in your cabin, when we had that early-morning interruption by a steward, supposedly wanting to make the room up . . . that was no steward . . .

that was Eric Spehl, sneaking a visit to his sweetheart."

She said nothing.

"Eric knew you were going to keep an eye on me, Hilda, but he didn't think sleeping with me would be part of the bargain . . . and he was furious with both of us. *That's* what I was being warned to stop doing—*seeing you* . . . sleeping with you. That's why Willy Scheef died . . . not to save the fatherland from Adolf Hitler. Just to cover up a petty little crime of assault, since it might lead to exposure of the bigger crime of sabotage, not to mention Eric Knoecher's murder."

She sighed heavily. "Eric was a simple, jealous boy."

"You and Colonel Fritz Erdmann and others in the resistance molded and shaped and manipulated Eric Spehl into doing your bidding. It's not that I don't sympathize with your cause—it's just that I don't like being molded, shaped and manipulated myself . . . or seeing big dumb clucks like Willy Scheef bumped off for no good reason."

"I had nothing to do with that."

"Of course you did—your young lover is risking everything to sabotage the ship he helped build, and he catches you in bed with another man. . . . All that stuff about needing adventurous men, wanting to live a larger life through a man of influence, that was the *real* you talking, wasn't it?"

"I suppose it was."

"And I was the perfect type to latch onto—sophisticated, successful, divorced. . . ."

"You flatter yourself."

He laughed again, managing not to cough this time. "What did Eric think your mutual future held? That he would sneak away from the ship, slip into America—that you and he would traipse through the flowers together, building a new life in the Land of the Free?"

"He would have worked as a photographer."

"And you would have been a photographer's wife? How long would that have lasted? It doesn't sound very . . . adventurous to me. Also, for a Communist, you seem to have rather refined tastes."

A tear rolled down her cheek, smearing the soot. "I did love him, in my fashion . . . and he died with me in his eyes."

"Looking up at an angel."

Another trickle of tear; a sniffle. "You're cruel."

"No. If I were cruel, I'd turn you in to somebody or other. Trouble is, I don't particularly care to see this thing get uglier than it already is . . . or to spend the next several months of my life in court proceedings and other inquiries, explaining what really happened to and on the goddamn *Hindenburg*."

She looked pointedly at him. "What *did* happen?"

Charteris sighed, shrugged; the drizzle was picking up again. "Eric figured out that Fritz was probably going to shoot him over the Willy Scheef blunder—they struggled, a stray bullet caught a gasbag. And the rest is history—or rather isn't history . . . because I'll never tell it."

Her smile had some sneer in it. "You will never tell it because I am right."

"You are, Hilda?"

"Yes—*you* caused this, Leslie. If you had not interfered—"

"I don't give a damn about that, because I don't believe it for a second. Those clumsy saboteurs might well have blown us up in any case. No, I won't tell this story because I wouldn't give Adolf Hitler the satisfaction of saying anarchist forces, opposing him, took all these innocent lives, on American soil."

". . . Oh."

A faint crackling of the burning ship could be heard from across the field—like someone was popping corn.

Quietly, he asked, "Is there a real Hilda Friederich?"

". . . No. She is an invention. People who share my beliefs, working within the Reich, arranged the false papers."

"And now you disappear into America. To start a new life."

"If you will allow."

"I'm not stopping you."

She swallowed; her lips trembled. "I did not mean to hurt you."

"You didn't hurt me, dear. A damn zeppelin blew up in my face—that's what hurt me."

"Then . . . we won't see each other again."

"How can we? You don't exist."

Then he turned away from her, his eyes reverting to the glowing, smoldering framework, as he waited for her to go.

Which, before too very long, she did.

Charteris stayed at the New Yorker Hotel for three days, before taking the train to Miami for his birthday festivities. A United States naval intelligence officer had taken a perfunctory interview with him, to see whether or not the creator of the Saint would be needed to testify at the upcoming American inquiry into the crash. The author told the investigator nothing of the plan devised by Erdmann, Spehl and Hilda/Beatrice, working hard to make it seem he had nothing pertinent to offer; and so he was not required to testify.

Reporters tracked him down at the hotel and, though he normally didn't shy away from publicity, he gave no interviews, and thus was barely mentioned in the press, though he did follow the story intently himself.

Joe Spah got plenty of publicity, posing with his pretty wife, his three tiny children and a police dog the kids had been led to believe was the late Ulla. Joe's acrobatic leap from the burning airship was heralded, though he had fractured his heel in the fall, and the Radio City Music Hall appearance had to be postponed.

Margaret Mather and the Adelts were widely interviewed, and it was revealed that Margaret would write her story for *Harper's* (prose, not poetry) and Leonhard's article (which now had an ending) would appear in *Reader's Digest*.

Other survivors—none badly harmed—were frequently quoted, including that rootin' tootin' Nazi George Hirschfeld (happily in the arms of some showgirl by now, Charteris hoped) and stockyard king Colonel Nelson Morris—though his businessman friends, advertising man Ed Douglas and perfume king Burt Dolan, had perished, as had Moritz Feibusch, though Moritz's crony Leuchtenberg, who'd been drunk most of the trip, made it. The Doehner boys also survived, and so did their mother, but they lost their father.

Among the surviving crew members were Chief Steward Kubis, who had jumped from the ship, then turned around and helped the American ground crew rescue passengers and other crew; Chef Xavier Maier and two other cooks; and Dr. Kurt Ruediger, who needed a physician's help himself, as he had broken his leg on his leap.

Mechanic Walter Barnholzer died in the Paul Kimball Hospital, as did Captain Ernst Lehmann, who on his deathbed spoke of sabotage causing the disaster. Captain Max Pruss survived, with disfiguring burns.

It was said Pruss was in far worse shape than Lehmann, but that the despondent *Reederei* director had simply lost the will to live.

Thirteen passengers were listed as dead, twenty-two crew members. Charteris noted with wry interest that Eric Knoecher's name was included on the former list, and Willy Sheef's on the latter.

Charteris never regretted his decision to keep what he knew to himself: the American commission blamed a hydrogen leak ignited by a spark of static electricity as the most probable cause of the explosion; and the German inquiry decided essentially the same thing. calling the terrible event "an act of God."

Sabotage never was seriously discussed in either tribunal, as America wished to avoid an international incident on her own shores, and Germany did not wish to acknowledge itself vulnerable to sabotage by a resistance movement within its own borders—a resistance movement its government claimed did not exist, at that.

Still and all, there were interesting scraps of testimony and evidence.

Such as a number of witnesses who felt they had heard a gunshot prior to the first explosion. A mechanic, Richard Kollmer, said he "heard the 'pop' of the firing of a gun, a small gun or rifle." Chicago stockyards magnate Morris, who had been in the writing lounge, also said he'd heard "a report, not loud," of a weapon.

Even Dr. Hugo Eckener, the father of the *Hindenburg,* had originally stated his belief that his airship was a victim of sabotage, saying, "Only the firing of a burning bullet into the gasbags from a distance would have accomplished it." But by the time of the official German inquiry, Eckener had changed his tune to the familiar gas-leak-and-spark scenario.

As the latter explanation settled uneasily into history,

Charteris began to think his mystery writer's mind had
imagined it all—at least until he read about two neglected
items of evidence found in the wreckage, given no serious consideration by either panel of inquiry:

A solid black chunk of residue identified by the New
York City Police bomb squad as the residue of a dry-cell
battery.

And a charred Luger—one shot discharged.

A Tip of the Halo

This novel is a follow-up of sorts to my previous historical mystery, *The Titanic Murders,* in which Jacques Futrelle—an esteemed detective-story writer of his day, and an actual passenger on the great doomed ship—solves two murders prior to a certain incident involving an iceberg.

So the most obvious question a reader might pose is: Was Leslie Charteris, creator of the Saint, actually a passenger on the *Hindenburg*? The answer is a resounding, absolute *yes* . . . sort of. As is indicated in this tale, Charteris (and his then-wife Pauline) were well-publicized passengers aboard the airship's maiden voyage; but history does not record his presence on the *Hindenburg*'s final run.

Every good mystery needs a detective, however, and—in the tradition of Futrelle's role in *The Titanic Murders*—I seized upon Charteris's *Hindenburg* connection and ran. Just as I was a childhood reader of Futrelle's "Thinking Machine" tales, so was I an avid fan of Char-

teris and his Saint—the Saint was my first big enthusiasm
as a reader of mysteries, and I was expelled from my
fourth-grade class at Grant School in Muscatine, Iowa,
for having in my little desk *The Saint and the Sizzling
Saboteur,* an Avon paperback with a wonderfully racy,
rather sadomasochistic cover. Numerous references in
this novel to that particular Saint tale can be found by
the keen-eyed Charteris fan, and of course my tongue-in-
cheek chapter titles are firmly in the fashion of what
Charteris referred to as his "Immortal Works."

The literate yet adventurous and even hard-boiled detective fiction of Leslie Charteris was my introduction to
a world of writers that included Dashiell Hammett, Ray-
mond Chandler, Erle Stanley Gardner and Mickey Spillane, and—for better or worse—set me on my life's path.
Any writer of mystery fiction might look with envy at
the gloriously successful career of this sophisticated, fascinating man, who saw the Saint reach radio, television,
the comics page and the silver screen; few doubt that
without the Saint, there would have been no James Bond
(and TV's "Saint" Roger Moore, of course, graduated to
Bondage). At the time of his death in 1993, at age eighty-
five, in Windsor, England, Leslie Charteris saw his Robin
Hood sleuth again heading to the screen for a big-budget
production (and he would certainly have been as dis-
pleased with the final result as he was with Hollywood's
previous efforts).

With the exception of Charteris's fanciful role, however, I have attempted herein to stay consistent with
known facts about the *Hindenburg* and her final voyage,
though the books and articles on this subject are often
inconsistent, particularly on smaller points, and the various experts disagree on all sorts of matters, trivial and
profound. When research was contradictory, I made the

choice most beneficial to the telling of this tale. Any blame for historical inaccuracies is my own, reflecting, I hope, the limitations of this conflicting source material.

Three nonfiction books were the cornerstones of my research. A. A. Hoehling's pioneering *Who Destroyed the Hindenburg?* (1962) first identified Eric Spehl as the probable saboteur; his book is a detailed, fascinating account of the trip and was extremely helpful to me. Hoehling's research was substantiated and somewhat expanded upon in Michael Macdonald Mooney's first-rate *The Hindenburg* (1972); though it covers similar ground, Mooney's book adds other details and perspectives, and was particularly rewarding in background information regarding passengers who became characters in this novel. A lavish coffee-table-style volume in the manner of their book on the *Titanic, Hindenburg: An Illustrated History* (1994) by writer Rick Archbold and illustrator Ken Marschall covers the golden age of the airship in general, and is less detailed about the *Hindenburg*'s final flight than the Hoehling and Mooney volumes; but its overview of the Zeppelin Company—and wonderful photos, paintings and diagrams, some of them elaborate foldouts—put it on the short list of volumes vital to my research. My sincere thanks to all of these gentlemen.

With an exception that will be noted, the characters in this novel are real and appear with their true names; the conflicts with Nazi Germany suffered by the subjects on Eric Knoecher's list are grounded in reality. There is no reason, however, to think that the real Eric Knoecher was a Nazi agent, that he was in fact anything but an innocent importer who died tragically on the *Hindenburg*. History records little else about him, or about Willy Scheef, who certainly did not attack Leslie Charteris in the night, since of course Leslie Charteris wasn't actually aboard the ship. These two were chosen from among the otherwise anonymous deceased because of the melodramatic felicity of their names and for purposes of verisimilitude. No disrespect is intended, and the characters wearing these real names in this novel should be viewed as entirely fictionalized. And—despite their real names and basis in history—these are all characters in a novel, fictionalized and doing the author's bidding.

Hilda Friederich has a basis in reality, though I am not privy to her real name: both Hoehling and Mooney cite her as Spehl's likely coconspirator, and both use pseudonyms. She was not aboard the flight, rather back home in Frankfurt, expectantly and continually checking in with the Zeppelin Company office on news of the flight.

The notion that Colonel Oberst "Fritz" Erdmann may have been party to the sabotage is suggested in the 1975 film version of Mooney's book, and Hoehling and Mooney both note Erdmann's strange, gloomy mood, with the latter indicating at least some discontent on Erdmann's part toward the Nazi regime; but the theory that his wife may have smuggled aboard the explosive device—in their well-documented last-second good-bye aboard the airship—is to my knowledge new to this book. I do not offer this as anything more than a theory that at least loosely fits the facts and possibilities.

Two books on the life and career of Leslie Charteris were enormously constructive: *The Saint and Leslie Charteris: A Biography* (1972) by W.O.G. Lofts and Derek Adley; and *The Saint: A Complete History in Print, Radio, Film and Television* by my friend Burl Barer, who is also the latest author to continue chronicling the Saint's adventures, including his first-rate novelization of the recent Val Kilmer–starring film. Also consulted was *The Saint* (1989) by Tony Mechele and Dick Fiddy, which focuses on the Roger Moore television series but does include material on the Saint's creator, as well.

Fans of the Saint and Charteris should run, not walk, to go on-line at www.saint.org, the phenomenally colorful, detailed Web site run by Dan Bodenheimer. Dan was incredibly generous with his time and knowledge, providing a copy of the long-out-of-print Lofts/Adley book mentioned above, sending photocopies of rare articles from obscure British and American fanzines, sharing personal anecdotes about Charteris, and pointing me to another remarkable Saint expert, Ian Dickerson. The benevolent Mr. Dickerson provided photos of Charteris and information he's gathered for a biography of Leslie Charteris, in progress.

Ian also shared a complete set of "A Letter from the Saint," a weekly letter written to fans by Charteris that ran from April 1946 through February 1947; this material—sixty-thousand-plus words of it—gave me a rather personal, inside look at the author's mind-set and lifestyle, and created much of the basis for his characterization in these pages—numerous throwaway lines in this novel, and stretches of interior monologue, are derived in part from this vital, vintage material. Should I ever be lucky enough to have fans as dedicated as Dan and Ian, I would be blessed indeed (haven't quite shaken this British thing yet—sorry).

A good deal of inspiration for the appearance and panache of Charteris-as-detective came from the May 1941 issue of *Life* magazine, which featured a six-page photo-illustrated mystery story by Charteris (celebrating the hundredth anniversary of the genre) in which the author portrayed his own character. Charteris posed as the Saint in monocle, mustache and dapper apparel including tuxedos and sporty ensembles. Those images seldom strayed

from my mind as I wrote this tale. Also productive in
this vein was "Meet the Saint," a chapter from *Meet the
Detective* (1935), edited by Cecil Madden, provided by
Dan Bodenheimer.

Numerous standard references, such as *Contemporary
Authors* and *Twentieth Century Authors,* were consulted
in regard to Charteris and his career. Specific reference
books used include *British Mystery Writers 1920–1939*
(1989) edited by Bernard Benstock and Thomas F.
Staley, and *Encyclopedia of Mystery and Detection*
(1976) by my friends Otto Penzler and the late Chris
Steinbrunner.

My fact-based novels about fictional 1930s/'40s era
Chicago private detective Nathan Heller have required
extensive research not unlike what was required of this
project. I called upon my Heller research assistants,
George Hagenauer and Lynn Myers, to help me in my
attempt to re-create the final voyage of the great ill-fated
airship. They both dug out numerous articles from sometimes obscure sources, and without them this journey
would not have been possible.

Among these articles were "The Last Trip of the *Hindenburg*" by Leonhard Adelt (*Reader's Digest,* November 1937) and "I Was on the *Hindenburg*" (*Harper's
Magazine,* November 1937) by Margaret G. Mather. Obviously, these two articles were essential to this book.
Leonhard Adelt, incidentally, survived the *Hindenburg*
only to die in the firebombing of Dresden; his wife, Gertrude (sometimes spelled Gertrud), survived Dresden and
her articulate, vivid remembrances of the airship and its
crash have been among the most important resources for
Hindenburg researchers.

Another helpful article (one of George Hagenauer's
finds) was "Aboard the Airship Hindenburg" (*Wisconsin*

Magazine of History, Winter 1965–1966) by Louis P. Lochner, actually excerpts from Lochner's diary of the maiden flight to the States, the same one Charteris was on. Also of interest were "What Really Downed the *Hindenburg*" (*Popular Science,* November 1997) by Mariette DiChristina, which reveals the little known fact of the flammability of the "doping" material that coated the airship; and "The First Airship Flight Around the World" by Dr. Hugo Eckener (*The National Geographic Magazine,* June 1930). On the Web (at www.airships.net) I discovered a detailed travel brochure from the *Deutsche Zeppelin-Reederei* company that included many details about life on the airship.

I would also like to cite the excellent History Channel documentary *The Hindenburg,* produced and directed by Don Cambou (no writer credit given). I also screened *The Hindenburg* (1975), the lavish Hollywood production based on Mooney's book, directed by Robert Wise from a screenplay by Nelson Gidding from a screen story by *Columbo* creators Richard Levinson and William Link; rather heavily fictionalized, and something of a soap opera in the manner of the then-popular disaster picture, legendary director Wise's film impeccably re-creates the ship's interior.

Other books consulted include *Dirigibles That Made History* (1962) by David C. Cooke, and *Airshipwreck* (1978) by Len Deighton and Arnold Schwartzman.

I would like to thank several editors: Natalee Rosenstein and Sara Carder of Berkley Prime Crime; my agent and friend, Dominick Abel; and of course my wife, Barbara Collins, on deadline working on a book herself during the writing of *The Hindenburg Murders* but still willing to lend a hand, to help try to guide this baby to the mooring mast . . . without any unexpected explosions.

About the Author

MAX ALLAN COLLINS has earned an unprecedented nine Private Eye Writers of America "Shamus" nominations for his "Nathan Heller" historical thrillers, winning twice (*True Detective,* 1983, and *Stolen Away,* 1991).

A Mystery Writers of America "Edgar" nominee in both fiction and nonfiction categories, Collins has been hailed as "the Renaissance man of mystery fiction." His credits include five suspense-novel series, film criticism, short fiction, songwriting, trading-card sets and movie tie-in novels, including such international bestsellers as *In the Line of Fire, Air Force One* and *Saving Private Ryan.*

He scripted the syndicated comic strip *Dick Tracy* from 1977 to 1993, is cocreator of the comic-book features *Ms. Tree, Wild Dog* and *Mike Danger,* and has written the *Batman* comic book and newspaper strip.

Working as an independent filmmaker in his native Iowa, he wrote, directed and executive-produced *Mommy,* a suspense film starring Patty McCormack, which made its debut on Lifetime in 1996; he performed the same duties for a sequel, *Mommy's Day,* released in 1997. The recipient of a record three Iowa Motion Picture Association awards of excellence for screenwriting, he also wrote *The Expert,* a 1995 HBO World Premiere film, and has recently written and directed a documentary on mystery writer Mickey Spillane.

Collins lives in Muscatine, Iowa, with his wife, writer Barbara Collins, and their teenage son, Nathan.

MARGARET COEL

THE EAGLE CATCHER

When tribal chairman Harvey Castle of the Arapahos is found murdered, the evidence points to his own nephew. But Father John O'Malley doesn't believe the young man is a killer. And in his quest for truth, O'Malley gets a rare glimpse into the Arapaho life few outsiders ever see—and a crime fewer could imagine...

❏ 0-425-15463-7/$6.50

THE GHOST WALKER

Father John O'Malley comes across a corpse lying in a ditch beside the highway. When he returns with the police, it is gone. Together, an Arapaho lawyer and Father John must draw upon ancient Arapaho traditions to stop a killer, explain the inexplicable, and put a ghost to rest...

❏ 0-425-15961-2/$5.99

THE DREAM STALKER

Father John O'Malley and Arapaho attorney Vicky Holden return to face a brutal crime of greed, false promises, and shattered dreams...

❏ 0-425-16533-7/$5.99

THE STORY TELLER

When the Arapaho storyteller discovers that a sacred tribal artifact is missing from a local museum, Holden and O'Malley begin a deadly search for the sacred treasure.

❏ 0-425-17025-X/$6.50

EARLENE FOWLER

introduces Benni Harper, curator of San Celina's folk
art museum and amateur sleuth

❏ FOOL'S PUZZLE   0-425-14545-X/$6.50

Ex-cowgirl Benni Harper moved to San Celina, California, to
begin a new career as curator of the town's folk art museum. But
when one of the museum's first quilt exhibit artists is found dead,
Benni must piece together a pattern of family secrets and small-
town lies to catch the killer.

❏ IRISH CHAIN   0-425-15137-9/$6.50

When Brady O'Hara and his former girlfriend are murdered at the
San Celina Senior Citizen's Prom, Benni believes it's more than
mere jealousy–and she risks everything to unveil the conspiracy
O'Hara had been hiding for fifty years.

❏ KANSAS TROUBLES   0-425-15696-6/$5.99

After their wedding, Benni and Gabe visit his hometown near
Wichita. There Benni meets Tyler Brown: aspiring country singer,
gifted quilter, and former Amish wife. But when Tyler is murdered
and the case comes between Gabe and her, Benni learns that her
marriage is much like the Kansas weather: bound to be stormy.

❏ GOOSE IN THE POND   0-425-16239-7/$6.50
❏ DOVE IN THE WINDOW   0-425-16894-8/$6.50